"Is it my imagination or are you trying to avoid me?"

Noticing how one of Wiliam's dark brows arched and how his eyes glittered down at her with derisive humor put Rachel instantly on the defensive, and she fixed him with a cool stare.

"Avoid you? Now, why on earth would I do that? Although for the life of me I cannot think what we could possibly have to talk about," she said, her voice strained.

"Oh—several things come to mind. I could begin by telling you how charming you look."

"Thank you, but I suspect that flattery is not your forte, Lord Kingsley."

AN ILLUSTRIOUS LORD

Helen Dickson

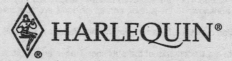

TORONTO • NEW YORK • LONDON
AMSTERDAM • PARIS • SYDNEY • HAMBURG
STOCKHOLM • ATHENS • TOKYO • MILAN • MADRID
PRAGUE • WARSAW • BUDAPEST • AUCKLAND

ISBN 0-373-30389-0

AN ILLUSTRIOUS LORD

First North American Publication 2001

Copyright © 1997 by Helen Dickson

This edition published by arrangement with Harlequin Books S.A.

® and TM are trademarks of the publisher. Trademarks indicated with
® are registered in the United States Patent and Trademark Office, the
Canadian Trade Marks Office and in other countries.

Visit us at www.eHarlequin.com

Printed in U.S.A.

HELEN DICKSON

was born and still lives in South Yorkshire with her husband and two sons on a busy arable farm, where she combines writing with keeping a chaotic farmhouse. And incurable romantic, she writes for pleasure, owing much of her inspiration to the beauty of the countryside. She enjoys reading and music. History has always captivated her, and she likes to travel and visit ancient buildings.

Chapter One

From a dry June day in 1785, the weather had suddenly changed to a biting wind and icy rain since Rachel Fairley and her two brothers, Stephen and Harry set out from London in the early morning to reach their home, Meadowfield Lodge, close to the village of Ellerton in the heart of Oxfordshire. Rachel found the journey long and tedious, made worse by thirteen-year-old Harry's coughing and sneezing.

He was far from well and she would be extremely relieved to reach their home where he could be put to bed. With his eyes closed, he sat huddled miserably in the corner of the coach, with rugs packed about his slender frame to keep out the invading cold. Rachel looked across at Stephen, two years older than her own one-and-twenty years. He had said little since the onset of the journey, seeming preoccupied with his thoughts.

"So, Stephen," she said, breaking into his reverie, "Lord Kingsley is to return to Mortlake Park. I have to say that I have no great desire to meet him."

"Then I must tell you that you are likely to do so, and very soon, for I believe he is expected to return to Mortlake this very day—so Aunt Mary informed me before we left for London last week. You are bound to meet at some event or other."

"Then I shall not look forward to it. From what I hear of his character, I think I shall find him a very disagreeable man indeed."

Although Stephen was himself in awe of the formidable Lord Kingsley's character, nevertheless he gave his sister a look of mild reproach. "You can hardly judge a man so severely when you have not made his acquaintance."

"And why not, pray? I have just cause to think ill of him, as well you know."

Stephen sighed, finding the cause of his sister's resentment towards Lord Kingsley rather tiresome. "Seeing that you constantly harp on about it, how can anyone fail to be aware of your ill feeling towards him? It is the source of his wealth that irks you, is it not?"

"Yes, I admit it, the source of his wealth does disgust me, for it is well known that his fine house and gardens are maintained by the profits he makes on his plantation in the Indies—from the misery of others."

Her brother scowled disapprovingly across at her. "The same can be said of others. There are many among the aristocracy and land-owning families who own plantations in the West Indies from which they derive much of their wealth."

"And without the Negro slaves, all of them would

no doubt face absolute ruin. Slavery is an abomination and should not be tolerated, Stephen.''

''You spend far too much time with Mr Nolan discussing the evils of the slave trade, Rachel,'' her brother rebuked her. ''Last year—as I remember— your opinion was raised against the rich Nabobs in India and their crimes against the Indian people'.

''That was before I was made aware of the evils that exist in the West Indies—which is surely the worst stain that exists on any area of British aristocracy.''

''That may be true, but Mr Nolan's views are too radical by far. I blame him for your aversion towards Lord Kingsley; if he were not forever putting his name forward as an example, then perhaps you would not have this larger-than-life image of him as being some kind of tyrant. It is not usual for a young lady to fill her head with such affairs, when her time would be better spent discussing more feminine matters, as our cousins Caroline and Emily do.''

Rachel grimaced. ''Much as I love my cousins, Stephen, they do little other than gossip over a dish of tea; their main preoccupation is their wardrobe. They are watched over twenty-four hours a day by Aunt Mary and talk of nothing more exciting than connections and the sort of company where good manners and breeding are essential.''

She sighed with annoyance. ''It all makes for exceedingly dull company. One cannot deny that reading and learning expands one's knowledge and enlivens any conversation.''

Stephen silently agreed with her. Their cousins, the Brayfield sisters, who lived at impressive Ellerton Hall, just two miles from their own, less imposing, home of Meadowfield Lodge, could not compete with Rachel's mental liveliness. She thrived on subjects that stimulated her mind and was forever reading political pamphlets and newspapers.

She was constantly occupied in lively discussion with Mr Nolan, Harry's tutor, which was a cause of annoyance to Stephen who preferred a quieter, imperturbable lifestyle. He had never possessed any enthusiasm for the rigours of learning, preferring instead—when he wasn't about the family business—to concentrate all his efforts and thoughts on his blossoming courtship with Miss Amanda Kingsley, the formidable Lord Kingsley's seventeen-year-old sister.

Stephen would be more than happy when Harry was of an age to continue his education at Oxford and they could dispense with Mr Nolan's services, for he considered that the alarming influence he seemed to have over Rachel was becoming quite disruptive to her state of mind.

Ever since his introduction into the household two years ago—at a time when she had been rejected in love by Ralph Wheeler and was nursing a broken heart—his mild-natured sister had undergone a transformation almost overnight into a confident and forthright young woman.

Her friendship with Mr Nolan was supported by intelligence and a mutual interest in endorsing the campaign against the slave trade, being championed in Parliament by Mr Wilberforce, the devout evangelical Member of Parliament for Yorkshire and Mr Nolan's mentor. Rachel's ardour and preoccupation with the evils of this trade in human misery was gradually turning into a crusade.

Their father was unconcerned by her avid interest; like most young ladies who considered they should have some cause or other to support, he was confident she would abandon it when she put the painful memories of her unhappy affair with Ralph Wheeler behind her and found herself a husband.

"It does indeed," Stephen agreed. "I must say that your strong mind and natural confidence dominates both our cousins."

"Strong-minded I may be, Stephen—and nothing would give me greater pleasure than to go out into the world as Kitty has done." She sighed, with a wistful look in her eyes, as she referred to their sister, who had left home to become an actress on the London stage—a disreputable profession, and frowned upon so ardently by their Aunt Mary.

"But one cannot deny that men's lives and decisions shape female destinies and will continue to do so for a good many years yet, I am sorry to say."

They fell silent as the coach continued on its way. Harry was overcome by a fresh bout of sneezing, and Rachel placed a hand to his forehead, concerned that he was still feverish and his eyes too bright, then passed him a dry handkerchief and secured the rug about his knees.

Glancing out of the window, she wished it was not so depressingly dull and extremely cold, with rain beginning to fall more heavily. They were to stop at the next inn for refreshments, but they could not take long about it, otherwise the roads would soon become rutted because of the rain.

They were travelling home in their own private coach after staying in their Aunt Mary's town house for the past week. Stephen had gone to London on some business for his father and, taking advantage of the opportunity to see Kitty, Rachel and Harry had accompanied him.

They had been unable to see her perform on the stage at Drury Lane, because the theatre was closed for the summer months. Unlike most actors who went on tour during the vacation, travelling with companies on regular country circuits, Kitty had chosen to stay in London.

This had puzzled Rachel at first because her sister lived for the theatre and she believed she would have taken any opportunity to continue her profession, but eventually she accepted her explanation that she was perfectly happy to remain in London and work in the fruit shop—above which she had rooms—until the theatre reopened in October.

To humour Harry, they had taken him on a sightseeing tour of the city, which included a visit to the Tower of London to see the wild beasts, and to watch the changing of the guard at St James's Palace. When Harry developed a streaming cold after taking a trip on the river, Rachel considered it best for them to return home.

"Lord Kingsley's return to Mortlake Park will spoil everything for you, Stephen, will it not?" she commented.

"I have to say it will, Rachel, but if Miss Kingsley and I wish to marry then we cannot do so without Lord Kingsley's consent. He is her guardian, after all, since the death of their father."

"Marry?" retorted Rachel, feigning surprise, for she had been aware for some time that their relationship was becoming more than mere friendship. "So— it has gone that far. I do hope you have not entered into any secret commitment with Miss Kingsley, Stephen?"

"No, of course not," he replied with a trace of indignation. "We are both of the same mind, but it is not my wish to place her in an awkward position until she has had the opportunity of speaking to her brother first." His expression, as did his brown eyes, softened. "But is she not the sweetest thing, Rachel, with the most gentle disposition? She does not possess one malicious thought or deed."

Stephen's voice was full of fondness when he spoke of Amanda Kingsley and Rachel could not deny that she was all he said of her. Not once in all the meetings she had had with her when they had met at Ellerton Hall—when she had been visiting her cousins and Miss Kingsley had been there also—had she seen the sweetness of her temper ruffled. They were well matched and of similar minds.

"Yes, I have to say she is, Stephen," she agreed with a smile, "and she does not hide the favourable impression you have made on her either. Although, I have to say that I have grave misgivings as to how her brother will react to all this. I do remember cautioning you on the affair when you first became acquainted with Miss Kingsley—but would you listen?"

"I have to admit the prospect of meeting with her brother does fill me with trepidation."

"Then do not let it," said his sister firmly. "You must stand up to Lord Kingsley. Do not let him bully you into submission."

Stephen looked at his sister with admiration. "Unfortunately, I am not like you, Rachel. You have always encouraged me by being the sort of person you are, but I do not possess your confidence or strength of character."

Rachel looked at him sharply. "And with *that* attitude, Stephen, you will be sure to lose her," she admonished gently.

There was no time to say more; the coach was pulling into the yard of a wayside inn where they were to partake of refreshment before continuing on the remainder of their journey to Meadowfield Lodge. The inn was crowded with other travellers but, after Stephen had spoken with the landlord, they were escorted to a private room on the first floor.

Having finished his meal, Stephen left to have a word with their coach driver while his sister and brother finished their stew. Harry was slow at eating, having little appetite for food, his cold seeming much worse.

Rachel was distracted when two gentlemen were shown into the room by the landlord. After furnishing them with tankards of ale, he left to fetch the food they ordered. They paid scant attention to Rachel and her brother, who sat quietly in a corner of the room. She observed them absently, watching as they removed their large coats and tall hats and sat at one of the tables across the room from them.

It was obvious by their manner and dress that they were gentlemen. The smaller of the two had light brown hair, a pleasant countenance and a soft, rather delicate mouth. However, there was nothing delicate about his friend.

Rachel judged him to be about thirty-one or two and he was tall and impressive—over six foot and broad-shouldered, yet lean of body, in the athletic sense. The darkness of his countenance was accentuated by the dazzling white silk neckcloth he wore.

She noted his dark eyes and the richness of his thick, black curly hair and sideburns that curled down to his jaw, which was square and firm and clean shaven, his mouth large and firm. He wore a dark green frock coat, its collar of dark green velvet. His waistcoat was of dove grey silk, the same colour as his trousers.

The landlord brought their food, which the smaller gentleman began to attack with a hearty relish, but the dark-haired gentleman stood up and moved restlessly towards the window, drinking deeply of his ale, his black brows drawn together in moody contemplation of the rain continuing to fall heavily from a sky the colour of pewter. His friend, Sir Edgar Mainwaring, cast him a look of annoyance.

"For heaven's sake, William, do come and eat. You have been downcast and disagreeable ever since leaving London. This beef is quite delicious," he said, packing a piece into his mouth. "Come—don't let it go to waste."

"Thank you, no. I have no appetite," he replied, his voice deep with resonance.

"Don't tell me you're still fretting over your brother's failure to turn up in London?" said Edgar.

"Yes, if you must know I am. We should have met up at Kingsley House on my return, but as you know he failed to appear. I have been informed by an acquaintance of mine that he's taken up with an actress—an actress, indeed—" he scoffed angrily, "and that most of his time is spent at the theatre. Why he has to consort with women belonging to such an unworthy, disreputable profession, whose situation in life is so definitely beneath his own, is quite beyond me."

"Why, you hypocrite," reproached Edgar, pausing briefly in his eating and showing some amusement, which only increased his friend's anger. "There is no one who likes the theatre more than you do. Come—admit it?"

William chose to disregard his friend's question as he turned and scowled at him.

''I have been away from England too long, Edgar. It would appear not only my sister but also my brother have been allowed far too much liberty. He has to learn he cannot live any way he likes. Oh, he has good qualities, that I grant. He is intelligent and does not lack common sense—but he is headstrong and has a tendency to resist authority—which at times makes him reckless and irresponsible.''

''Good heavens! I see nothing wrong in your brother enjoying the favours of an actress, if they are freely given. He is only involved in a romantic liaison with the girl. Where is the harm in that, pray? It's not as if he were planning on marrying her.''

''And how can I be certain of that? These actresses exhibit themselves shamelessly for money, cavorting with every male member of the audience. The vulgarity of their profession bars them from any respectability. No doubt to hook a gentleman of my brother's calibre from the audience is the grand finale of the show.''

His words had an aggressive ring to them and, turning suddenly, he put down his tankard on the table in a way that betrayed his suppressed anger. He moved once more to stand by the window, looking out, his body taut, his hand resting high against the wall, clearly quite put out by his brother's seemingly irresponsible behaviour and his friend's easy tendency to condone it.

''Your condemnation is unnecessarily severe, William,'' Edgar demurred. ''Why—theatres are growing in popularity all the time and there are some refined, extremely talented and highly versatile actors and actresses on the London stage. I know several myself—and so do you, come to think of it. There's many a time you've taken a box at Drury Lane.''

"They can be an amusing form of diversion, I grant you—both versatile on stage as well as off,'' William replied with irony. ''During my absence, it appears that my brother has become an ardent visitor to the gaming halls as well as the theatre, and an expert in dispensing his favours and his money with merry abandon. I have a distinct feeling that he is about to plunge the whole family into a frightful scandal.''

Having finished her own meal, Rachel was sitting quietly in the corner of the room with Harry, patiently attentive as she tried to coax him to eat some of the mutton and vegetable stew the landlord had recommended, hoping it would dispel his pallor and help revive his spirits a little.

All the while, she had been unable to do other than listen to the angry discourse between the two gentlemen across the room. The tall dark gentleman was clearly angered by his brother's behaviour, while the other gentleman was trying hard to placate him.

Rachel considered that the content of their discourse was hardly a matter to be discussed with such loud fervour in the presence of a thirteen-year-old boy. He was clearly listening to them, and they were succeeding in distracting him from the food she was so anxious he should eat.

Her own anger was rising and she felt victimised; her sister could well be one of the actresses of whom the tall gentleman spoke with such biting censure. Unable to sit and listen to him a moment longer, she stood up quickly and crossed the room, addressing herself to the gentleman by the window.

"I would be obliged, sir, if you would kindly keep your opinions to yourself. You are upsetting my brother."

William turned his head and looked her full in the eyes, fixing her with a gaze of angry indifference. "I am? Then I am sorry to hear it. Perhaps, if your brother has such sensitive ears and is so easily offended, it would be best for all concerned if he were to leave the room—then we could all air our opinions without danger of giving offence."

"No, sir, he will not leave the room. After learning that your brother is some kind of accomplished Lothario with a penchant for actresses, then I myself have no wish to hear more, either—so I would be obliged if you would either voice your opinions in a more temperate manner or leave the room yourself. The cold air might go some way to banishing your ill humour."

The young woman's anger and deep blue-eyed animosity might at any other time have amused William, and he might have taken time to admire her slender form and the flawless beauty of her face, but now he did not smile. His temper was not improved by her bold attack, which caused his lean face to darken and his lip to curl scornfully across his even white teeth.

"And I, madam, would be obliged if you would see fit to mind your own business."

"At least I keep my own business to myself, sir, and do not air my opinions so vociferously in public."

William's mouth was tight and his black eyes snapped fiercely as he fixed her with a savage look. There was a murderous expression on his face and it was with a great deal of effort that he restrained himself. "You are extremely outspoken, madam."

"Not usually," she replied, looking at him with a cool hauteur that belied the anger mounting inside her to match his own. "Only when I find myself in the presence of someone as insufferable as yourself. No matter what your station in life, sir, I have seen better manners among the meanest born.

"The vulgar and incomprehensible remarks you made against the women who choose the stage as their profession were harsh indeed—and decidedly unjust. It is with opinions such as these that there is little wonder your brother chose to relinquish his meeting with you. I cannot say that I blame him."

William's face paled significantly beneath his dark countenance, although he was furious with himself more than with her—for he seldom betrayed his feelings in this manner. Before he could reply to her scornful remarks Edgar, sensing the unpleasantness crackling between the two of them, stood up to intervene.

"I say—there is no need for this unpleasantness, surely," he said in an attempt to take the heat out of the situation. "This young lady is quite right, William. You are being extremely boorish. I apologise for my friend if he has upset you in any way, madam. It was not intentional, I do assure you."

For the first time Rachel unlocked her gaze from that of his friend and looked at Edgar, a softness entering her eyes and her face breaking into a warm smile—which Edgar found absolutely enchanting and went a long way to infuriating his friend further.

"Thank you, sir—but I am quite sure your friend is more than capable of making his own apologies—should he think fit, of course. However, I would advise you to be more selective in your choice of friends in future."

Aware that Harry had left the table and was crossing the room to where she stood, she again fixed the tall gentleman with a look of cool contempt. "You, sir, are the most conceited, ill-mannered person I have ever met and I sincerely hope I do not have the misfortune of doing so again." She smiled at his friend. "Good day to you, sir." Turning quickly, she moved towards her brother. "Come, Harry. Let us go and see what is keeping our brother."

Picking up her reticule, Rachel left the room with Harry. A low whistle escaped Edgar's lips as he watched her go, his eyes full of admiration, while his friend glowered at the doorway through which she had disappeared.

"My—what a termagant and enchantress she is. I would not have missed that for the world. It would seem you have finally met your match, William. But I must say she was right, you know," he admonished. "It was quite discourteous of you to speak to her as you did—it is not like you—and the young lady was justified in asking you to moderate your tone. Clearly she was quite concerned about her brother, who seemed far from well to me."

"Really! I have to say I failed to notice."

"Clearly. It is not like you to let your anger get the better of your discretion, William. It was most unwise of you to enter into a quarrel with such a charming and attractive young woman. You do not need me to tell you that the gentlemanly thing to do would be to go after her and offer your most sincere apologies."

William regarded his friend with genuine astonishment. "I most certainly will not."

"Then you are not the man I took you for," said Edgar, quite disgruntled and returning to do justice to his roast beef, which was in danger of going cold.

At last some of William's anger relaxed its grip. Aware of his friend's deep displeasure caused by his failure to do the decent thing and apologise to the young woman, and knowing he would get no peace between here and his home unless he did so—and beginning to feel a sense of shame for his unforgivable conduct—he strode across the room and went down the stairs, seeing the young woman crossing the yard to a waiting carriage.

"Please wait," he commanded, stepping out into the rain.

Rachel paused at the sound of his voice, her anger touched with surprise. Harry, eager to be out of the rain, ran quickly to the carriage and clambered inside for shelter. She turned and looked at the tall gentleman striding towards her with astonishing agility and grace for all his height, having to tilt her head slightly to meet his eyes.

Some deep-rooted feminine instinct made her breath catch in her throat on being suddenly confronted by a man of such powerful physical presence. Unexpectedly, she found herself the victim of an acute attack of awkwardness and momentarily at a loss for words, for out here in broad daylight—and in such close proximity—his overwhelming masculinity seemed more pronounced.

Despite her outward calm, inside she was quaking, but she did not lower her gaze beneath his penetrating assessment of her face as he continued to study her for a long, uncomfortable moment.

For the first time, William took full measure of her beauty and he looked with interest, drawn to it, feeling a stirring of admiration. Her face was both beautiful and intelligent and there was a defiant and determined thrust to her small chin as she squared up to him—at odds with her generous mouth, with lips tantalisingly soft and trembling and asking to be kissed, hinting at unimaginable, passionate delights.

Her brows were arched and sleek, her eyes, searching his in a cool and candid manner, a wonderful shade of dark blue with pupils as black as jet, slanting and slightly tinged with shadows beneath the brim of her bonnet. He began to regret the angry words they had exchanged, spoken in the heat of the moment.

"Please allow me to offer my apologies. My friend was quite right. My behaviour towards you was unpardonable."

The words were harsh but the anger had gone. Rachel continued to meet his gaze directly, sensing his apology was offered with reluctance rather than willingness, and that he had been urged to do so by his friend.

"You are correct," she said, her voice unrelenting and colder than she intended as she struggled to overcome the effect he was having on her, arousing sensations she had thought never to feel again, "but you have wasted your time. Your behaviour *was* unpardonable, your manners atrocious.

"Did I not know that you have been prompted by your friend to follow me out here to apologise, then I would have believed you to be sincere—but as it is—I cannot. Good day to you, sir."

William's face stiffened into a hard mask and he gave her a long, incredulous look. Then his anger returned and he was irritated by her obstinacy and in no mood to indulge in further argument.

"Then forgive me—I shall trouble you no further. Good day, madam."

He bent his tall frame in a curt bow and without another word spun on his heel and went back inside the inn, leaving Rachel to walk to the coach. Stephen joined her, observing her vexed countenance.

"Why—Rachel—what is it?"

"That insufferable man!" she exclaimed, climbing inside the coach.

Stephen climbed in after her. "I saw you talking to him. What did he say? You are upset."

"Not upset, Stephen. I am angry. I have to say he is the most arrogant, conceited man it has ever been my misfortune to meet."

"Then I can only regret that he was shown into the same room as yourself—for I have to tell you that the gentleman who has so clearly vexed you was none other than Lord Kingsley."

Rachel stared at him in amazement, momentarily rendered speechless. "Lord Kingsley!" she said at length. "But you must be mistaken."

"Sadly—no. I've just been speaking to his coach driver, who confirmed his identity."

"Then I was not favourably impressed. His ungentlemanly behaviour does not surprise me in the slightest. I despise him and I despise everything he stands for. I apologise if our angry interchange has ruined any chance you might have of securing his sister's hand in marriage—and I have to say that if I were you I would not have Lord Kingsley for a brother-in-law for a gold crown."

As the coach gathered pace on the increasingly slippery roads Rachel turned away from her brother's dejected countenance and gazed out of the window, recollecting what Lord Kingsley had said about his sister, who she knew must be Amanda—he did not have another. He had said that she, as well as his brother, had been allowed far too much liberty while he had been away from England.

What had he meant by that? Was it possible that he had heard of Amanda's association with Stephen and disapproved of it? If so, then she found herself feeling extremely sorry for her brother.

No matter how hard she tried, she was unable to banish the insufferable Lord Kingsley from her mind. She had been prepared to dislike him—and she had not been disappointed, for he was everything she had imagined him to be.

Her first impressions of him, now she had become acquainted with him, had been justified—but no one had told her how strikingly handsome he was, or that he possessed an overwhelming, physical masculinity that had the power to render her defenceless, to make the blood run warm in her veins.

Their meeting had been brief and emotive, but she had felt his magnetism and knew he was capable of arousing emotions and sensations inside her—painful and disturbing, though pleasurable, sensations that she had fought to suppress ever since her unhappy affair with Ralph Wheeler two years ago. His rejection of her had been harsh and cruel indeed, causing her to lock her heart and vow never to fall in love again.

But that was before she had met Lord Kingsley. Dislike him she might, but he had the power to remind her that she was still human, still a woman of warm flesh and blood, and not as immune to the physical allure of the opposite sex as she thought she was—as she wanted to be. *This* she had been quite unprepared for.

Chapter Two

Harry was put to bed the moment they arrived at Meadowfield Lodge, a large manor house in a wooded, picturesque setting just two miles from the small market town of Ellerton. Leaving Mrs Armstrong, the housekeeper, fussing about him like a mother hen, Rachel went down to find her father, his silver head bent over some ledgers, in his study.

George Fairley was a thin man of medium height, with an abiding and gentle nature, who cared deeply for all his children—although how he wished Stephen, his heir, possessed some of his two daughters' strength of mind and they some of his compliance. His dear wife—dead these past three years had been self-willed and in possession of a sharp intelligence, which both Kitty and Rachel had inherited.

Both were headstrong and impetuous young ladies—Rachel having become more so of late; in fact, ever since the death of her mother and Kitty's departure for the theatre. Because of his own increasing ill health—which he knew worried her a great deal, however hard she tried not to show it—she had now taken on the problems of the whole family.

Rachel crossed the room towards her father, deeply concerned about him. His face was seamed and lined, his skin like parchment. His heart was weak and he was frequently racked with a troublesome cough that would sap his strength. The doctor visited him frequently and, thankfully, the medicine he prescribed usually helped for a short while, offering him some relief.

Rachel loved her father with all her heart and worried about him all the time. Her mother's death and Kitty's leaving had taken something out of him; she felt a strong need to protect him from any further worry. She was thankful that of late he had placed most of his business affairs in Stephen's capable hands, relieving himself of a great burden.

He looked up when she entered.

"Well, Rachel—" he beamed at her "—it's good to have you home again. You enjoyed your visit to London, I hope?"

"Yes, very much," said Rachel going to him and placing her arm affectionately about his thin shoulders, thinking sadly how frail he had become. Trying not to show her concern, she planted a light kiss on his brow. "Although I regret taking Harry on the river, for I fear that was where he caught his chill."

"I dare say he'll get over it now he's home with Mrs Armstrong and yourself to fuss over him. He's a strong boy with a good constitution and will not be down for long. I wonder how he will take it when I tell him that Mr Nolan is to leave us," he said.

Looking at his daughter from beneath lowered lids, he chose his words with care for, considering the friendship that had developed between the two of them over the past months, he knew this would come as something of a surprise to her also.

He was right in his thinking; Rachel stared at him in shocked amazement. "Mr Nolan is leaving us? But what on earth for?"

"As well you know, he has never made any secret of his interest in politics—in which area he is ambitious to carve himself a career—although I find his views slightly too radical myself. I believe he has been tempted up to Yorkshire by Mr Wilberforce to assist in bringing voters to the polls. I do not doubt that we shall see him as a Member of Parliament before very long."

Rachel was saddened by this news, for she would miss Mr Nolan and their interesting debates sorely. Although, from the outset, when he had come to Meadowfield Lodge to be Harry's tutor, she had not been deceived: Kitty had been the true object of his interest.

Kitty, with her head high in the clouds, with never a thought of marrying anyone and settling down, her whole being and reason for living captivated by the idea of becoming an actress, had hardly been aware of it. She had treated him with amusing indifference, in direct contrast to the seriousness of her admirer, and saw no necessity of making herself agreeable to him.

Recovering from a shattered love affair with Ralph Wheeler and reluctant to become romantically involved again with any man and to risk being hurt a second time—as well as having to endure pity and sympathetic kindness from family and friends once more—Rachel's own interest in Mr Nolan was confined to his intellectual capacity; she was not in the least jealous of the interest he had showed in Kitty.

Hemmed in, and often oppressed by the restrictions imposed on the female sex by the society of that time, he had opened Rachel's mind to worldly affairs, making her realise just how ignorant she was.

Since Kitty had left Meadowfield Lodge twelve months earlier, Mr Nolan had endured her absence in a sad and dignified manner. But Rachel was deeply conscious of his inner suffering, so it did not surprise her that he had decided to give up tutoring to enter politics.

"But what about Harry's education? You will have to set about finding him another tutor—although you will be hard pressed to find one as competent and likeable as Mr Nolan."

"I am considering sending Harry away to school—if the idea appeals to him, that is. It will be good for him to be in the company of other boys. But tell me how you found Kitty? She is well, is she?"

"Kitty is very well," Rachel replied, smiling fondly at her father, knowing he had been waiting anxiously for news of his eldest daughter ever since their departure for London, although, when she had seen Kitty at her lodgings, she had noticed a change in her.

Rachel had thought she had seemed preoccupied and had looked a little pale, which she had put down to her working too hard at the theatre, for Kitty had explained that being an actress was an extremely demanding profession and she had often been compelled to keep late nights because of either the lateness of the show or rehearsals.

Since the closure of the theatre for the summer months she had worked long hours in the fruit shop, for Kitty had been determined to support herself from the outset, refusing to accept the offer of an allowance from her father. Rachel had been a little concerned about her, but said nothing to her father, not wishing to worry him unduly.

"And has she still got her head set on carving out a profession for herself in the theatre?"

"Very much so. Although I have to say that, by all accounts, she appears to be extremely talented— more so than any of us have given her credit for. As yet she has to be given a major role—but she is certainly a rising star."

"From the moment I took her to London on her eighteenth birthday to see a play at Drury Lane she fell prey to the allure of the theatre. I've often wished we had remained at home instead."

"She would have found her own way there eventually, Father," said Rachel gently. "You have nothing to reproach yourself with. Kitty was determined to become an actress. You did everything in your power to dissuade her, but your objections and pleas for her to think again fell on deaf ears.''

Her father nodded, a deep sadness entering his tired grey eyes, knowing Rachel spoke the truth. He had done his utmost to discourage Kitty from leaving home to become an actress. He was an honourable man of high principles, loving and caring, and he had always been available for all his children. He was not likely to turn away should one of them decide to stray from the fold.

When Kitty had told him of her decision to become an actress—regardless of how outrageous and degrading the profession was considered to be for a gentleman's daughter by the standards of the time, by most of their neighbours and the small, closely knit community of Ellerton—it was not in his nature to banish her from his home.

Even though the sort of life she had chosen to lead would be like poison to a decently brought-up young woman's mind, daily he hoped that she would see the error of her ways, come to her senses and return home.

At the time Rachel, who was three years younger than Kitty and extremely fond of and close to her sister, had said little; her own private opinion was one of criticism, for she had been irritated by what she had considered to be her sister's selfishness and utter disregard to the pain her decision to become an actress had caused their father—and so soon after their mother's demise.

True to his nature, there had been no thought of recrimination on his part as he had watched her go to serve her apprenticeship with a provincial theatrical company in Bath, before being spotted for her talents and recruited to the company of the theatre in Drury Lane. He had known that she would go with or without his blessing and so, loving her as he did, he had given it.

But Kitty, regarded by her family as being headstrong and unpredictable, had given no thought to the fact that her actions could damage or bring shame to her family, and especially to Rachel's own prospects of making a decent marriage. It had ruined her chances of ever marrying Ralph Wheeler, a young well-to-do gentleman who had lived in Oxford, with whom she had fallen deeply in love with all the passionate ardour of youth.

The moment his family had found out about Kitty's attachment to the theatre, Ralph had ceased to call on her at Meadowfield Lodge. No explanation had been given, but Rachel had known that for this reason his parents had been set against any union between them. In no time at all, she had heard that he had married a young woman of equal wealth but with no scandal attached to her name, wounding Rachel more deeply than anyone had realised.

"Have you seen anything of Aunt Mary while we've been in London, Father?" Rachel asked in an attempt to steer the conversation away from Kitty and dispel the sad, sombre look in her father's eyes.

"Yes—as a matter of fact, I have. My dear sister

called just this morning. She's very excited about Lord Kingsley's expected return to Mortlake Park and has been in quite a flap for days now. She intends entertaining more than usual in the hope that he will notice one of her girls.''

He smiled, looking lovingly at Rachel and lowering his tone to a conspiratorial whisper. ''Although neither of them can hold a candle to you, Rachel—even though I do say so myself. With your looks, you'll no doubt dazzle our noble neighbour and steal him from right under their very noses.''

Recollecting the unpleasant encounter she'd had with the aforesaid gentleman, Rachel gave him a wry smile. ''That I very much doubt, Father.''

''It's strange that we have lived at Meadowfield Lodge for the past five years and the only members of the Kingsley family we have met are Miss Amanda and her brother James—who, I believe, is in London at this time and whose reputation is described as being somewhat dubious.

''His elder brother, Lord Kingsley, has always struck me as being an elusive sort of character, spending much of his time in the West Indies as he does. Although my dear sister has informed me that he now intends settling at Mortlake Park for good.''

''Yes, I have heard that, also.''

''I wonder when we will have the pleasure of meeting another member of the family,'' her father mused.

''I already have—this very afternoon.''

Her father looked at her curiously. ''Oh? Then I assume you are referring to Lord Kingsley himself—

seeing as his stepmother never leaves the house. Although why a woman should want to keep herself cooped up inside such a great house—grand though it is—is quite beyond me.

"There are some who say she is of a somewhat eccentric nature and docs not enjoy the best of health—for which I must sympathise. Her father owned a plantation on Antigua, I believe, which was where Lord Kingsley's father met her. She was an only child and her family no longer own any property on the island—but my sister has led me to understand that both James and Amanda will become extremely wealthy on her death."

"Yes—so I believe. A good catch for anyone. However, it was James's elder brother, Lord Kingsley, I encountered at the inn where we stopped for refreshments on our journey from London."

"I see," said her father with interest. "And what did you make of him? Was he the formidable gentleman he is reputed to be? Or was he quite the opposite?"

"I suppose he could be, if the mood took him, but I have to say I found him to be the former—and full of his own importance. Lord Kingsley did not endear himself to me in the slightest. I found him wanting in both manners and civility. He did not conduct himself with the dignity worthy of a member of the peerage."

Her father looked at her with some surprise. "Dear me, such harsh censure. What has the poor man done to warrant your low opinion, Rachel?"

Quickly Rachel gave her father an account of her meeting with Lord Kingsley. When she had finished, he shook his head, a deeply troubled expression having appeared on his face as he listened to his daughter recount Lord Kingsley's reference to the lowliness of an actress's profession.

"If people make such disparaging remarks as these, then Kitty will have to be a determined young woman indeed to withstand them. Where was Stephen while this unpleasant encounter was taking place?"

"Outside with the coachman."

"Then, taking into consideration his fondness for Miss Kingsley, I do not suppose he was well pleased. Were you introduced to Lord Kingsley?"

"No."

"Then if you should meet again—for it is certain you will at some time, given your aunt's extensive programme of social events at which Lord Kingsley will be top of her invitation list—it seems I shall have to be present in order to keep the peace." He chuckled. "Now come, my dear, let us go in search of Stephen. I'm sure you must both be quite ravenous after your journey."

Before coming to Meadowfield Lodge, the Fairleys had lived in London. They were a family of considerable wealth, their fortunes lay in the coal which had been mined up in Newcastle, going back to the time of Charles II when one of their ancestors—as a reward for his loyalty to the King—was awarded an annuity of one thousand pounds and a small royalty on coal dues in the north. Over the years as manufacturing increased, so did the demand for coal and the Fairleys' wealth.

However, their wealth was not as considerable as that of George Fairley's widowed sister Lady Mary Brayfield, who had made a prestigious marriage. Because of the Fairleys' lack of rank, George's daughters could not expect to make such esteemed marriages as their cousins, Lady Mary's daughters, Caroline and Emily.

Living so close and both having lost their partners in life served a mutual purpose for George Fairley and his widowed sister. On occasion she would act as chaperon to his daughters—although since Kitty's departure for the stage there was only Rachel—and he as his sister's companion.

This was seldom of late, for, sadly, the deterioration in his health did not allow him to move far from Meadowfield Lodge or to partake in the exhausting excitement of many social events.

On Lord Kingsley's return to Mortlake Park, after being in the West Indies for the past six months, his sister's visits to Ellerton Hall to see Caroline and Emily—where, by design, Stephen would also happen to be—had become less frequent. Deprived of the pleasure of her company, he had become sunk in gloom and despondency.

Because Rachel had been kept busy nursing Harry through his severe chill, she had been unable to visit Ellerton Hall. It had been after one of Stephen's dutiful visits to their aunt Mary that she had asked him about Miss Kingsley.

"According to our cousins," he told her, his mood one of dejection, "she spends a great deal of time with Lord Kingsley's friend, Sir Edgar Mainwaring, who is staying at Mortlake for a few weeks. He is very attentive towards her, by all accounts, and Caroline told me herself that she is sure Lord Kingsley has marked him out for Amanda.

"He has been a close friend of her brother's for many years and thinks very highly of him. Clearly he is a most suitable connection; both Caroline and Emily are certain that if anything comes of it they will be very happy together. I fear I have been slighted, Rachel," he finished miserably.

"From what I can remember of Sir Edgar, he was quite charming, but not for one moment do I think you have been slighted—especially not by Miss Kingsley. Such an insult is not in her nature. It will be her brother's doing—that you can be sure of."

"Then what is to be done, Rachel?"

"You must go to Mortlake Park and confront Lord Kingsley. If you value his sister's friendship and wish to win her over, then you must be firm and decisive in this matter, or by your complaisancy it is certain you will lose her."

"But maybe she no longer cares for me."

"Having observed the two of you together, Stephen, by her very look I can see she has more than a hint of affection for you. If you already have her heart, then she will not so easily give it to another—

even if that other happens to be a man of her brother's choosing.''

''But you can hardly expect him to approve of his sister allying herself to a man of my station—without rank or breeding. I feel I am a little out of their class.''

''The Fairleys are a highly respectable family, Stephen,'' Rachel chided him. ''Our connections may not be aristocratic, but they are certainly not to be ashamed of. Why—you and our father are each as much a gentleman as Lord Kingsley. Besides—a title does not make a man a gentleman in the literary sense of the word. Anyone who is acquainted with you could not doubt your respectable reputation and dependability.''

''Nevertheless, I cannot compete with Sir Edgar Mainwaring who, like Lord Kingsley, can claim connection to some of the greatest peers in the land.''

Rachel turned from him to go in search of Harry. ''Go to Mortlake Park and face Lord Kingsley,'' she said, pausing and looking back from the doorway at his downcast face, ''and who knows—he may prove to be a more amiable man than the ogre he has been depicted. Although,'' she said, her tone taking on a note of gentle teasing, ''after my own disagreeable encounter with him at the inn on our journey from London—I am sorry to have to say that I very much doubt it.''

It was at Ellerton parish church, three weeks after their return from London, that Rachel had her second encounter with Lord Kingsley. As usual, she was attending Sunday morning matins, seated between her father—who was feeling well enough to attend the service—and her aunt Mary on the hard wooden bench of the pew. Her cousins Emily and Caroline were seated with Stephen and Harry—who had recovered from his severe chill—in the pew in front.

Just before the ageing pastor began the service, she was aware of a stir among the congregation. Turning slightly, she saw that two gentlemen and a young lady had just entered the church and were seating themselves in the Kingsleys' family pew towards the back of the church.

A ripple of whisperings spread throughout the congregation, for it was quite an event to see any member of the eminent Kingsley family present at a church service—only Miss Amanda on occasion.

Over the years, the present Lord Kingsley's father—who had not been a particularly likeable man—had possessed little time for the church and, in consequence, the family pew had remained noticeably empty—although the ancient marble tombs inside the humble church were occupied by several of their ancestors.

Rachel recognised Miss Amanda Kingsley, who knelt demurely, bowing her head over her hands clasped in prayer. She also recognised the pleasant countenance of Sir Edgar Mainwaring, but when her eyes came to rest on Lord Kingsley, nothing could have prepared her for the unimaginable thrill that shot through her, a quivering excitement that almost took her breath away.

He was exactly as she remembered him—tall and darkly featured and just as incredibly handsome. His hat was held in his gloved hand and his head proudly set. His expression was alert and one of highly charged emotion, as if he battled with some inner thought.

It was not until he met her gaze, his eyes widening in recognition and total surprise, that she realised she was staring at him across the yawning abyss that separated them. Observing the stern set of his features and remembering the unpleasantness of their previous encounter, whether it was the time that had elapsed since then which had softened her anger, or the aura of godliness which filled the ancient church, Rachel's opinion of him had softened slightly.

Was he always so serious, she asked herself, so severe? But then, she thought with mild amusement, since returning to Mortlake Park, perhaps the poor man had little to smile about. Maybe allowances should be made and she should not judge him too harshly, for what right had she when she was neither acquainted with his manner nor the peculiarities of his nature?

She turned from him, giving her attention to her prayer book, although throughout the service as she tried to keep her eyes fixed on the altar and the pastor in his white surplice, and recite the holy words of the prayers she knew by heart, she could feel Lord Kingsley's dark eyes burning holes into her back. She was certain he observed her every move.

When the final amen had been said, the congregation slowly drifted outside into the bright glare of the morning sunlight. From where he was standing, Lord Kingsley observed Rachel coming out of the church, clutching her prayer book in her gloved hands.

She stopped to speak to someone, smiled and began to walk along the path in his direction where he had paused to speak to the pastor, who was effusing at length on the honour it was to see him and his sister among the congregation. Rachel had no alternative but to pass close by him in order to reach the gate which led out on to the road.

Lord Kingsley saw that she moved with dignity and grace and was quite tall and perfectly proportioned. As she came closer, he saw that her skin was flawless, her hair beneath her bonnet of a dark and lustrous quality and her eyes, filled with animation and intelligence and dominating her face, as he well remembered, were of a deep shade of blue, slanting attractively upwards.

Her lips were pink and delectable, hovering between a pout and a wickedly attractive smile, her eyes unable to hide some amusement caused by an inner thought. He lowered his head in acknowledgement and watched her pass on, observing her turn her head slightly and glance back at him, her mouth turning provocatively up at the corners.

With the pastor's words falling on his deaf ears, William stared after her, his features as expressionless as one mesmerised. He watched her walk down the path towards the road, curious as to who she could be and determined to find out more about her.

Rachel stopped by their carriage standing outside the church gate. With Harry by his side and his hand resting on his son's narrow shoulder, her father had stopped to speak to his sister, who was hovering outside the church porch with Caroline and Emily in the hope of having a word with Lord Kingsley when he had finished speaking to the pastor.

Stephen, she saw, was in happy conversation with Miss Kingsley, who was dressed in dark blue. She had a graceful slenderness and was quite tall with fine-boned, sharp features and a poetic countenance. Her hair was fair, her eyes soft and brown.

Rachel smiled suddenly when she saw a beaming Sir Edgar coming quickly towards her.

"Why—this is a surprise—and a very pleasant one too, I might say. You do remember our meeting at the inn, I hope?"

"Of course I remember." She smiled.

He frowned suddenly, recollecting the unpleasant circumstances of that encounter. "Yes, you would, wouldn't you? I imagine such a meeting would be difficult to forget. I'm afraid my friend Lord Kingsley was not in the best of humour that day."

"Now that I do remember." She laughed. "I can only hope that his temper is much improved."

"Yes, indeed it is. Tell me, do you live in Ellerton?"

"About two miles outside—on the Oxford road."

Edgar turned slightly to Lord Kingsley who, drawn towards the young woman who, regrettably, had experienced the violent impact of his temper on the day he had returned to Mortlake Park, had come to stand beside him.

He was so aloof, so superior, so carelessly confident and aware of his power and masculinity, making Rachel acutely conscious of his presence. She bobbed a curtsy and, with a formal inclination of his head, he acknowledged her coolly, a barely perceptible smile playing on his lips, but Rachel was aware that, quite deliberately, he was turning on her the full force of his powerful personality.

His dark eyes, which she remembered had been filled with anger on their previous encounter, were cordial now, but she felt the pull of their magnetism and was in danger of being overthrown by it, for not since her association with Ralph Wheeler had a man looked at her in such a way as this.

Why she should think of Ralph just then she could only guess at, for she had suppressed all thought of him for so long, but the bold assessment of Lord Kingsley's gaze had brought unwanted memories back to haunt her, and she felt the chains that imprisoned her in the past begin to loosen. Lord Kingsley looked the perfect gentleman—but to Rachel's vulnerable and unhappy heart, he spelt danger.

After polite introductions had been made, he addressed her. "So, Miss Fairley, we meet again."

He spoke with the same deep resonance that Rachel remembered, each word exact, the tone and level of his voice conveying to her the measure of his self-control.

"Yes, we have met," she admitted, her voice cool

though not hostile. "Although I have to say that I am surprised you remember me."

"You made quite an impression on my friend," laughed Sir Edgar. "It's a rarity indeed for a young lady to have the courage to stand up to him when she is not accustomed to his temper."

"I am not afraid of Lord Kingsley," she said, meeting the aforesaid gentleman's direct gaze once again. His eyes were powerfully compelling, almost refusing her permission to look away. "Nor am I afraid to speak my mind when the occasion warrants it."

"You made that perfectly clear," he said. "Having had time for reflection, Miss Fairley, am I now forgiven? My behaviour to you then was unpardonable. I have reproached myself many times on my conduct that day. It was quite inexcusable."

"Your behaviour did not recommend you to me in the slightest, Lord Kingsley, but yes—" she relented, unable to prevent her lips from curving slightly in a smile, and not wishing to jeopardise further any chance Stephen might have of securing the hand of his sister "—you are forgiven."

"Thank you. Tell me, Miss Fairley, do you live locally?"

"Yes."

"And have you lived in Ellerton long?"

"Five years—no more."

"That long? I do not recall having seen you."

"Perhaps that is because I live about two miles outside Ellerton, Lord Kingsley, and also because you have been absent from these parts for long periods over the years."

"Unfortunately, that is so—but I hope to rectify that in the future."

"You are acquainted with my aunt, I believe," Rachel said, looking towards her aunt Mary who had been waylaid by the pastor as she had been hurrying to approach Lord Kingsley before he left the churchyard.

He followed her glance. "Ah—Lady Brayfield! She is your aunt?"

"Yes."

Lord Kingsley nodded. "Charming lady—with two fine daughters."

"Yes, indeed," reiterated Sir Edgar, glancing towards Caroline and Emily standing dutifully beside their mother, his eyes resting appreciatively on Caroline in a way that contradicted any suspicions Stephen might have that he had any designs on Lord Kingsley's sister. "Lady Brayfield has very kindly invited us to attend a party at Ellerton Hall next week, Miss Fairley—is that not so, William?"

"She has, indeed."

"It promises to be a fine evening—amusing and diverting. Are you to attend, Miss Fairley?"

"Yes—I believe so."

"I say," said Sir Edgar, his gaze suddenly diverted. "Who's that fellow your sister is conversing with, William?"

Simultaneously Lord Kingsley and Rachel looked to where Amanda was still talking to Stephen. They stood apart and Amanda's face was raised to his, her lips parted in a smile. There was a look of utter absorption on their faces, a look which told the onlookers that hidden emotions and the forces of nature were at work between these two—a look which excluded all else.

The meeting was a casual one, unexpected yet welcome to the two people under observation, but not, apparently, to Amanda's brother, whose sleek black brows were drawn together in a deep frown of disapproval. Rachel heard him take a deep breath and saw his eyes darken with anger.

Lord Kingsley watched as his sister, becoming suddenly aware of their scrutiny, turned and walked towards them with Stephen by her side. He frowned, clearly displeased.

Rachel saw that Amanda's eyes were aglow, her face pretty and pink—whether it was from the cool wind that blew in the churchyard, snaking its way between the thick dark yew trees and tall tombstone slabs, or Stephen's presence, was a matter for conjecture.

But one could not help noticing how close she stood to his side, how lovely she looked and how radiant—and how Stephen gazed at her with unfeigned admiration. However, Rachel could not help feeling sorry for Amanda; it could be no easy matter having Lord Kingsley for a brother.

Observing the tightening of Lord Kingsley's features when he looked at her brother, Rachel felt a stirring of anger inside her.

"Allow me to introduce my brother," she said with a note of defiance that no one could fail to be aware of. "Mr Stephen Fairley. Stephen, may I present Lord Kingsley and Sir Edgar Mainwaring?"

The atmosphere was formal, the moment one of awkwardness. It was plain to Rachel that Lord Kingsley was most displeased that his sister had been allowed to form such a close attachment with a man not of his choosing during his absence—and it was also plain that he would do all in his power to discourage it.

Taking his sister's elbow, Lord Kingsley bowed. "I am pleased to make your acquaintance," he said abruptly. The tone of his voice was impatient; it was plain that he was eager to be away. "Please—excuse us." His dark gaze swept over them in a dismissive manner, lingering for a moment on Rachel's face, which was open and defiant, before they moved on to their waiting carriage.

Standing beside the stiff form of his sister, Stephen sighed deeply. "Lord Kingsley is a fearsome-looking gentleman—don't you agree, Rachel?"

"So he seems. But I am not afraid of him, Stephen. My opinion regarding Lord Kingsley remains unchanged. The man is intolerable."

And yet, staring after him, Rachel saw his features in her mind's eye and felt an emotion, overwhelmingly at variance with the conclusion she had made as to his character, that troubled her greatly—an emotion she was reluctant to revive and did not wish to acknowledge.

Chapter Three

With his hands clasped lightly behind his back, William Kingsley stood looking out of the long window in the grand drawing-room at Mortlake Park, letting his eye wander appreciatively down the gentle sweep of velvety lawns towards the black waters of the slender lake glistening in the valley below. Several acres of woods and low rolling hills surrounded the house and valley.

After spending many years of his adult life in the West Indies overseeing his family's business affairs, it was good to be back in England—back at Mortlake, which had mellowed over the years, the golden yellow stones of which it was built streaked with reddish brown.

Mortlake Park was a perfect product of centuries of redesign and development, as each generation of Kingsleys had adapted it to fit their needs. William's inheritance was both ancient and beautiful, and he considered it a privilege to call it his home, where he hoped he could now settle down.

However, there was a dark cloud hanging over his family that could not be ignored. Ever since the demise of his father two years earlier, leaving him to care for James and Amanda, his father's children by his second wife—his first wife having died when William was in his infancy—his family had been beset with troubles that were a constant worry to him. Now, his most outstanding concern was his stepmother's health.

He turned from his quiet contemplation of the lake when one of the footmen announced the arrival of Mr Stephen Fairley. With interest, he watched the newcomer walk stiffly towards him, a nervousness about his manner. Whether it was from awe at finding himself in such magnificent surroundings, or fear at the reception he was to receive from its owner, was a matter for conjecture.

He stopped before William, who could see how he strove to overcome his nervousness, yet there was a simple pride in his upright bearing and the way Stephen looked him straight in the eye, which William admired, despite himself. Before he had returned to Mortlake—having received, from James in his letters, an account of Amanda's attachment to this young man—he had been determined to put an end to the relationship, but that was before he had made the acquaintance of his sister.

No matter how hard he tried, he could not banish Rachel Fairley from his thoughts. He was fascinated and drawn to her. She intrigued and tormented him in such a way that his instinct told him to tread with care where the Fairleys were concerned—especially with regard to the delicate matter of his sister's friendship with her brother.

His own half-brother, James, was no saint, being a wild young hoyden with a reputation for gaming, drinking and wenching with an assortment of mistresses from the theatre. William had come home with the intention of curbing James's wild ways, but as yet he had failed to locate him since returning from the Indies, and he could not return to London to search him out until this tiresome matter with his sister was settled.

On learning of Stephen Fairley's close friendship with his sister, he had made it his business to find out as much as he could about the Fairleys. They were well to do—of that there was no doubt, their money having been invested wisely and successfully by George Fairley's forebears in coal and in the manufacture of textiles in the north of the country.

Maintaining a modest lifestyle, the Fairleys lived without ostentation. Nothing but good was said of George, whose manners bespoke good breeding, and his son's behaviour and duty to his family could not be faulted.

The Kingsleys were members of one of England's oldest and wealthiest families and William could claim close acquaintance with many peers of the realm, whereas Stephen Fairley was of little consequence and with no suitable connections to recommend him—and yet he had the look and bearing of a gentleman.

Through his enquiries, William had learned that, against her family's wishes, George Fairley's eldest daughter had left home to carve herself a career on the stage. Because of it, her younger sister, Rachel, had suffered a broken romance, which, by all accounts, had wounded her deeply and from which, some said, she would never recover.

With their aristocratic background, the young man's family, finding it unacceptable for their son to be joined in an alliance to a young woman whose sister—though the family were prominent members of society—indulged in such low behaviour, had steered him in the direction of another, more suitable young woman.

William strongly suspected that this was Miss Fairley's reason for being on the defensive whenever they met, why she tried to appear unapproachable—when all the while, beneath her cool façade, there beat the heart of a woman with a burning desire to be loved.

As the two men faced each other, each remembered their meeting in Ellerton churchyard. Stephen was the shorter of the two, his body fine-boned and slender, with eyes that glowed deep blue—the only similarity he had to his wilful, bold and beautiful sister, William observed with a keen eye. He could feel the blood run warm in his veins when he thought of her, and was determined to be the one to exorcise the ghost of her lost love.

He received Stephen Fairley with cool politeness, his manner brusque but not hostile. "I am happy to welcome you to Mortlake Park, Mr Fairley. To what do I owe the pleasure?''

''Thank you for receiving me. I have a serious matter I wish to discuss with you, sir.''

''Let me be the judge of that, Mr Fairley.''

''Of course. It—it concerns your sister, sir.''

''Yes—I thought it might. I understand that during my absence you have formed an attachment to her—is that correct?''

''Yes.''

''So—what is it that you wish to see me about?''

''I—I am aware that what I am about to ask will take you by surprise, sir—but I would consider it an honour if you would consent to Miss Kingsley becoming my wife.''

Having fully expected this, William showed no surprise. There was a moment's silence before he spoke, his face remaining expressionless.

''Honoured! Yes. Considering your situation in life I am sure you would be,'' he replied with a touch of irony that was not lost on Stephen. ''However, Amanda is very young and extremely naïve in such matters. The romantic attachment she feels for you I put down to youthful infatuation.''

Stephen stiffened. ''There I have to contradict you, sir.''

William's eyebrows rose. ''Do you, indeed?''

''Your sister and I have come to care for each other deeply, sir—and whatever you may have heard, I must tell you that our friendship has not advanced beyond conversation. It has all been conducted in a decent and proper manner.''

''So I should hope. However, I have to say that the overtures you made to her during my absence do not meet with my approval. It is my wish that any acquaintance between you should cease—for the time being, at least.''

''I see. Then, does that mean I can hope?''

William seemed to consider his question carefully before favouring him with a reply. He nodded ever so slightly, looking him directly in the eye, speaking softly. ''Everyone is allowed to hope, Mr Fairley.''

''I have no title to offer her—no grand estates or family connections to match your own—but my family's wealth and the fact that I am my father's heir would guarantee that your sister lacked for nothing. The deep love and devotion I feel for her is unequalled.''

Remembering the look that had passed between his sister and this young man in the churchyard—a look that had told him there was true affection between them—William did not doubt his words. But, for reasons of his own—family reasons, whether right or wrong, that were best left unsaid—in all conscience he could not give his consent to an alliance between them at this time.

He could not deny that he liked and approved of Stephen Fairley. He was a fine, intelligent young man who would make Amanda a good husband and be an asset to the family. It pained him greatly to refuse his request; by doing so, he knew how deeply his refusal would hurt his sister. But he had no choice. He turned from him, finding it exceedingly difficult to continue looking into his deep blue eyes—eyes filled with hope and desperation.

"I am sorry, Mr Fairley. I cannot give my consent to your request at this time."

"What of Miss Fairley's mother? Should she not be consulted on this matter?" Stephen dared to venture.

"No," William replied quickly—much too quickly, Stephen thought. "Her mother is of the same opinion as myself—and besides, I do not wish to trouble her at this time. She is not in good health."

"Then am I to understand that you do not consider me a suitable match for your sister because my family circumstances do not meet with your approval?"

"It is not my intention to be disrespectful towards your family, Mr Fairley; from what I have heard of your father, I hold him in the highest regard. His reputation as a gentleman and a businessman is unequalled and, I regret to say, as yet I have not had the honour of making his acquaintance."

Stephen's face had taken on a youthful dignity as he looked at the older man. His age and inexperience were evident, yet he was prepared to stand his ground to defend his good name if required. "My father is a private man, Lord Kingsely, and benevolent, with a rational and cultivated mind. There is no one better."

"Yes—I am sure you are right, and your loyalty towards him is to be commended. Should I give my consent for you to form an alliance with my sister, then I fully understand the value of such a connection to your family, but I have to tell you that it simply cannot be. Amanda has been too long at Mortlake without company, her only companions being Lady Brayfield's charming daughters, for which I am grateful.

"But it is my wish that she leaves England for a while to travel—to broaden her mind. She is to accompany her aunt, who resides in London, on a tour of Europe very soon. She is to introduce Amanda into society. It will be good for her."

Trying hard not to show his wretched disappointment, Stephen paled and swallowed hard. "I see. May I enquire as to how long she will be gone?"

"Six months to a year, I think. Maybe longer."

"I see," Stephen replied with stiff politeness. "Then there is nothing more to be said. I bid you good day, sir, and thank you for sparing me a few moments of your valuable time."

On returning to Meadowfield Lodge, Stephen recounted his meeting with Lord Kingsley. His refusal to give his consent to an alliance between Stephen and his sister made Rachel upset and consumed with a disappointment that she could not quite analyse. She considered Lord Kingsley's treatment towards her brother to be harsh, indeed, and, seeing the pain and hurt filling Stephen's eyes, her response was immediate and one of anger.

"I have to say it, Stephen, but his refusal does not surprise me in the slightest. Lord Kingsley would not tarnish the ancient noble line of Kingsleys with the blood of a commoner. Was he impolite to you?''

"No. Not in the least."

"Then, perhaps if he were not so sure of his position and himself, it would have been a different matter entirely. It would be interesting to see how fast our proud neighbour would have consented to your proposal if his family were not quite so wealthy." She sighed, placing her hand comfortingly about his waist with sisterly affection in an attempt to banish the look of total dejection from his countenance.

"Do not be too downhearted, Stephen," she said gently. "Who knows what the future holds? Why—if the love between yourself and Miss Kingsley is as deeply committed as you say it is, then a trip to Europe is hardly going to change her mind. When Lord Kingsley sees this, and if he cares for his sister and can see that she will be happy with no other, then maybe he will relent."

Rachel tried to sound reassuring, but her words lacked conviction.

Stephen made the effort to force a smile to his lips. "I very much doubt it—and I believe you do, too." He sighed deeply. "Oh, Rachel—you can have no conception of what it is like to lose the person you love."

So lost was he in his own misery that he spoke without thinking, forgetful that his sister's loss of Ralph Wheeler had been as great, if not greater, than his own, which brought a painful stab to her heart.

* * *

Still smarting with wounded pride over Lord Kingsley's refusal to give his consent for him to marry Amanda, filled with an aching, awful sense of loss and unable to live at Meadowfield Lodge and not see his beloved Amanda—and having no wish to attend his aunt Mary's party where he would again have to face Lord Kingsley—Stephen left for London.

Seated beside her father in the carriage carrying them to Ellerton Hall one week later to attend the supper party, Rachel regretted her brother's decision not to attend, wishing he'd had the courage to stand and face Lord Kingsley despite his refusal to allow him to marry his sister.

Her father observed her closely, aware of how deeply Stephen's absence affected her. It was one of the reasons why he had struggled to overcome his weak and weary state in order to accompany her to the party.

"I am sorry Stephen is not with us," he said.

"So am I, Father. Although I do believe we have Lord Kingsley to thank for that."

Her father frowned. "Come now, Rachel. Do you have to be so inclined to think the worst of him all the time?

"From what Stephen told me of his visit to Mortlake Park, Lord Kingsley was in no way offensive and merely told him that any relationship between him and Miss Kingsley must cease for the time being. From that, one can only conclude that he did not refuse his consent for Stephen to marry his sister outright. There is some hope for the future. I must say that you have developed an unreasonable dislike for Lord Kingsley, Rachel.''

''Not so unreasonable, Father,'' she countered. ''Not when you consider the source of his wealth—which is an abomination in itself—and now this insult and humiliation, not only to Stephen, but to our family as a whole.''

Her father sighed, shaking his head wearily. ''Oh, dear. You do seem to have a propensity to go through life determined to dislike all men, my dear.''

''No—not all men,'' Rachel said, her eyes clouding with painful and bitter memories. ''Only those who bear a resemblance to Ralph Wheeler.''

Her father patted her hand, knowing just how painful it was for her to be reminded of her former love and how deeply hurt and humiliated she had been by his rejection of her. ''I know, my dear,'' he said gently, ''and I know just how much he hurt you—but Lord Kingsley in no way resembles Ralph. Try to be a little more tolerant towards him, will you?''

She smiled, squeezing his hand gently. ''Yes—I will try.''

''And whatever your feelings happen to be on the matter of his wealth—let us not make an issue of it. And, you know, Lord Kingsley may have just reasons not to give his consent for Stephen to marry his sister—and it is not for us to enquire into them. Why—had Miss Kingsley been my own daughter I, too, might have refused. She is young, after all, and a trip around Europe with her aunt will do her the world of good.''

"Then why not with her own mother? Do you not think it strange, Father, that no one ever sees her?''

"No, not in the least; it is no secret that Miss Kingsley's mother does not enjoy the best of health. But, Rachel,'' he said with a note of gentle warning, frowning and looking quite stern, ''I will not be on the cross with Lord Kingsley.

"Knowing your low opinion of him and how quickly your temper is roused, I will not have you being unpleasant to him at my sister's party tonight— or at any other time, come to that. You will behave in the manner in which you were raised. Let good manners and common sense prevail. You will be charm and politeness personified. Is that under-stood?''

His eyes looked directly into his daughter's, with a note of authority in his tone that he had often used in the past, but she had not heard in a long time since his illness had taken hold; it left her in no doubt as to his meaning. He was telling her there would be no long faces, no unladylike behaviour, and no words of recrimination or outraged family pride if she were to find herself in the company of Lord Kingsley.

"Yes, Father,'' she acquiesced softly, a slow flush tinting her cheeks as she lowered her eyes, giving no indication of the turbulence the prospect of meeting Lord Kingsley was having on her emotions.

The sun was declining when they reached Ellerton Hall, a warm breeze heralding the first breath of summer. The elegant house was set on a slight rise above water meadows on the edge of the town. A cavalcade of carriages carrying local dignitaries filed up the drive, depositing their dazzling occupants at the bottom of a short flight of steps.

Dressed in emerald green satin, with diamonds at her throat and her hair arranged in a mass of silver-grey curls, Lady Brayfield, supported by her brother, Rachel's father—who felt able to do so—received her guests.

Lady Brayfield was of medium height, slender and regal looking, with warm brown eyes and a welcoming smile, who loved entertaining. Her two daughters, Caroline and Emily, excitement lighting up their faces at the prospect of the long evening ahead of them, hovered behind her.

They were lively young ladies of similar stature. Caroline, the eldest and darker than Emily, was dressed fetchingly in lavender-coloured silk, while her sister was dressed in white with yellow trimmings.

Lady Brayfield enquired after Stephen and as usual avoided speaking of Kitty. She had been shocked and horrified by Kitty's decision to become an actress, considering her behaviour to be totally unacceptable. It had scandalised the entire neighbourhood and she refused to speak of her, being unable to forgive her complete disregard for the shame and disgrace she had brought on her family.

In high spirits, Caroline and Emily claimed Rachel immediately, whisking her away to enquire after Stephen, eagerly insisting on her telling them everything that had taken place on his visit to Mortlake Park to see Lord Kingsley.

The house was steadily filling up with guests, the atmosphere beginning to take on a joyous atmosphere as people greeted each other. Footmen moved among them, offering refreshment; voices were harmonious, with laughter rising above the conversation. The hall and downstairs reception rooms to be used during the evening were decked with flowers and the dining-room gleamed with brightness—of silver and crystal and pristine white tablecloths.

Rachel, who had felt uneasy about the evening for days, was relieved to find the party was larger than usual—about sixty guests in all—because of the expected presence of Lord Kingsley. Hopefully, with so many people milling about, she would escape having to converse with him.

He was the last to arrive, accompanied by Sir Edgar Mainwaring, who immediately left his side to dance attendance upon Caroline—she had become quite besotted by him after their meeting at Ellerton church.

Lord Kingsley entered Ellerton Hall with an air of utter assurance. Highly conspicuous, he seemed oblivious to the ripple of curiosity and excitement that swept among the already assembled guests, and the admiring feminine glances and appreciative whispers behind unfurled fans.

Exuding a strong masculinity few women could resist—and giving them the impression he was a man of lusty, unashamed appetites—with merely a look and a cynically humorous smile he had the ability to charm his way into most of their rapidly beating hearts.

His tall and lean, yet athletic, stature had a splendour to it, with which few other men in the room could compete. Casually taking a glass of wine from the tray of a passing footman, he moved among them with ease, tall and exceedingly handsome in his black frock coat. His neck tie was dazzling white, as was his damask waistcoat, its raised satined pattern catching the light from the many candles.

Rachel was quite unprepared for the way her heart gave a sudden leap, and she could not prevent a certain excitement from sweeping over her, making her realise that she was not as immune to his powerful masculine personality as she had thought.

All the other guests faded into the shadows beside him. His presence was like a positive force. His glance idly swept the crowded room until, drawn by her beauty, his eyes met hers, wide and direct. There was a cool impertinence on his face when he looked at her, his eyes bold and black, with a twinkle of appraisal in their depths. His lips curved in a crooked smile.

Rachel caught her breath, and for a brief moment experienced the same pleasurable feminine sensations as all the other women on whom he bestowed his enigmatic gaze. Scarcely aware of her actions, she made a little curtsy as he inclined his head in her direction, before dragging his eyes away and giving his hostess his full attention.

* * *

The evening was far advanced when, after doing her utmost to avoid him, they came face to face. During a break in the dancing, and flushed from dancing one of the country dances with an exuberant partner, she had retired to a quiet part of the room and was fanning her glowing cheeks, when suddenly he appeared in front of her.

She started violently, feeling her heartbeat quicken alarmingly. Surprise registered in her eyes and there was a sharp intake of her breath, but when the initial awkwardness of the shock of seeing him so close wore off—and she resolved not to let him see how much his presence disturbed her—she favoured him with a little curtsy before turning, about to walk away, but he halted her.

"Miss Fairley," he said, having no intention of letting her escape so easily. Having observed her moment of discomposure at his sudden appearance with an amused and satisfied eye, he would have to be blind not to see the torrent of emotion he unleashed in her whenever they met—and which she would, no doubt, hate him for.

He hadn't stopped thinking about her since he'd first seen her, when she'd bestowed on him a look that had declared war. But, he thought, with cynical amusement, he didn't imagine for one moment it was going to be war all the way between them—though it was a fight he was determined to win—knowing from many an impassioned experience that neither of them would be dissatisfied with the outcome.

''Is it my imagination or are you trying to avoid me?''

Noticing how one of his dark brows arched and how his eyes glittered down at her with derisive humour put Rachel instantly on the defensive, and she fixed him with a cool stare, trying to ignore the aura of confidence that surrounded him, the impact his closeness was having on her, and how his potent masculine virility was making her feel altogether too vulnerable. When she spoke, she tried to sound assertive, which wasn't easy, especially when she saw his lips curve in a slow smile.

''Avoid you? Now, why on earth would I do that? Although for the life of me I cannot think what we could possibly have to talk about,'' she said, her voice strained, the promise she had made to her father earlier to be charm and politeness personified in her dealings with Lord Kingsley instantly forgotten. She was angered by the way his dark penetrating eyes provoked in her a welter of disturbing emotions that threatened to discompose her completely.

William had been an interested observer throughout the evening, watching Rachel integrating herself in the dance—whether it was the fast rhythm of a jig or the slower steps of a progressive country dance. He had found her pleasing to watch as she had smiled and had talked to her partner when they had come together in the dance, throwing back her head and laughing delightedly at something he had said, the long slender column of her throat arching like the curved white throat of a swan.

She had moved with a mysterious grace and a sensuality that had the power to set a man's soul on fire, her eyes shining with a brilliance like sunlight on water. William thought how radiant she had looked, how she had outshone every other woman in the room in her dress of deep blue silk gauze—the same colour as her eyes—that provided a fluttering, floating effect, giving her a look of vulnerability.

That look was misleading, he thought with wry amusement, when he remembered how he had experienced the volatile nature of her temper and the quickness of her tongue at first hand. But he wasn't deceived, for he sensed that, hidden from the inquiring eyes of the world, was a soft defencelessness about her just waiting to be assailed.

"Oh—several things come to mind," he said lightly. "I could—by telling you how charming you look."

"Thank you," Rachel replied with unsmiling resentment, snapping her fan shut with a sharp click, "but I suspect that flattery is not your forte, Lord Kingsley. Your sister is well, I hope?"

"Yes, thank you. She is very well."

"I am surprised not to see her here this evening. The music and dancing are quite exceptional and I know how she loves to dance."

"So she does, but she is in London with her aunt at present. And your brother? He is not here either, I see."

"How observant you are, Lord Kingsley. No, Stephen is also in London—on family business. Your sister is to leave for the continent very soon, I understand?''

''Yes, that is so.''

''Then it is to be hoped that, when she returns to Mortlake, her ardour for my brother will have cooled.''

''Yes—let us hope so. She is young—she'll get over it.''

''And if she doesn't?'' Rachel asked softly, directly, her eyes challenging his.

William's handsome mouth became compressed and his expression unreadable. He fixed her with his imperious dark gaze and his tone was measured when he answered her. ''We shall see. It would seem that, during my absence, they formed quite an attachment—causing their passions for one another to dissolve any social distinctions which should have applied. Unfortunately, there was no one at Mortlake to prevent the relationship from developing the way it did.''

Once again Rachel's curiosity concerning Lady Kingsley, Amanda's mother, was roused, but she declined to enquire as to why she had not tried to halt the relationship.

''But it was all quite innocent,'' she said in defence of the couple. ''I can see nothing wrong in two people forming a romantic attachment. How can you defend yourself on this matter? Can you not put your sister's happiness above your pride, Lord Kingsley?''

''I am not ashamed of what I have done, Miss Fairley, and I do not feel that I have to defend what I do to you or anyone. My sister's happiness is all important to me. I would not hurt or distress her in any way. That is why I must make sure her choice of husband is the right one."

"Her choice?" Rachel exclaimed with slight emphasis. "Or yours? It would seem to me that you consider my brother's connections too little and his presumption too great. Perhaps you are contemptuous of his lack of rank—that because he does not spend his time in leisure or possess a title, then he does not possess the proper credentials required to be considered a gentleman."

"You have formed a harsh opinion of me, Miss Fairley. However, your assessment of my character means little to me—and the things you speak of bear little truth."

"Then I am puzzled."

"Puzzled! Do forgive me. I would not wish to be the cause of any discomfort you might feel. My reasons for refusing to consent to an alliance between your brother and my sister are not open to discussion."

"But you do oppose the match?"

"Naturally I oppose it—although it may surprise you that it affords me little pleasure. My sister is but seventeen years old."

"And for that reason you will not consent to their marriage?"

"No—since you ask. Not entirely for that reason."

"Then—recollecting the conversation I happened to overhear between yourself and Sir Edgar at the inn on our first encounter how you spoke of actresses with such severe censure—could it be that you know of my own sister's involvement in the profession?

"Let me see," she said, making a pretence of trying to remember his exact words when all the while she could recite every one of them by heart, so indelibly were they printed in her mind, "I believe you said that the vulgarity of their profession bars them from any respectability—that they cavort with every member of the audience and shamelessly exhibit themselves for money."

A spark ignited in the dark depths of William's eyes and his black brows knit together. "It is clear you have a remarkable memory, Miss Fairley, and I would be lying if I retracted anything I said that day."

"Dear me. Poor Stephen. With a sister belonging to such an unworthy, disreputable profession, he is hardly good social material. It would seem there is too much against him to be considered a suitable match for your sister. Although—I have to say that, from what I have come to know of her, she does not share your prejudice, sir."

Rachel had hoped to shock Lord Kingsley with her forthrightness, but he gave no sign of being disturbed by her words in the slightest. His eyes, full of disdain, remained fixed on hers.

"It seems to me, Miss Fairley, that it is you who are prejudiced, for I do not remember uttering one word in condemnation of your family's situation—it is none of my concern, in any case."

"No, you did not have to. Your manner and expression on being introduced to my brother outside the church in Ellerton were far more eloquent than any words you might have uttered.''

"I think you do me an injustice, Miss Fairley. You seem to have formed a firm opinion of my character before having acquainted yourself with me. However, I am flattered to learn that you have spared any of your time to think of me.''

"Don't be. I have long been acquainted with your character by those who have described you.''

"To my merit?''

"So you would hope—but quite the contrary, I assure you. Nothing I have heard regarding your character has been agreeable, Lord Kingsley.''

"I must say, Miss Fairley, that you seem well opinionated on the imperfections of my character—and I am not ashamed to admit that I have many faults. But…perhaps if you were to take the time to look into your own character instead of examining mine, then you might find that your own faults far outweigh my own.''

He stepped back just as the music was starting up again and couples were beginning to assemble on the floor. "I shall detain you no longer; it is plain that my presence clearly offends you. Excuse me, Miss Fairley.''

Rachel watched him walk away, hoping she would never have to speak to him again, for each meeting was like open combat between them—a clash of wills that only inflamed her smouldering resentment for him.

Her cousin Emily came to stand beside her, watching his retreating figure with such calf-like admiring eyes that she failed to notice Rachel's angry discomposure caused by her altercation with Lord Kingsley.

"Oh, Rachel," she said breathlessly, holding her heart with her clenched hand. "When I heard Mother had invited Lord Kingsley to the party, I very nearly died. How I wish he would dance with me, but he has not danced the whole evening."

"Perhaps that is because Lord Kingsley does not care to dance, Emily."

"Maybe if I were as beautiful as you, Rachel, then he would have asked me—but I would have seemed so silly to him."

"Nonsense, Emily," said Rachel, looking at her cousin with smiling fondness, despite the anger still beating in her heart. "Lord Kingsley does not know what he has missed by not asking you to dance."

"Is he not a fine gentleman—and so handsome?"

"Yes," she admitted absently, watching as he paused to speak to her father. They had been introduced to each other earlier in the evening and, she had observed, they had already been involved in a lengthy discussion. "He is very handsome, although I suppose being the proud owner of Mortlake Park and one of the richest men in the country makes him seem more attractive."

"You must be on the best of terms—otherwise he would not have talked to you for so long."

"There you are mistaken, Emily. It is just the opposite, in fact. Lord Kingsley and I are not on the best of terms. We do not get on.'' She sighed deeply, wondering why she felt so deflated all of a sudden. She spoke so softly that Emily almost didn't hear her. ''We do not get on at all.''

''Then you can count yourself the only one—for there isn't a woman in the whole of Ellerton who would not die for a single rendezvous with such a charming man.''

Rachel looked at her with condescension. ''Charms he might have, Emily—and it is clear from the rapturous effect he has on you and every other lady in the room that he is well practised in their arts—but I find him all arrogance and conceit, and altogether too full of himself.''

Noticing that he left the room with her father, who was bearing up to the evening better than she had anticipated, she turned away sharply, irritated by the enjoyment they clearly derived from each other's company and wondering what they could possibly have in common that allowed them to get on so well.

Chapter Four

The days following the party at Ellerton Hall found Rachel in low spirits. She was restless and dejected, which she put down to Stephen's absence and Mr Nolan's imminent departure although, since making the acquaintance of Lord Kingsley—and the disquieting effect he had on her emotions and sensibilities—of late Mr Nolan's passionate outpourings on matters of public concern did not hold her attention quite so much.

In fact, never had her thoughts been in such confusion. Whenever she remembered the bitterness of her conversation with Lord Kingsley at Ellerton Hall, she felt a stirring of regret that she had been so outspoken and had behaved in an undignified and unladylike manner in the company of a gentleman with whom she was hardly acquainted.

Her dejection could also be put down to a letter she had received from Kitty, a letter which held disheartening news which concerned her greatly, for

Kitty wrote that she was feeling extremely unwell of late.

Reading between the lines, Rachel suspected there must be something very wrong, for her sister had always enjoyed the best of health and had never been one to complain. She also remembered thinking she did not look her usual exuberant self when she had last seen her in London with Stephen and Harry.

Kitty begged Rachel not to distress their father with this news and went on to say that there was a matter she wished to discuss with her of some importance. She urged her to travel to London so that she might see her as soon as she was able. Puzzled as to why she should wish to see her and concerned by the urgency of her request, Rachel was determined to go as soon as it could be arranged. Her aunt Mary was to take Caroline and Emily to London very soon and she hoped her father would permit her to go with them.

She was alone in the house, her father and Harry having gone into Ellerton on an errand, when one of the maids came to inform her that Lord Kingsley had arrived and was asking to see her father. Rachel's heart gave a leap of surprise and, she had to admit, a certain delight, not having seen him since her aunt Mary's party at Ellerton Hall three weeks ago.

Although why she should feel such tremulous delight when she remembered their last ill-fated meeting—and all she held against him—filled her with bewilderment. Nor could she escape the overpowering effect he seemed to have on her whenever they met, which increased at their every meeting, or the fact that, where he was concerned, her emotions were all at war within her.

She rose from where she had been sitting and writing a letter to Kitty, smoothing her skirts with slightly trembling fingers as she watched him enter, her face set in cool, but not unfriendly, reserve as she forced herself to ignore the churning inside her.

William's eyes never faltered from her face as he crossed towards her calmly, bowing his dark head with innate graciousness, his expression devoid of any of the ill humour that Rachel had come to associate with him.

She was wearing a simple low-necked dress of apple green, her dark hair hanging loose. There was a demure, almost virginal appearance about her pale features, and a quiet beauty and innocence in the luminosity of her wide blue eyes.

"I came to see your father, Miss Fairley," he said, when he looked down into the clear depths of her eyes, thinking there was little wonder he was attracted by her, "but I understand he is not at home."

"No, he—he's gone into Ellerton with Harry, Lord Kingsley, although I expect him to return at any time, should you wish to wait." She moved towards a chair, discomfited by his closeness, feeling altogether too vulnerable beneath the directness of his gaze and experiencing its full power and provocation.

"Thank you. I am happy to find he is well enough to get about. I understand he does not enjoy the best of health."

"No—sadly, that is so. His weak heart gives us all cause for concern. Can I send for some refreshment while you wait?" she offered when they were seated opposite each other.

"No—no, thank you. Please, do not trouble yourself. I apologise for calling uninvited, but I chanced to be riding this way and thought I might have a word with your father on a certain matter."

"Of course. I-I'm glad you called, Lord Kingsley," she said hesitantly, meeting his eyes unwillingly, finding the moment one of awkwardness as she prepared, as graciously as possible, to apologise for her behaviour on their previous encounter.

"Oh!" His face inscrutable, William leaned back in his chair and looked into her tense face, quietly waiting on her words.

"Yes—you—you see, it gives me the opportunity to apologise to you for my behaviour when we last met at Ellerton Hall. I was too outspoken. It was quite wrong of me and I should not have said the things I did."

"Please do not feel the need to apologise, Miss Fairley," he said with a faint smile and a touch of gallantry. "I also said some things I regret for which I, too, apologise."

Rachel could feel the colour rising in her cheeks as she dropped her eyes; although his expression was grave, his eyes were as teasing as a small boy's. It was with a feeling of relief when, at that moment, there was the sound of a commotion out in the hall, of someone lifting a heavy object down the stairs.

William glanced at Rachel enquiringly and she smiled.

"Do not be alarmed, Lord Kingsley," she said. "The commotion you hear is Mr Nolan bringing his trunk down the stairs."

"Mr Nolan?"

"My brother Harry's tutor. Sadly, he is leaving us today."

"To take up another tutorial post?"

"No—I think not. He—he has always been interested in public affairs—I suppose it is inevitable that he will eventually be drawn into politics."

"Is he to leave for London?"

"No. Yorkshire. His home is in Hull. He—he is a close associate of Mr Wilberforce. Have you heard of him, Lord Kingsley?" she asked purposefully, watching his reaction to her question, asked in a casual manner, carefully; but, apart from a slight tightening of his jaw, his expression remained unchanged.

"There are few who have not heard of the illustrious Member of Parliament for Yorkshire, Miss Fairley. I believe he has been asked by the Abolition Society to take up the cause for the fight against the slave trade."

"Yes, so I have heard. It is a subject you should understand well, Lord Kingsley—owning a plantation in the West Indies and being a slave owner yourself."

"That is correct," he admitted without any sign of embarrassment. "Being an acquaintance of Mr Wilberforce, I suppose Mr Nolan shares his views?"

"Yes. Mr Nolan is an intelligent, responsible gentleman who deeply disapproves of slavery and has strong feelings about the cause.''

"You, too, it would seem, Miss Fairley. No doubt all your information comes from the knowledgeable Mr Nolan.''

"Of course, and it is through his teachings that I have been able to form my own opinion on the subject.''

He nodded slowly. "You have a right to your opinion—however misguided it may be.''

"Misguided? No—I do not think so.'' Rachel bristled, annoyed because he clearly thought she was easily influenced. "Slavery is an abominable practice and should be abolished. To make one's fortune based on something as evil as slavery is quite indefensible. Does it not bother you living off the oppression and misery of others, Lord Kingsley?''

"The opinions of others do not bother me unduly, Miss Fairley, and it would seem that your values are greater than mine—and others who belong to the aristocracy with plantations in the West Indies.''

He sat perfectly still and spoke as calmly as his emotions would permit—as if he were discussing nothing more serious than the weather, but each was aware of the tense undercurrents vibrating between them. Rachel's instinct, and his expression, told her it would take very little to turn his indolence to anger, but she refused to be deflected.

"You are not alone, I do know that. A great number of the aristocracy build their magnificent mansions—designed by only the finest architects—living a civilised life as all nobles and peers understand it—while the slaves who work their plantations in the West Indies struggle in what can only be described as some kind of jungle for survival.''

''It would seem the affairs of your own family are hardly a well-kept garden, Miss Fairley,'' he replied drily. ''I would not attempt to defend slavery, and, regrettable though it is, it is a fact as well as an exercise in human failing that most of the leisured classes enjoy their standard of living by exactions on others. But do not forget that, here in England, the lot of industrial workers is as bad as anything that can be found on the plantations in the West Indies.

''I hardly think you are in a position to preach to me on the way I conduct my family's affairs—or on the evils of slavery—when your own family obtains its wealth from the exploitation of children as young as five years old, who work down the coal mines and in the textile mills being built with incredible speed in the north.''

''I very much doubt that. There is a difference.''

''And you are certain of that, are you? Have you seen for yourself?''

''No—I—I—'' she faltered.

''Well—there you are, then.''

''But there is a difference,'' Rachel persisted, irritated by the smug tone of his voice and the curl of his lips, which she thought resembled a sneer rather than a smile. ''The people who work in the coal mines are legally free to do as they choose. They are not beaten or whipped. Slavery is an abominable practice and should be abolished.''

''And what would be the solution in your opinion? At the moment, the Anti-Slavery Movement is too weak to overcome the system.''

''It will not always be that way. The argument should be carried through the press and any other means to attract public opinion.''

''And what then? Do not forget that the trade is a legitimate form of commerce that only an Act of Parliament can put an end to.''

''Then Parliament must be lobbied.''

William sighed, vexed by her propensity to argue whenever they met. ''I'm afraid it is not that simple, Miss Fairley, and,'' he said, getting up from where he sat and going to stand by the window, letting his gaze travel beyond the garden towards the river which threaded its way through the very heart of Ellerton, ''I do not intend arguing on the moral aspects of it just now—not on so fine a day as this.''

He turned and looked at her. ''I wonder if, while I am waiting for your father to return from Ellerton, you would walk with me through your garden to the river?''

''Why—I—I—'' she faltered, taken completely by surprise. She was weak, suddenly, at a loss to know what to say and she wondered why, for she was usually in command of herself.

''Do you like walking?''

''Why—yes—I enjoy walking very much. It is a healthy exercise—but I—I don't know if I should.''

"If you are afraid that your reputation is in danger of being ruined should you be seen walking alone with me, then do not be concerned. From the house, the river is only a short walk beyond the garden, and there are windows enough for your servants to keep you in view at all times to ensure I do not compromise you."

Rachel smiled, beginning to warm a little towards him now he was not quite so formal. "It is considerate of you to be so concerned for my reputation, Lord Kingsley."

His dark eyes twinkled merrily. "I am well aware that once a young woman's reputation is lost it can never be retrieved, Miss Fairley."

"Then my reputation must be protected at all cost. I shall see to it that Mrs Armstrong, our housekeeper, does not let me out of her sight for a moment."

"Does that mean you agree to walk with me?"

"How can I refuse?"

"Then that is settled. However, before we leave the house, there is one thing I must ask of you."

"Oh?"

"That we declare a truce. Agreed?"

His eyes were gently enquiring and Rachel was intrigued by this confounding man. Never had she met a man who perplexed her more. He smiled and she felt her own mouth begin to follow, feeling her antipathy towards him start to melt. The arrogance she had come to know so well was gone. However, suspecting this to be only a temporary state of affairs, she was determined to make the most of it.

Still smiling she nodded. "Yes, it is agreed."

It was not without a certain pleasure that Rachel accompanied Lord Kingsley down to the river. He was in a thoughtful mood as they walked along a wide sunny path flanked with high laurels and rhododendrons, flowering generously in rich, lush colours of purple, white and brilliant red.

They reached the sun-splattered river, which tumbled over its rocky bed. Along its way to Ellerton, small tributaries left the main flow to feed the lake in the grounds of Mortlake Park. Birds were industriously nesting in the trees; the gnarled branches reached out over the water, some so low their leaves brushed the surface, the glancing drops of water catching sparkling, dancing crystal clear prisms of light.

They paused on the rise of the old stone bridge, the silence inhabited only by the flowing water tumbling over stones and disappearing beneath the narrow arch.

William leaned indolently against the low wall of the bridge and looked at Rachel, the sun shining on his bare head. He was a man not unaccustomed to the attractions of a beautiful woman, having admired and loved many in a casual way—and because of his looks and his immense wealth he had never had to work very hard at getting them to part with their favours, for those assets alone made him desirable to them.

But he had never been impressed with emotions of the heart. Romantic love was something he was unaccustomed to, for never had he met a woman who had impressed him with her intellect, wit and dignity, a woman who possessed an equal agility of mind to his own enough to make him want to spend the rest of his life with her. But that was before he had met Rachel Fairley.

For the first time in his life he found himself responding to a woman's intelligent individuality, making him both captivated and intrigued—although she had made it quite plain from the outset that in her opinion there were certain unfavourable aspects to his character that did not endear him to her in the slightest.

However, he did not believe this for one moment and felt that her demure, almost prim exterior hid a woman of passion. She drew him like a magnet. He wanted her, despite the cool reserve she always adopted whenever they were together, which, he suspected, was her way of fending off predatory males.

He meant to capture her, to turn this calm, proper young lady into a tantalising creature of desire, who, when aroused, would breath a sensuality she was not even aware of, to take her to the very heights of passion.

He studied her profile as she looked down at the river. Her dark hair rippled and lifted in the gentle breeze, and he found himself imagining how it would feel to run his fingers through the silken strands. Sensing his eyes on her, she turned and met his gaze and smiled, her teeth gleaming white between her softly parted lips.

"So," he said at length, "your father will have to find another tutor for your brother?"

"No, we are done with tutors. Harry is to go to school. I believe Father is considering sending him to Harrow."

"Ah—my old Alma Mater," he said. "I have fond memories of my own schooldays spent at Harrow. And what of you? I suspect you will miss Mr Nolan and his excellent mind," he said, with slight ironic emphasis on the last two words.

"An excellent mind is not the only aspect of Mr Nolan's character I shall miss when he leaves us."

William arched a sleek black brow quizzically. "Then I would say that youth—and maybe romance—has coloured your perceptions."

His voice was low and seductive, yet not without a hint of teasing. His dark eyes were persuasive and compelling and he was standing close, so close, that Rachel's eyes were drawn to his as sunlight played lazily about them.

"Romance!" She smiled, a slow, teasing smile, while giving him a sidelong glance from beneath her lashes, thrusting away an image of Ralph as he intruded into her thoughts—Ralph, who had issued words of love and words to betray. Her father was right—Lord Kingsley did not resemble Ralph in any sense. His tone was light, teasing, almost, and she was surprised to discover that she did not mind, that she was flattered by it, in fact.

The gentle, flirtatious play with words was quite new to her and, for the first time in over two years, she found herself warming to the attentions of a man again, a handsome man, with wickedly dancing dark eyes, and she wanted to savour all the delights she had denied herself for so long. "I did not say anything about romance, Lord Kingsley."

"No—but you must have encountered such a weakening state of affairs, surely?"

"Not that I've noticed. But you must have encountered it yourself to describe its effects. And if, as you say, it has such a debilitating effect on one, then I must strive to remain in control of my emotions at all times and keep my eyes wide open."

William suppressed a smile. "Are you usually so forthright, Miss Fairley?"

"Yes. Does it offend you? Would you prefer it if I were all simpers and smiles like my cousins Caroline and Emily?"

"Heaven forbid." He laughed. "Now *that* is not in your nature. But you will miss your brother's tutor, will you not?"

"Yes, I shall. I shall miss his friendship but—not as much as he misses my sister."

"The one treading the boards at Drury Lane?"

"Yes—the same."

"And how does it affect you having a sister belonging to such a notorious profession?"

"Many families in our situation would see it as a disgrace but neither I nor any member of my immediate family see it that way—except for Aunt Mary, who has refused to speak of her ever again. In fact, I rather envy my sister her freedom. Her profession we have never tried to conceal—and how it is viewed by others is a matter for them,'' she said firmly and with meaning, meeting his gaze squarely, for she already knew of his low opinion where actresses were concerned.

"Mr Nolan admired Kitty a great deal and was quite devastated when she left. Which, I suspect, is why he is returning to Hull.''

"Then perhaps you should go with him,'' William said, his firm lips curving in a teasing smile, hoping to steer the conversation away from the subject of her sister's profession, for he had no wish to become embroiled in another heated discussion. "With your strong mind and firm opinions, you would no doubt prove to be quite an asset to Mr Wilberforce.''

"Unfortunately, there are those who would not be so tolerant of a woman playing the political game, Lord Kingsley—even those among my own sex who do not share my radical views.''

"And how radical are you?''

"In an ideal world I could be as radical as I please,'' she said, laughing exquisitely, unconsciously, "but unfortunately this is not an ideal world, Lord Kingsley. I have to say that my father—who is open minded in many things—considers it right and proper that girls should be well educated, which is why he always employed the best governesses for Kitty and myself.

"Unfortunately, women who have had a good education and are accomplished in languages and mathematics are generally frowned upon and deprecated if they try to assume independence—or show any ambition other than how to excel at needlework and manners in order to make themselves fit for marriage.''

''Do not undervalue your sex. There are many strong-minded women of this age who are not afraid to stand up and be counted. You are a clever woman, Miss Fairley, and in my opinion a clever woman can do almost anything she puts her mind to.''

''And achieve nothing but ridicule from both sexes, I shouldn't wonder,'' she smiled, her eyes bright and her cheeks glowing.

''It would take a brave man to ridicule you, Miss Fairley. A brave man indeed.''

His voice was smooth, almost like the finest silk. He looked at her for a long moment and then he smiled, a wonderfully engaging smile, making their previous altercations suddenly seem petty and small. Without knowing it Rachel had become vulnerable and approachable—which was what he had intended, for he had succeeded in lightening a dark corner in some unknown part of her mind, causing something to stir.

Her eyes, vividly blue in the sunlight, looked into his, intrigued by this strange and open conversation they were having, but hastily, almost shyly, she averted her gaze, her cheeks burning, perplexed and quite astonished by her own bewildering thoughts.

Her father and Harry had returned from Ellerton and, being informed by one of the servants that Lord

Kingsley had come to call and was at that moment outside with Miss Rachel, Harry immediately came in search of them as they were about to walk back to the house.

He came running along the path and almost immediately Lord Kingsley began telling him all about Harrow and his own days spent there as a schoolboy. Quite unfazed by the rank and importance of Lord Kingsley, Harry listened with enthusiasm, his eyes wide with interest.

They sauntered back to the house where George Fairley met them in the hall. Thanking Lord Kingsley for a pleasant walk, Rachel left them alone and went upstairs to her room, strongly stirred by emotions she was finding extremely difficult to ignore.

She found the softening to Lord Kingsley's nature both puzzling and enlightening, and could not for the life of her think what had brought about this transformation. Had she misjudged him? she asked herself, because for the first time she had had a glimpse of a different person beneath that cool, arrogant exterior.

He had been unusually charming towards her on their walk, which was strange after their previous, caustic encounters, and she found herself softening towards him—even when she brought to mind his involvement with his family's sugar plantation in the West Indies, worked by African slaves, from which he derived much of his wealth.

His harsh refusal to consent to a marriage between her brother and his sister, which Rachel firmly believed he did because he considered the Fairleys' situation in life inferior to his own—she found this latest discovery clouded the initial judgement she had formed as to the nature of his character.

Rachel was puzzled as to why Lord Kingsley had come to Meadowfield Lodge to see her father, who was in no hurry to enlighten her as to the reason, even though he was quietly aware of her curiosity. It was when they were sitting quietly after their evening meal, after the departure of Mr Nolan for his native Yorkshire and when Harry had gone up to his room, that he spoke to her from behind the newspaper he was immersed in.

"So, Rachel, how did you get on with Lord Kingsley this afternoon?"

She looked up from the book she was reading. "Well enough, I suppose, considering the unpleasantness of our previous encounters. In fact, he was polite and quite charming, which I have to say I found puzzling."

"Good. I'm glad to hear it. Considering every young woman in Ellerton swoons at a mere glance of him—did such intimate contact not raise any romantic thoughts in that head of yours?"

"Father!" Rachel chided in a shocked tone, looking towards where he sat, although she was unable to see any of his features other than the top of his silver head above the sheets of the newspaper.

"Now don't sound so missish. Why should you be any different to all the other young ladies? It is a known fact among them that Lord Kingsley is quite the handsomest man in the district. It isn't right to have your head set against him in this manner.

"Is it that business over Stephen and his sister that still upsets you? Or is it that you are still smarting over your affair with Ralph Wheeler—refusing to let a gentleman get close to you again lest he treat you in the same despicable manner?"

Rachel looked at her father sharply. "I no longer think of Ralph in the romantic sense, Father—and it is not that I refuse to become close to any other man—it is that I am reluctant to do so in fear of being hurt a second time," she said, not wishing to raise her father's hopes by telling him she might be about to have a change of heart where Lord Kingsley was concerned. An invisible thread had appeared between them, invisible and fragile, drawing them together in a way that astonished and bewildered her, and until she was able to sort out her confusing thoughts, then, that was how it would remain.

"And, of course," she went on, "knowing how hurt Stephen is feeling, naturally it upsets me. But that is not the only reason. You know I do not endorse the way Lord Kingsley makes his money to maintain his grand house and life style."

"I see," he said, lowering his newspaper and looking across at her. "And you told him that, did you?"

"Why, yes, I did."

"Then I can only hope you were not too outspoken. Faced with determination such as yours, Lord Kingsley would not have a prayer. And what did he say?"

"Very little."

"Well I hope you allowed the poor man to defend himself?"

"Of course. But he said nothing in his own defence. In fact, he refused to be drawn on the issue, only to liken it to the industrial workers' plight here in England, implying they had much in common with the African slaves."

"Did he now? Well—he may have a point, you know. The lot of the workers in the coal mines and in many more industries can be as cruel as it is on any of the plantations in the West Indies. The profits from the cultivation of sugar are much greater than any other cultivation in Europe and America so one cannot blame the planters for defending it."

He paused, thoughtful for a moment, and when he continued his voice was serious.

"I hope you did not behave in an impertinent and presumptuous manner, Rachel, for if you did then I am sure Lord Kingsley would have been too much of a gentleman to contradict you in your own home. However," he said with a sudden mischievous twinkle in his eye, again lifting his newspaper, "I find it strange that he did not make his opinions on the issue of slavery known to you."

Rachel stared across at him in bewilderment. "Why—what can you mean, Father?" she asked, beginning to feel distinctly uneasy that he was about to tell her something concerning Lord Kingsley that she did not know.

"Only that his views regarding the plantation system are not much different from your own. Lord

Kingsley is seriously considering selling his plantation on Barbados, and he came to see me today to pick my brains regarding investments in industry here in England.''

Rachel's eyes widened in undisguised astonishment and a wave of colour flooded her face. She stared at him, unable to move. "He—he what?"

At last her father put down his newspaper and smiled placidly. "Oh dear. It seems this has come as something of a shock. Are you all right, my dear?"

"Yes—yes, of course," she said, her voice sounding unsteady, for she was unable to think straight—so confused were her thoughts just then. "But why did he not tell me this? Oh, Father—I feel such a fool. But why is he selling his plantation? Why, if, as you say, the profits from the cultivation of sugar are so immense?"

"Why should he uphold a system he does not agree with—that goes against his conscience? He, too, wants to see the end of slavery—with a dedication and passion that would surprise even you. After all, he does have first-hand knowledge of it.

"But, tell me, Rachel," he said, watching her expression closely as she struggled to come to terms with what he had just divulged, "how do you feel about him now you know he is not what you thought him to be—now the man you thought of as your enemy has revealed himself to be your friend? Not quite the ogre you once thought, eh?"

"No, perhaps not," she confessed reluctantly. "But I still have some reservations. However, I have to say that I do not look forward to our next meeting.''

''In my view, the only way you can redeem yourself is to apologise—although it will have to wait; he is preparing to leave for London within the next few days.''

''Apologise?''

''Yes,'' he said, smiling as he folded his newspaper. ''Although, just think, perhaps he might refuse to accept it—considering your harsh opinion of him. And I'm sure you deserve it. However, Lord Kingsley is a gentleman and I am certain he will forgive you graciously.''

In her room later that evening, Rachel stared moodily at her reflection in her dressing-table mirror as she still battled to come to terms with what her father had told her concerning Lord Kingsley. She had always believed first impressions to be important and from the very first moment she had set eyes on him he had not impressed her in the slightest—until today.

All that she'd held against him, she now realised, had been founded on nothing more than gossip and, she was forced to admit, she was beginning to feel very foolish and somewhat ashamed of her assertions. How could she have accused him so readily when she had so little to furnish the evidence?

But when she remembered their conversation when he had come to call on her father that very day, why, when they had discussed the issue of slavery, had he not told her of his own revulsion for the trade? Why had he let her chatter on in a somewhat accusing and superior manner about the injustice of it?

Unless, she thought, with a stirring of anger, he had smugly refrained from telling her so he could enjoy her humiliation and embarrassment, for he would know how foolish she would feel when she found out.

Her father had asked her how she felt now he was no longer her enemy, but her friend. Well, how did she feel? she asked herself. How could she answer that question? When she remembered the way it had been between them down by the river, of the intimacy of the conversation they had shared, when, for the first time since their acquaintance there had been no rancour between them, then at that moment the issue of slavery was far from Rachel's thoughts.

Looking back, she remembered how their conversation had been almost flirtatious and she knew it was pleasure she had felt at being in his company—pleasure and something else, something she did not recognise, for it was so dissimilar to anything she had felt about him before.

She trembled slightly, feeling the blood pumping strongly through her heart when she remembered the unique power of his dark eyes, which had remained fastened on hers the whole time, as if reading her inner most, most intimate thoughts.

Afraid of the weakening she felt within her when dwelling too long on his image, firmly fixed in her mind, which she now realised was stronger than anything she had felt for Ralph, she quickly blew out the candle on her dressing table, certain of one thing as she crossed to her bed—she and Lord Kingsley could never be friends in the ordinary sense of the word.

Chapter Five

With reluctance Rachel had to admit that her father was right. The correct and decent thing to do was to apologise to Lord Kingsley for having elected to judge him so readily and so wrongly. However, knowing that he was to leave for London shortly, she was relieved that she would not have to face him just yet. She intended leaving for the city herself with her aunt Mary and her cousins, but considered it unlikely they would meet.

However, the little comfort she had derived from anticipating that their next meeting would be later rather than sooner and thinking to delay her offer of an apology was wasted, for along with her father and aunt Mary and her cousins she was invited to dine at Mortlake Park before Lord Kingsley and Sir Edgar Mainwaring left for London.

No matter how she struggled to find a suitable excuse to get out of going, she had to resign herself to it; there was no way out that she could think of. She would have to go.

It was not the first time Rachel had seen Mortlake Park, the grand country residence of the Kingsley family, but it was the first time she had been invited to enter. The house, with two wings embracing a central court, was situated on the crest of a low hill, and with its many turrets and courtyards it rose over the still waters of the lake, presenting a stirring sight which could be seen all over the surrounding countryside.

Rachel and her father—who was honoured to be invited to Mortlake Park as Lord Kingsley's guest, and thankful he was well enough to accept, having just endured a debilitating few days in bed—travelled to Mortlake Park alone in their carriage, approaching over a graceful bridge that spanned the narrowest part of the lake and proceeding up a long curved drive to the front of the house.

The closer the carriage carried Rachel to Mortlake Park the more vulnerable and weakened she became, feeling that this was very much Lord Kingsley's territory, where he was master and reigned supreme. Since their last meeting at Meadowfield Lodge, he had figured persistently in her thoughts, and the closer she got to meeting him again, the prospect brought on a fit of nervousness.

Liveried footmen assisted them out of the carriage and escorted them into the house. Unconsciously, Rachel's feet carried her forward. Looking around her, she finally stood against the marble columns inside the great hall, seeing a fine oak staircase rising from the centre to form a gallery up above.

She was relieved to find other guests had already arrived—ten or a dozen, maybe more. Some she recognised as neighbours, among them her cousins and aunt Mary, whose eyes lit up on seeing her brother and niece and who immediately crossed over to them.

Rachel's nerves were already at full stretch as she watched Lord Kingsley come towards where she stood, in an agony of apprehension, with her father. He was unsmiling, his dark hair and the immaculate black clothes he wore making him seem like a sinister-looking figure indeed. He walked with an easy stride until he stood before them, inclining his head in polite greeting.

Rachel dropped a conventional curtsy, lowering her eyes, her eyelashes touching the soft flush which had suddenly sprung to her cheeks. For a moment they looked at one another without speaking; for some indefinable reason she began to feel uneasy. Even though a faint smile now touched his lips, his behaviour was so unpredictable—and she knew it was going to be no simple matter apologising to him.

He was at once courteous and attentive as polite greetings were exchanged. His eyes came to rest on George Fairley.

"Welcome to Mortlake, Mr Fairley. I am so glad you were able to come this evening. Lady Brayfield tells me you have not been well of late. I trust you are feeling better?"

"Thank you—yes. It was kind of you to invite us, Lord Kingsley," replied George Fairley. "However, I have to say I was somewhat surprised to receive your invitation. I was under the impression you were to leave for London.''

''That is still the case. Sir Edgar and I are to leave first thing in the morning—but we thought a little dinner party would not go amiss before we left.''

''And will your stay in London be a lengthy one?''

''I hope not. I have been absent from Mortlake Park too long as it is. There is much to be done.''

''I, too, leave for London within the week,'' said Lady Brayfield, ''with my daughters, of course—and Rachel is to accompany us.''

Once more Lord Kingsley's dark gaze became fastened on Rachel's which seemed to be watching him in fascination. ''Really?'' he said in a soft voice. ''Then no doubt we shall meet at some occasion or other, Lady Brayfield.''

''Yes—I very much hope so.''

''And are you to accompany the ladies to London, Mr Fairley?'' asked Lord Kingsley.

''Heaven forbid, sir. Unfortunately, my health will not permit it—and I regret to say I do not possess the stamina to keep up with the amount of parties and assemblies my dear sister is planning on attending. No,'' he chuckled, ''give me the solitude of Meadowfield Lodge any day.''

''There I cannot blame you,'' smiled Lord Kingsley. ''I have no mind to stay long myself.''

''Tell me, are we to have the pleasure of Lady Kingsley's company this evening, Lord Kingsley?'' asked Lady Brayfield.

''I'm afraid not. My stepmother does not enjoy the

best of health, as you know. She keeps to her room most days.''

"Then I am sorry to hear it. Please convey to her our good wishes.''

"Thank you." He looked across the hall to where the butler was announcing that dinner was shortly to be served, before looking at Rachel and offering her his arm. "Miss Fairley—may I escort you into dinner?''

"Yes, thank you,'' she said, overcoming her nervousness, surprised she was able to answer audibly. She placed her gloved hand on his arm, feeling the sinewy muscles beneath the cloth of his coat and the warmth and power within him.

As everyone began to move in the direction of the dining-room, Lord Kingsley looked down at her. "You look entrancing," he said quietly, his dark eyes boldly sweeping over her in appreciation—at the deep pink satin gown she wore with a low bodice and two flounces on the skirt that parted to display the underskirt of rows of cream and pink lace ruffles. "That colour pink certainly becomes you.''

There was a caressing note to his voice that caused Rachel to look at him inquiringly. What she saw in his eyes sent a quiver through her and she felt her heartbeat quicken alarmingly; she was certain his penetrating eyes could lay bare the soft flush that covered her body from head to toe beneath her dress.

She experienced some consternation and dismay— and at the same time a certain amount of pleasure at the effect he was having on her, but she was resolved not to show it. It was clear there was to be a continuation of the intimacy that had existed between them when he had called at Meadowfield Lodge, showing her a softer side to his character—which she considered to be far more dangerous to her sensibilities than what she had at first imagined him to be.

The whole house was elegantly designed and decorated with great taste. On leaving the hall, they passed through a fine suite of rooms, all tastefully and expensively furnished, the walls displaying a mixture of equestrian, military and landscaped paintings. Elaborate gilt-framed mirrors glittered everywhere.

The dining-room was large, the ceiling and walls of exceptionally fine stucco work and heavily gilded. Portraits hung on the walls of various members of the Kingsley family, and over the chimneypiece a huge portrait of one of Lord Kingsley's ancestors with his wife and children dominated the room.

A long, splendidly arrayed table, decorated with roses and silver candelabras and fine china and silver, was set for sixteen people. Because everybody was already well acquainted, each having much in common, the conversation was interesting and lively.

Lord Kingsley presided over the meal with aristocratic courtesy. Looking down the table from where she was sitting between Sir Edgar and the vicar of Ellerton, Rachel was confused as she watched him entertain his guests, for he was all charm and politeness—so very much at variance to the character she had built up of him in her mind.

Because he was not at all like she had imagined

him to be, she was angry with herself for having allowed herself to be influenced so easily by what others had said of him.

With imposing servants in attendance, a variety of dishes was served and the longer the meal progressed, the louder and more lively the conversation became. Apart from exchanging the conventional pleasantries, Rachel joined little in the conversation, preferring to listen instead. Matters of local interest were discussed at length and society gossip, before moving on to the politics of the day.

When America was mentioned and its independence discussed, it was inevitable that someone would bring up the subject of Lord Kingsley's sugar plantation on Barbados.

"Rumour has it that you are considering selling your plantation in the Indies, Lord Kingsley," said Lady Brayfield sitting on his right. "Is this true?"

"I can confirm the rumours, Lady Brayfield. It is true that I am to sell my plantation on Barbados."

Lord Kingsley's gaze flickered to where Rachel sat and she lowered her eyes, becoming swamped with a sickening feeling of embarrassment and confusion, knowing by his look that the conversation they had had at Meadowfield Lodge was uppermost in his mind. She also knew that she would have to face him eventually to apologise for having misjudged him so readily—and that he would show her no mercy.

"Then does that mean we will see more of you— that more of your time will be spent here at Mortlake?"

"It does."

"But why sell when sugar is one of the world's most lucrative commodities? For what reason?" asked the gentleman sitting across from Rachel.

"A moral one," he answered, simply.

"Oh—I see. So you have not been pressured into it by the abolitionists—who, I hear, are gathering strength since Mr Wilberforce voiced his own opinion that slavery should be ended."

"No. My own conscience tells me it is not right. To make one's fortune based on something as evil as slavery is quite indefensible," William said, reiterating Rachel's own words, his eyes once again coming to rest on hers, giving her the impression that he was addressing her and no one else.

"Because my father supported slavery as being a natural and unquestioning condition for black people, it does not necessarily follow that I should agree with or approve of everything he did. It is an appalling practice—inhuman—and I agree absolutely with the abolitionists that it must end."

There was a ripple of agreement from everyone around the table.

"I have to say," Lord Kingsley went on, still looking at Rachel, "that it is an issue I have discussed with an acquaintance—whose opinion is equally as strong as my own, and who made no attempt to conceal her own abhorrence regarding the evils of slavery and the disgust it arouses in many people.

"However, I suppose it's fine for everyone in England—who have never seen a black person in their lives—to moralise on the rights and wrongs of such a practice, but who never lift a finger to change things other than utter self-righteous proclamations.''

Rachel became scarlet to the roots of her hair, for his eyes conveyed to her the message that she was the acquaintance he spoke of. She could not remember having felt so foolish or so humiliated—just when everything was beginning to assume different proportions, when she knew that everything she had thought in relation to his concerns had been wrong and was prepared to swallow her pride and apologise for having misjudged him.

Oh, she thought angrily, if she were not in the presence of so many people, what wouldn't she say to him? He had no *right* to imply that she was one of those self-righteous moralists! She met his eyes when they came to rest on her tight features and she was furious to see that he was aware of her discomfort and seemed amused by it.

At that moment servants began placing decanters of port and brandy on the table, which was a sign that it was time the ladies withdrew. Rachel was relieved to escape to the adjacent salon, hoping that before the gentlemen joined them she would have had time to compose herself. The gentlemen were not absent too long, but thankfully, by the time they were all seated and cards were produced, her fury had abated.

Being an accomplished musician, Emily sat at the fortepiano and her nimble fingers began to pass over the keyboard as she played a lively piece. A footman appeared and stepped towards Lord Kingsley, who bowed his head to listen to what he had to say.

Observing him from across the room, Rachel saw a troubled frown crease his forehead before he turned towards his guests. He smiled and with what she thought to be an assumed lightness, excused himself, telling them there was a small domestic matter that required his attention, before following the footman out of the room.

Replete after a such a splendid meal, everybody abandoned themselves to playing cards and listening to the soothing tones of the music. With languishing dark eyes, Caroline sat beside Sir Edgar Mainwaring on one of the elegant settees. Sir Edgar was an irresistible charmer whose attentions towards Caroline had plunged her into a state of romantic excitement.

Wanting to secure a good match for both her daughters, Lady Brayfield did not oppose the interest he was showing in Caroline—in fact, she was evidently well pleased with the way things were moving in that direction. Caroline may not have captivated the attentions of Lord Kingsley, as her mother had hoped, but Sir Edgar Mainwaring would do very well indeed.

Standing close to the French windows, having no desire to join one of the card games in progress and drawn by the coolness the terrace offered, Rachel slipped outside into a twilight haze. The magnificence of the house contents and decoration was well matched by the view to be seen from the terrace, of well-planned gardens and acres of parkland stretching all the way to Ellerton.

Passing empty rooms, she began to stroll along the length of the terrace, lifting her face to allow the light breeze to cool her cheeks. Reaching the end, she paused on top of a short flight of steps that led to the gardens below.

The evening was warm, the air filled with the scents of summer flowers. She breathed deeply, listening to the notes of the music as they floated out to her through the open glass doors. She looked towards the lake in the distance, its waters still and dark. On the horizon the sky was a blaze of crimson, shot through with threads of blue and silver.

Sighing deeply, she was about to turn and go back, but became rooted to the spot when, quite by chance, she happened to glance through a slightly open French window that she was close to and saw a woman standing in the centre of the room.

Unable to prevent herself from doing so, Rachel moved closer to the window and stared at the woman, for she looked so strange and the scene was quite bizarre. She was a slender woman of medium height with an air of respectability, and yet her appearance was rather odd.

She was elaborately overdressed and her face painted—outrageously so. Her lips were as brightly crimson as the dress she wore, her cheeks coated with rouge and powder. Her hair was almost white; an attempt had been made to arrange it, but without success, for untidy strands hung limply down the sides of her face—which was somewhat haggard, but still bore traces of great beauty. Rachel had the strange suspicion that the lady was Lady Kingsley, but if so, then what was wrong with her?

A maid was in the room with her. From their actions, Rachel could see she was quite distressed and trying to coax the woman towards the door. But the strange-looking woman was resisting and was clearly angered by the maid's persistence—she began throwing her arms wide and shouting at her in a hysterical manner. There was something about her behaviour that was beginning to seem increasingly odd.

At that moment the door opened and, transfixed, Rachel watched as two footmen entered, followed by Lord Kingsley. He appeared to be quite calm when he spoke to the woman and his presence seemed to have a calming effect on her, for gradually she became quiet, looking suddenly weary. Her shoulders drooped and she hung her head, as if overcome by a deep sadness, as she allowed herself to be led from the room.

Lord Kingsley was about to follow but at that moment his eyes fell on the partly open French window. Whether he sensed her presence or looked by chance, Rachel had no way of knowing, but she saw his face quicken and his eyebrows draw together in anger when his eyes fastened on her still form standing there.

At once she retreated a step, her heart pounding uneasily at being caught out witnessing something he would not have wanted her to see. He strode across the room quickly and out onto the terrace, firmly taking hold of her arm and guiding her away from the glass doors. His face was grave and his lips pressed together in a firm line when he stopped and released her.

Swamped with guilt at having witnessed something not meant for her eyes, her cheeks became flushed with embarrassment.

"I—I am so sorry," she stammered, regretting having walked so far along the terrace. "I was merely walking along the terrace-I—I did not mean to—"

"I'm sure you didn't, Miss Fairley," William interrupted curtly.

"Was—was the lady I saw Lady Kingsley?"

"Yes. My stepmother is ill—that you already know. Earlier today she considered herself to be too ill to attend the dinner party this evening, but thought she felt much recovered suddenly. However—as you saw for yourself—she was not and her maid has taken her back to her room."

"Oh, I see," Rachel murmured, strongly suspecting his explanation was merely an invention to pacify her. But the matter was clearly one of a delicate nature and she was not one to pry, although her curiosity concerning Lady Kingsley had increased considerably.

"I would appreciate it if you did not discuss this matter with the other guests, Miss Fairley, and urge you to forget what you have seen."

Rachel swallowed hard and she nodded. "Yes—of course. You can be assured of my discretion."

His expression relaxed. "Yes—I'm sure I can. Now," he said, with an assumed lightness, falling into step beside her as they walked back towards the Salon and his other guests, "tell me, do you like Mortlake, Miss Fairley?"

"Oh, yes," she breathed, relieved to see his features soften and more than happy to put what she had just seen behind her for the time being. "Who would not? It is very beautiful. One advantage of severing your interests in the West Indies is that it will enable you to spend more time here. You must miss it very much when you are away."

"Yes, I do. The West Indies are extremely beautiful—and I do not deny that I have become extremely fond of Barbados and its people—and yet I leave it without regrets for what I have here at Mortlake Park."

"Who would not be happy in surroundings such as this?"

"I hope you are enjoying the evening."

"Yes, very much. You are a generous host, Lord Kingsley."

"Oh—I can be quite charming when I am in such delightful company. You were very quiet during dinner, Miss Fairley," William said softly, thinking that in the diminishing light her face looked like an icon—with her pale skin and large dark eyes.

"I was?"

"Yes. Considering the topic being discussed earlier I would have thought you would have favoured us with your opinion."

"You already know my opinion, Lord Kingsley—and, besides, perhaps I had nothing much to say and preferred to listen instead."

"And did you find what you heard interesting?"

"Since you ask, no. I did not care for the conversation at all. Especially when you implied that I was one of those people who utter self-righteous proclamations. Why did you not tell me of your decision to sell your plantation on Barbados when you called at my home that day to see my father?" she reproached him. "Was it your intention to make me feel foolish when I found out the truth?"

She asked the question lightly, without rancour, for, this being his home and she his guest, good manners prevented her from arguing.

William shrugged slightly. "I saw no reason to. I do not feel I have to justify my aims or reveal my intent to anyone—and you must believe me when I say that it was not my desire to make you feel foolish. If I have done so, then I apologise most humbly."

"Thank you."

"It was plain when I called on your father that day that you thought the worst of me, Miss Fairley, but why should I have enlightened you in order to alter your opinion of me? Although in the light of the evidence you had to hand, I can well understand why you must have thought me a tyrannical slave owner.

"When I referred to those who moralise on the evils of slavery without lifting a finger to change things, I was not applying the accusation to yourself—and I am sorry if you thought that. But, sadly, there are many in England—and especially in the Government—who fit the description.''

''Am I to understand you refer to those who hold high office and also own plantations in the West Indies—who will not show support to the abolitionists for fear of losing a large proportion of their wealth should slavery be abolished?''

William nodded. ''The same. But if I may refer to your initial assessment of my character, your reaction towards myself, to what you understood to be correct, was severe and complete—but as I remarked on our last encounter, it was somewhat misguided.

''Maybe the knowledgeable Mr Nolan was responsible for that,'' he said quietly, with a trace of sarcasm, ''who, it would appear, was so ready to malign my character—who set himself up as judge and jury where I am concerned, and who seemed to have such a passionate interest in my affairs.''

''With the evidence on hand, he would hardly have sung your praises,'' Rachel said with a little smile.

''Perhaps if he had inquired a little further into my affairs, he would have discovered that I was considering selling the plantation long since. It was no secret.''

''Then what can I say, Lord Kingsley? Except that, whatever your reasons for waiting until your father's demise to unburden your sins is really not my concern.''

William frowned and seemed to consider the word thoughtfully before replying. ''Sins! Yes—I suppose

that is how you would look at it—and you are right—
I should have done something about it before he died.

"However, I am not a saint, Miss Fairley, and like
all men I have many flaws. I do not deny that I've
done my share of wrongdoing and attracted much criticism—from myself, mostly, but, considering the savage nature of the times, I saw to it that the plantation
was run in a decent and proper manner."

He sighed suddenly, looking ahead towards the
gathering darkness. When he next spoke, his tone was
one Rachel hadn't heard before, his expression when
he next looked at her possessing a yearning quality,
as if at some time during his life he had been affected
by some unsupportable distress.

"All my life I have looked after the Kingsleys'
interests on Barbados. It was my grandfather who
started our plantation and bought the first slaves. He
died shortly afterwards, leaving my father to inherit.
From being a relatively poor man, sugar made him
wealthier than any of his forebears. He would not lay
such wealth aside for any moral grievances people
might have against slavery."

"And you are different?"

"I am. My father was aware of my views and dis-
content—he even sympathised with them—in his own
grudging way. But he was a firm man and would not
be gainsaid. He was convinced his way was right.
When he died I could live with it no longer."

"And now?"

"Now I want something that does not include the
enslavement of others. Oppression is never right."

"Even if that something merits less—after all the years of plenty?"

William smiled down at her upturned face, watching her closely. "If I invest wisely, then I believe I shall be able to stave off the years of famine, Miss Fairley."

Looking into his eyes, Rachel thought what a curious and fascinating man he was. There were so many conflicting sides to his nature that astonished her. It was clear to her now that she had been quite wrong in her assertions and was mature enough to admit it.

"It seems I owe you an apology, Lord Kingsley. I had no right to judge you. I am sorry if I offended you."

William's lips curved in a slow, teasing smile and his strongly marked brows were slightly raised, his dark eyes suddenly glowing with humour.

"I am not usually one to forgive an injury—especially when that injury has been directed against my character. When I recollect my own apology to you on our first encounter and your harsh refusal to accept it—then you could hardly blame me if I chose to to take a similar stance.

"However, I consider myself to be a gentleman—regardless of your low opinion of me—and if I wish to improve your opinion and settle this matter amicably, then I can see I must accept it."

His words kindled wrath in Rachel's deep blue eyes. "How noble of you," she replied with barely concealed sarcasm, her face set in stiff lines and her voice steely. "But if you cannot accept my apology willingly, then I would prefer it if you did not accept it at all."

She noticed an irritating spark of mischief dancing in his dark eyes and she knew he was playing with her, delighting in vexing her, and she flushed with indignation.

"I beg you not to mock me, Lord Kingsley."

The mischief disappeared from his eyes and his expression above the snowy whiteness of his cravat became serious.

"Mock you? You are mistaken if you think that. I would neither mock nor offend someone I hold in such high regard as yourself. You, Miss Fairley, are so much at variance and a complete contradiction in terms of appearance. Not only are you beautiful, but you also have a frail vulnerability—and yet beneath it all there is a strong, wilful determination which belies your outward appearance.

"I admire you greatly. I admire your forthright character and strength of mind. If you had been born a man, without the restrictions imposed on your sex, I believe you would achieve anything you so desired."

Rachel was filled with astonishment; he never failed to surprise her. She stared at him, her eyes wide in her pale face, more than a little shocked by what he had said.

"You—you jest," she murmured.

"I am not jesting. I never jest about serious matters. Whenever we meet, you always succeed in get-

ting on the wrong side of my character. No woman
has ever done that. As a man you would make a formidable adversary, Miss Fairley. A man would be
proud to do battle with such a worthy opponent.''

Rachel stared at him, at a complete loss for words.
She told herself that, despite the changes she had discovered to his character, he was still arrogant and
conceited, the kind of man she disliked most, and yet
he was unlike any man she had ever known; she
found herself drawn to him against her will. He had
succeeded in making a definite impression on her
which was both stimulating and exciting.

But she should be warned; she already suspected
he was a man adept at getting what he wanted, that
he was a man of power, and she sensed an element
of danger in becoming too well acquainted with him.

He was standing very close, looking down at her
penetratingly. The silence stretched between them,
lengthening and becoming dangerous, but Rachel
could not move, and, feeling herself to be in the grip
of some powerful emotion, she did not want to
move—even though it was an emotion that threatened
to destroy her sensibilities and overwhelm her.

The moment was one which saw a heightening of
both their senses and involuntarily William took a
step that closed the distance between them, his eyes
darkening and letting his gaze drop to her lips, moist
and slightly parted. His closeness made Rachel feel
too vulnerable, but she was unable to move away. She
caught her breath, able to feel the heat emanating

from his body, to feel the power within him and the warmth of his breath on her upturned face.

Just when she thought he was going to lower his face to hers, to place his mouth on her lips, to her relief and dismay the moment was broken by her aunt Mary coming out onto the terrace.

"Why, here you are," she remarked, walking towards them, having noticed their absence and judging it advisable to seek them out—and on observing the hasty steps they took away from each other, and the look that passed between them when she stepped out onto the terrace, then she thought it was not a moment too soon. "I came to find you to see if either of you would care to partner me at whist."

Rachel flushed scarlet and gave an embarrassed, shaky laugh, trying, but without success, to hide the confusion she so clearly felt at being caught alone with Lord Kingsley in what had almost been a compromising situation.

"Why—I would love to, Aunt Mary. I—I just stepped on to the terrace for some air and became quite distracted by the view."

"Apparently so," her aunt replied drily.

"I—I'd better go inside. Excuse me, Lord Kingsley."

His eyes glowed warmly down at her, feeling none of the embarrassment which so clearly gripped her. "Of course. I must go inside, also. I am neglecting my other guests."

Followed by her aunt and Lord Kingsley, Rachel walked back into the brightly lit salon to join the other guests. The rest of the evening passed in some kind of blur. Lord Kingsley did not address her directly again but his eyes trailed over her continuously.

She was aware of his presence, of his eyes, which had an unsettling effect on her heart. She could not think coherently, and from the way every pulse in her body throbbed intolerably, how every time their eyes met she felt all the power of his gaze, it made her realise that something was happening between them. There were forces at work in her mind she found almost impossible to understand.

Chapter Six

What Rachel had seen at Mortlake Park disturbed her greatly. What was wrong with Lady Kingsley? she asked herself. It was well known she did not enjoy good health, but from Rachel's own observations her behaviour had been most peculiar. In addition, Lord Kingsley's request that he would prefer her not to discuss what she had seen, to try and forget it, puzzled her further. Why? What did it all mean?

She turned all these questions over in her mind, but no answer was forthcoming. In the end, she tried concentrating her thoughts on other matters, for, after all, it really was none of her concern. But she had a curious feeling that Lady Kingsley's condition was somehow significant to Lord Kingsley's refusal to allow his half-sister to marry Stephen.

Her own feelings towards Lord Kingsley were confused. She felt guilty, ashamed, even, of her premeditated opinion of him, and yet, recollecting his harsh treatment of her brother, then she believed she still had every reason to think ill of him. Although, she asked herself—when she considered his manner towards her father and herself since their first encounter, which could not be faulted—was it possible that she had misjudged him in that also? Perhaps rank and connections were not as important to him after all; it was a reasonable enough explanation for him to consider his sister, at seventeen years of age, too young to marry.

But there were other conflicting emotions churning around inside her that added to her confusion where he was concerned, which were of a more personal nature, emotions she was reluctant, but which she knew she would have, to face, if she hoped to have any kind of future. She had no wish to remain at Meadowfield Lodge all her life, pining for a lost love who had found happiness with another.

Ralph Wheeler had entered her life at a time when she had been young and vulnerable, when she had wanted nothing else from life but love and passion, but he had played her false. He had lied to her, deceived her when he had said he loved her, and destroyed all her hopes, all her ambitions for the future, leaving her with nothing but anger and a bitter memory of betrayal.

But under the layers of resilience and cold reserve she displayed to any predatory male who turned his attentions on her, determined never to allow anyone to hurt her as Ralph had done again, there still lurked the same young girl who had fallen in love with Ralph, a girl who had laughed and teased in the summer of her youth, who had been full of all the joys that life had to offer.

And now, since Lord Kingsley had entered her life, she felt he had the power to make her think once more of that same young girl, to revive her spirit and to renew her faith in a world in which she thought love had been denied her, and to help her to view life once more with the same carefree emotions.

With a warm glow flowing through her, she thought repeatedly of their conversation on the terrace at Mortlake Park. Remembering how much sincerity there had been in his voice as he had described his own views with regard to her character, she had a curious longing to hear him repeat what he had said.

They were not the words of an enemy and, remembering the strange and serious expression in his eyes and the compelling way in which they had been spoken when he had said, "I would neither mock nor offend someone I hold in such high regard as yourself" and "I admire you greatly", neither were they the words of a friend in the ordinary sense.

After much heart searching and emotional upheaval, now, to her consternation, her feelings for Lord Kingsley were so very different to what they had been. He filled her with a warmth and excitement otherwise unknown to her—and she knew it was going to be difficult to dislike him the way she had been able to before she had made his acquaintance.

There was an intensity of feelings between them that developed increasingly with each encounter, and also a physical attraction they were each aware of.

When she thought, with a certain amount of pleasure and embarrassment, of the intimate moment they had shared on the terrace, there was no doubt in her mind that he would have kissed her but for her aunt's untimely—or timely—arrival for she was unsure how she felt about it in the light of this self-revelation, when she had been profoundly conscious of his nearness and all her control had almost left her.

Not even Ralph had provoked such a debilitating effect on her senses. She had never felt so weakened by him. In fact, looking back, Ralph now seemed to have been so young, still a youth, and dull in comparison to Lord Kingsley. Their's had been a shared, gentle passion—which made her ask, now she had made the acquaintance of Lord Kingsley, if it really had been love?

She found there was an element of danger in knowing Lord Kingsley that secretly excited her, however hard she tried to fight against it, for in her quiet moments she kept seeing his amused, dark, sardonic eyes.

She did wonder if he were set on a course of seduction, which she found disturbing, but on reflection she did not suspect him of being a philanderer; being an aristocrat, he was ruled by the gentleman's code of behaviour that demanded self-control and prevented him from making advances towards the innocent daughter of a friend—however much he may desire to do so.

He had given her an insight into the serious side of his nature; she realised that, in contemplating this, she was in danger of becoming his victim—which, she suspected, was what he intended. But if so, after alienating her over his harsh treatment of Stephen, why would he think she would succumb to his powers of persuasion?

Not for one moment had the word love entered into her thinking; it was not an emotion she wanted to familiarise herself with just then, and anything of that nature between herself and Lord Kingsley she considered to be quite out of the question. A man who was as rich, powerful and incredibly attractive as he was could have any woman he desired.

He had been right when he had said that she succeeded in getting on the wrong side of his character whenever they met. Whenever she was with him, his presence affected her greatly in a way she could neither contemplate nor understand; she felt that, to cover her confusion, she had to be on the defensive.

If they were to meet again—as they surely must, given his friendship with her aunt Mary and his acquaintance with her father, and as she ardently hoped—then she was determined to tread carefully in a way that showed restraint.

After receiving another letter from Kitty, which informed her that Kitty's situation was a good deal worse, making it impossible for her to resume her career with the company at the Drury Lane theatre when it reopened, and honouring Kitty's request that she said not a word of the dire straits Kitty found herself to be in to their father, it was an extremely worried Rachel who set off for London with her aunt Mary and her cousins.

She hoped that, when she arrived, she would be able to confide in Stephen, who, like the rest of the family when they were in London, always resided at Brayfield House, but she was disappointed to find he had left for Newcastle on business.

Lady Brayfield's fashionable house in Hanover Square soon became a hive of activity, with an endless stream of visitors. Ever since her marriage to Lord Brayfield she had been a popular figure on the London scene. She loved entertaining and enjoyed most social events. The table in the hall was permanently full of calling cards.

With tremendous excitement, Caroline and Emily planned all the social functions they were to attend. Their time spent in London was to be one long round of balls, assemblies, masques, picnics and other events which would exhaust even the most energetic young lady.

However, Rachel, who was in no mood to enjoy such an active social life, did not share their exuberance, for when she thought how miserable Kitty appeared to be from the tone of her letters, then she made up her mind to see her as soon as possible.

Lady Brayfield, who had a natural affection for her niece, and had been kind and supportive since her mother's death and Kitty's departure from Meadowfield Lodge to follow her acting career, was not so busy that she did not notice a change in her. When her daughters were visiting the shops, leaving Rachel, who preferred not to accompany them, at home, she managed to speak to her alone in the drawing-room.

"I cannot help noticing that you have not been yourself of late, Rachel," she said with a touch of concern. "I strongly suspect you are concerned about Kitty. Am I correct?"

Rachel stared at her, for usually her aunt meticulously avoided any mention of Kitty.

"Yes—I am. I—I believe she has not been well of late and I shall not be content until I have seen for myself that she is all right."

"It's a pity she did not show the same concern for yourself when she took it into her head to become an actress," retorted her aunt, unable to keep the abrasive note from her voice.

"She has done me no great wrong that I can see," Rachel replied softly, not wishing to become embroiled in any conflict with her aunt over Kitty.

"You are too forgiving, Rachel. Your loyalty and love for your sister are to be commended, but Kitty, ruled by her emotions, has selfishly taken your devotion for granted. She has certainly done you no favours. That business with Ralph Wheeler is sure proof of it."

"I have no regrets over that, Aunt. By all accounts, Ralph is happily married now."

"He would have been married to you had Kitty given you any consideration. Your chances of procuring a suitable marriage have been reduced considerably. No man of rank and substance will ally himself to a woman who claims such close kinship with an actress.''

''Oh, one never knows, Aunt,'' said Rachel lightly, keeping to herself the fact that Kitty's actions often led her to think with a gnawing anxiety of her own future, but refusing to let it worry her unduly or to pity herself, ''there may be someone who will choose to overlook that when they learn my father has settled on me a substantial dowry.''

''Maybe—but somehow I doubt it—unless, of course, his estates are so encumbered he has to marry a woman with sufficient means.''

''If that were to be the case, then I would not accept such a situation. I would sooner not marry at all.''

''Spinsterhood is not for you, Rachel—that is a poor outlook and is unthinkable.''

''Oh, I think I could reconcile myself to it very easily, Aunt.''

''Why should you? You have assets to attract a husband—maybe not an earl or a lord—but a respectable gentleman just the same.''

''Who would do just as well,'' smiled Rachel, amused by the importance her aunt and women like her placed on a title. ''I care little for people with titles who have nothing else to recommend them.''

She would have liked to add—with nothing better to do other than dress up in the latest fashions and fritter their money away on entertainment and clothes, but thought better of it, not wishing to give offence to her aunt, for it came very close to attacking her own way of life.

"But there is no denying a title would be very nice all the same. You have good looks to recommend you and you are proficient in most things—better so than my own daughters, though I do say so myself.

"I love them dearly, but how I wish Caroline and Emily had just a little of your sense, Rachel—I suppose it's my own and my dear late husband's faults. They have been spoilt and indulged all their lives and, as a result, have turned out to be rather silly young women. Caroline, in particular, is vain of her prettiness."

"But she does appear to have captured Sir Edgar Mainwaring's heart, Aunt Mary. Anyone seeing them together cannot fail to see there is true affection growing between them."

Her aunt brightened suddenly. "Yes—now that would be a good match, and he is in London at this time with Lord Kingsley."

She looked at Rachel with sudden interest, remembering the look that had passed between her niece and the aforesaid gentleman when she had come upon them on the terrace at Mortlake Park, which had piqued her curiosity. "Speaking of Lord Kingsley, Rachel, he seemed to be much taken with you when we were at Mortlake Park."

Deliberately rejecting any notion of her aunt's, that Lord Kingsley and herself would one day become attached to one another, Rachel smiled, shaking her head slowly. "No, Aunt, not really. I know I can hope for nothing from Lord Kingsley other than his acquaintance. I shall never lose sight of my own inferiority where he is concerned,'' she said with wry humour. "And—anyway, there are other things in life apart from marriage."

"Unfortunately, to hold a place in society, a woman must be married, Rachel. It is a fact of life. Maybe we will see something of Lord Kingsley before he returns to Mortlake Park. As I understand it, he is in London to locate his brother.

"Although, from what I know of James and his intemperate desire for pleasure—having lived so long on the liberties of his family—his presence is to be found wherever there is popular entertainment. Lord Kingsley will not have to look very far. Now—what is all this about Kitty not being well?"

Unable to keep up with the pretence that all was well with her sister any longer, Rachel sighed.

"When I received a letter from Kitty before we came to London, she informed me that she has been quite unwell of late—and that she is unable to resume her career with the company at the Drury Lane theatre."

"I am sorry if her health is not as it should be, Rachel, but I, for one, am relieved to hear she is no longer exhibiting herself on the stage," said Lady Brayfield. She looked at Rachel sharply. "Is your father aware of this?"

"No. Kitty begged me not to say anything for the time being. And besides—you know yourself, Aunt, how frail he has become of late. With his weak heart—and the doctor's advice that he does not over-tax himself unduly—I fear any further anxiety over Kitty might prove too much for him. I really must spare him this if I can.''

Her aunt's eyes softened. ''Your sense of obligation and duty to your father is commendable, my dear, and…I suppose you are right. His worries over Kitty are great indeed. But what is she doing? What does she live on? I know—in her foolish desire to be totally independent—she refused any offer of an allowance from my brother.''

''Unfortunately, until I have seen her, I am no wiser than you are, Aunt.''

''Then I suppose you will have to go and see her,'' remarked her aunt crossly. ''Although I have to say that I am ashamed and disappointed by Kitty's behaviour. Your father allowed her too much licence—I said so at the time, but would he listen? What on earth possessed her to do something so extreme as to become an actress? Did she not realise that we were the ones who would have to live with the scandal? She has brought nothing but disgrace and embarrassment to the whole family.''

Rachel could not deny that there was much truth in her aunt's words; nevertheless, she was hurt by the severity of her condemnation of Kitty. She rose immediately to her sister's defence.

''Being the kind of person you are, Aunt, it is natural that you should feel disappointment, but I cannot help admiring Kitty's Bohemian attitude to life—and her contempt for society's ways. Despite the embarrassment you say she has brought on us all—which I am sure was unconsciously done—I am very proud of Kitty.

"When Stephen and I were in London in the spring and went to Drury Lane to see her on the stage, before the theatre closed for the summer months, I have to say that she shows great talent and works very hard. The acclaim she receives is well deserved."

Her aunt's lips curved in a slow, disdainful smile. "Kitty was always susceptible to flattery and adulation and it would seem that little has changed. However, knowing of your fondness for her, I shall make no further disparaging remarks. When do you plan on visiting her?"

"As soon as possible. Kitty has always been a rather complex person—but she has always been decisive and known what she wanted. That is why the contents of her letters of late have given me cause for serious concern. It is so strange—so unlike her."

"Yes—I can see that you are worried, Rachel, and have cause to be. She is your sister, after all, and it is only natural that you feel concern. But I will not accompany you—you do understand that, don't you?"

"Of course. I shall go alone."

"No. You must take my maid Celia with you. I cannot permit you to travel about London by yourself. My dear brother would never forgive me."

Kitty rented two rooms above a fruit shop in Catherine Street, close to the Drury Lane theatre. Rachel

shuddered to think of her sister living in such a disreputable area with its sinister maze of courts and
dark abodes, and where harlots paraded nightly. Since
the theatre had closed for the summer months and she
had declined to go on tour, Kitty assisted her landlady, Mrs Gilbey, in the busy fruit shop.

After instructing Celia to remain with the carriage
until she had seen her sister, Rachel went towards the
shop. Usually, she would have paused to look around
her, marvelling in the throng of people strolling about
in a carefree, casual way in the warm sun.

Distracted by concern for her sister, however, today
she was unable to delight in the wonders of the capital—to take note of the whole area ablaze with colour
and a cacophony of sounds as barrow boys and cos-
termongers, milkmaids and the songs of ballad sing-
ers, to name but a few, rose above each other to compete with the sound of iron-rimmed wheels of
carriages and carts rattling over the cobble stones.

Inside the shop she saw a buxom woman of middle
years, with florid features and copious double chins.
A large, stained apron covered the front of her dress
and she was serving a customer, which told Rachel
that this must be Mrs Gilbey. She looked towards
Rachel, whose face was bright with hopeful anticipation that at last she was about to see her sister.

"Are you Mrs Gilbey?" Rachel, not having met
the woman on her previous visit with Stephen, inquired when she had finished serving the customer.

"Yes, dear. And what would you be wanting?"

"I have come to see my sister, Miss Kitty Fairley. Is she at home, do you know?"

The smile faded from Mrs Gilbey's lips and she wiped her hands down the front of her apron. "I think you'd best step into the back for a moment, Miss Fairley," she said, moving towards the back of the shop and leaving her assistant to serve a young couple who had just come in from the street to purchase some succulent-looking strawberries on display.

Mrs Gilbey parted a curtain covering a doorway, through which a narrow wooden staircase rose to the rooms above. She turned to face Rachel, fixing her with a steady gaze.

"Your sister has gone," she said directly, "two weeks back."

Rachel was so surprised she could only stand and stare at her in disbelief.

"Gone?" she repeated. "But—that is not possible. You must be mistaken."

"No, she's gone all right," said Mrs Gilbey, offended that this young woman should doubt her word.

Rachel's confidence at seeing her sister had been so great that this blow made her heart sink.

Seeing the spontaneous shock and disappointment on Rachel's face, Mrs Gilbey relented and spoke more kindly. "I'm sorry. This is a shock for you, I can see."

Rachel looked at her in bewilderment. "Where—where did she go?"

"I don't know, dear. But I have to say I was most disappointed in her. Left without a by your leave, she did—all of a sudden one night. Took her things and left owing two weeks' rent.''

''Oh—I'm so sorry, Mrs Gilbey. I—I shall recompense you, of course.''

''Thank you. That would be appreciated.''

''Do you have any idea where she might have gone? Are there any friends you know of whom she might have gone to stay with?''

Mrs Gilbey shook her head. ''I couldn't say. Besides—she's hardly likely to tell me, is she, owing me two weeks' rent?''

''No—I'm sorry. Of course not. Did her friends often call on her?''

''Oh, aye. They did that. Popular was your sister—with most of the company from the theatre.''

''Was—was there anyone in particular, Mrs Gilbey? I—I mean—''

''Was there a gentleman?'' Mrs Gilbey finished for her, nodding. ''Yes—and a proper gentleman he was, too, if you ask me. Handsome he was—and always dressed in the finest clothes.''

''Do you remember his name?''

''No. He came but seldom—but she was quite struck by him—you could tell. He came to call a couple of days before she left—and they had a right proper argument, they did. Not that I was in the habit of listening, mind, but a person would have to be stone deaf not to have heard them.''

''What did he look like?''

''Oh—quite tall, he was, very fair and handsome.''

"And you really have no idea where she might have gone?"

"No. Although you may find out more at the theatre. Her friends might know."

"You may be right—although I was under the impression she was no longer with the company at Drury Lane."

"That's right. She left some time ago and helped me in the shop until she up and went."

"She wrote telling me she was not feeling well, Mrs Gilbey. Was she ill?"

Causing her chins to wobble, Mrs Gilbey shook her head and appeared to give Rachel's question some thought. "I don't know about that, Miss Fairley. If she was poorly, then she never said a word to me—but come to think of it, she did look a bit peaky and wasn't her usual cheery self."

Feeling Mrs Gilbey could be of no further help, Rachel sighed, wanting to run up the stairs and look in the room above the shop to make sure Kitty wasn't there. After giving Mrs Gilbey the rent Kitty had left owing, she moved back into the shop, pausing in the doorway.

"Thank you for your help, Mrs Gilbey. You have been most kind. If—if my sister should return, please tell her that I have called and she must contact me."

"Aye—I'll do that," she said, but as Rachel walked back to the waiting carriage she shook her head, knowing full well that she had seen the last of Miss Kitty Fairley.

* * *

The fear and anxiety over Kitty's whereabouts gripping Rachel's heart was so great that she was swamped with hopelessness and despair, remembering nothing of the journey back to Hanover Square. She was hopelessly confused as she struggled with many unanswered questions.

Where was she? Who was the man Mrs Gilbey had referred to? Was she in love with him? Had she gone to live with him? Dear Lord, she hoped not. Her sister had already stepped outside the bounds of propriety by becoming an actress—but for her to live openly with a man would ruin her reputation completely.

If only Stephen had not left for the north—he would know what to do. It would be so much easier for him to make enquiries into Kitty's whereabouts than for her.

She was in such a dilemma when she climbed the steps of the house that she failed to see the elegant black carriage and four waiting in the road.

She saw Lord Kingsley through the open door to the drawing-room the moment she entered the house, even before her aunt, having heard her come in, came into the hall to announce his presence. He looked so handsome, so full of vigor and so perfectly turned out in his dark green frock coat and pristine white cravat, his curling black hair gleaming brightly.

Caroline and Sir Edgar Mainwaring conversed together, Sir Edgar having taken a seat beside Caroline, who looked calf-like into his eyes and smiled prettily, listening to all he said and holding on to his every word, while Emily, seated opposite, occasionally put in a word or two. Lord Kingsley was standing by the fireplace, seeming to be unconcerned about making conversation. After removing her bonnet, Rachel moved slowly into the room.

As if he felt her presence, by some sixth sense William turned and saw her watching him. The strangest sensation passed between them and Rachel suddenly had a peculiar feeling that here was someone who could help her, that he was so strong, so self-assured. How good it would be, she thought wearily, to put the burden Kitty had presented her with on to someone else, someone she could rely on to help her locate her wayward sister.

But why should she imagine for one moment that Lord Kingsley would come to her aid? He was in London to locate his own brother who, according to her aunt, was equally as troublesome as her sister.

"Rachel, my dear," her aunt welcomed her, "I am so glad you are back. We have visitors—Lord Kingsley and Sir Edgar Mainwaring."

"Yes, so I see."

Lady Brayfield disappeared to arrange for refreshments to be brought for her visitors while Rachel stepped into the room—and it seemed to her that Lord Kingsley's gaze never left hers. She lowered her eyes as she bobbed a polite curtsy and then raised them slowly, looking up at him fully.

His eyes were sharp and observant, and all the anxieties she was feeling leapt towards him. He frowned slightly, detecting all was not well with her, that she was putting on a show of politeness for his benefit.

His expression was grave and inquiring. "It is a pleasure to see you again, Miss Fairley. Are you enjoying London?"

"Since we arrived scarcely two days ago, sir, I have hardly had time to attend any of the functions my cousins are so busy planning. And what of you? Have you managed to locate your brother or does he continue to elude you?"

"For the present. Although I understand he is staying with an acquaintance in Kent and is due back in London any day now. Sir Edgar and I are to visit the Drury Lane theatre tomorrow evening. I have taken a box and Lady Brayfield has honoured me by accepting my invitation that she, your cousins and yourself, be my guests."

Overhearing what he said, Caroline gave a little squeal of delight. "Oh, that will be wonderful," she enthused. "I have heard they are putting on Mr Garrick's play, *The Country Girl*—and that Mrs Jordan is to play the lead."

William smiled at her obvious pleasure. "She is indeed. And if she is as successful here in London as she was in Dublin then we are in for a treat."

"I have heard that her morals are quite outrageous—for I do believe she has not one, but several illegitimate children. Is that not so, Lord Kingsley?" asked Emily suddenly, in wide-eyed innocent curiosity.

"Emily!" chided Caroline sternly. "You must not let Mama hear you say such things—especially not in the company of gentlemen."

Unrepentant, Emily ignored her sister's stern rebuke, her flushed expression and bright eyes revealing her eagerness for a little scandalous gossip. "Nevertheless, it is so, is it not, Lord Kingsley?" she persisted. "And is it not quite shocking and shameful?"

Frankly amused, William laughed outright, his strong white teeth flashing from between his parted lips. "I have to say it must be both shocking and shameful indeed for a lady to find herself in such an unfortunate predicament once—but several times is quite insupportable. Mrs Jordan's affairs have been fodder for gossip for some time. It would seem she has not been ungenerous in dispensing with her favours.

"I do feel you will enjoy seeing *The Country Girl* and as it is the first night of showing—the theatre having been closed for the summer months—then I imagine every seat will be taken."

"Then thank heaven you have hired a box, Lord Kingsley," said Emily. "I would not want to miss it for the world."

Turning, Rachel saw by the expression in Caroline's eyes and the note in her voice as she animatedly discussed the event with Emily, that the prospect of an evening spent at the theatre with Sir Edgar delighted her.

She searched frantically in her own mind for a reason not to go, in no mood for such frivolity until she had found Kitty. She knew her aunt would not have accepted Lord Kingsley's invitation had she not been aware that Kitty was not to resume her career with the company.

Lord Kingsley smiled with polite indulgence at the two sisters, but then turned his full attention to Rachel, again fixing her with his dark, inquiring gaze. ''And what does Miss Fairley say? Does the prospect of seeing the opening night of *The Country Girl* not excite you as much as it does your cousins?'' he asked quietly.

''I—I thank you for your kind invitation, Lord Kingsley, but—I—I—''

''Come now, I know on our first encounter I gave you the impression that I abhorred the theatre and had a low opinion of anyone connected with it—but I assure you that is not the case. On quieter contemplation, I have re-examined my behaviour of that day and remember your abhorrence to my remarks that you found so offensive. I recollect on it often and have every reason to reproach myself. My behaviour to you then was unpardonable.

''I do want you to come—the reason for my invitation being that it would give me the chance of proving to you that I do have some redeeming qualities. Once ill thought of, I have to find some way of gaining your favour.''

There was no mistaking that he was in earnest and Rachel felt a stirring of warmth in her heart and—not for the first time—a dawning of respect. He was making it extremely difficult for her to refuse his invitation. ''You—you do not have to prove anything to me, Lord Kingsley.''

"But I believe I do."

"Why should you? Why should you feel it necessary to have such sentiments? Forgive me if I seem surprised, but on three of our previous encounters we did not get on at all well.

"I say this without being cruel or unkind, but I realise now that my manner must have seemed impertinent and presumptuous to you and, having a tendency to let my tongue run on without restraint, I did not believe I had impressed you in the slightest and had only succeeded in convincing you that not only am I inferior to you in social standing but also of mind."

"Not inferiority of mind. Never that, Miss Fairley—and I believe I am not so self-opinionated as to think it," he said gravely. "It is food to my soul to find someone, like yourself of equal mind, both refreshing and stimulating to converse with.

"I should have made an attempt to suppress any uncivil behaviour I might have shown—and if I exposed my anger and frustration then it was directed more at myself than with any intention of wounding you. Is it too much to hope that eventually you might view my character in a more amiable light?"

Rachel looked at him steadily. "No—it is not—but, in truth, I do not understand you. You are quite surprising."

"If you knew me better you would know I am full of odd surprises," he smiled. "I am paving the way with good intentions for the future, Miss Fairley. You see, with the sale of my plantation on Barbados, my life and associates are going to be somewhat different from what they have been.''

Rachel was silent, declining to ask if she could be named among his new associates. It was not without a certain wild pleasure that she hoped she would be, although she would not allow herself to think of him in any light other than an acquaintance—pleasant or otherwise remained to be seen.

''You have a sister on the stage at the Drury Lane theatre, I believe?'' he said on a lighter note. ''If she is in the play, then you will have the opportunity of seeing her perform—unless, of course, you will find it an embarrassment watching her in our presence.''

''No—of course not, but my—my sister is no longer with the company at Drury Lane, Lord Kingsley.''

''I see,'' William said, seeming to detect from the way her words faltered and she avoided his gaze that all was not as it should be with her sister. ''So—you will come?''

''Yes—thank you,'' she replied, smiling softly into his eyes. ''How can I refuse?''

''Then it is settled.''

There was a note of finality in his voice which told Rachel there was nothing more she could say on the subject.

''Forgive me, Miss Fairley, but I cannot help but observe your despondency. Is there anything the matter? Is there something wrong?''

''No. If I appear despondent, then it can only be put down to my outing and the awful congestion of

the traffic on the streets. I have to say that because
of it my errand took twice as long as it should have
done.''

''I believe it is something other than the traffic
which troubles you. You have been to see your sister,
have you not?'' He smiled when she glanced at him
sharply. ''Forgive me, but your aunt mentioned it.''

''Yes—yes, I have.''

''Then that must have given you certain pleasure
to see and talk to her again.''

''It would—but sadly I was denied that pleasure. I
did not inform Kitty of my visit, you see, and she was
not at home.''

They were distracted at that moment when Lady
Brayfield returned to her guests, and it was only when
they had departed and Rachel had given her an account of her visit to Kitty's lodgings, relating all that
Mrs Gilbey had told her, that her aunt relented in her
attitude towards Kitty and became almost as concerned as to her whereabouts as Rachel was.

''You are right, of course, Rachel. Kitty is your
sister and no matter what she has done, however foolish, she must be found. I am afraid your father must
be told at once.''

Rachel's eyes flew to hers in alarm. ''Oh, no, Aunt.
Surely not. I dread to think of the effect such news
will have on him.''

''Nevertheless, he must be told. It is our duty to
tell him. We can only pray it does not prove to be
too much for him.''

Chapter Seven

The street in front of the Drury Lane theatre, which provided an unfailing source of entertainment for Londoners, was congested with carriages and people alike long before the doors were opened for, being the opening night after the long closure over the summer months, the only sure way of securing a seat in the gallery or the pit was to arrive at the theatre early.

It was Emily's first visit to the theatre and she was in a state of euphoric excitement, her eyes positively agog as she absorbed everything—from the elegant and fashionably attired gentry and nobles in the gallery and private boxes, to the disreputable-looking raucous mob down in the pit.

"Good gracious," she said in shocked amazement. "It hardly seems a reputable place to be when one observes the scandalous behaviour of the people down below."

"Nonsense," laughed Sir Edgar good-humouredly, glancing over the edge of their box at the subject of her attention. "Theatres are much improved and quite respectable places nowadays.

"Only ladies of a certain low character, as seen down in the pit, attend without a male escort," he said in a conspiratorial whisper to Emily, indicating several ladies of dubious reputation, with over-painted faces and garish, extravagant head-dresses and huge nosegays on the bosoms of their provocative low-bodiced gowns.

"And do you enjoy the theatre, Sir Edgar?" asked Caroline.

"Yes, enormously, although one of my chief delights when I am in London is to visit the pleasure gardens on the south bank of the river."

"We've never visited any of them as yet, but Mama has promised to take us to Ranelagh next week. She says they are far superior to Vauxhall and one cannot move a step without coming upon a prince or an earl."

"Then you must allow me to be your escort," offered Sir Edgar, "and Lady Brayfield is quite right. Ranelagh may be more expensive at two shillings and sixpence for admission as opposed to Vauxhall's one shilling, but I consider it to be well worth it. Yes—I shall be happy to escort you, Lady Brayfield," he said, looking to where she sat next to Rachel at the other side of the box.

"Thank you, Sir Edgar. We shall look forward to it," she acknowledged with a gracious smile.

"Of course, I cannot speak for Lord Kingsley," said Sir Edgar, "who, I dare say, will be otherwise engaged—but it will be my pleasure to show you the Rotunda and the canal—and the flower gardens are a constant delight—is that not so, William?'' he enthused, turning to his friend, who acknowledged his question with a smile.

''They certainly are. And if it is possible to see them by moonlight, then Ranelagh is a magical place to be.'' He looked across at Rachel, who seemed unusually quiet. ''Are you to visit Ranelagh also, Miss Fairley?''

She seemed to start and caught his gaze. Clearly something other than the pleasure gardens occupied her thoughts. Secretly she was wondering how she could possibly get to the back stage of the theatre to make enquiries about Kitty, for there must be someone who would remember her and know something of her whereabouts.

''Why—yes, of course.'' she replied absently. ''I am looking forward to it.''

Rachel fell silent, fixing her gaze on the closed curtains that hid the stage. Deeply apprehensive, she hadn't slept the previous night through worrying about Kitty; as a consequence, she was pale and her expression strained. On arriving at the theatre, Lord Kingsley had given her an anxious look and had spoken to her quietly as he had taken her arm and had escorted her up the stairs to the box he had hired for the evening.

''You seem to have a great deal on your mind this evening, Miss Fairley.''

''Yes,'' she had replied, meeting his gaze, seeing

no reason to deny what must be obvious. "You are very perceptive, Lord Kingsley."

"I merely observe that you are not your usual self," he had said.

"I beg you not to concern yourself on my account. I am sure my problem will resolve itself."

By the time the performance began, the theatre, seating about two thousand people, was packed, the audience becoming quiet with expectancy as the curtain rose and the footlights blazed—but whether it would remain so when the play began, when the ineptitude of any of the actors did not meet with the audience's approval, then it would respond with a loud stamping of feet and hissing and booing to show its displeasure.

The box next to Lord Kingsley's was full of fashionable fops, loud with idle chatter, constantly making forward comments to the ladies on the stage— much to the displeasure of the more refined, intelligent theatre goers, who took a genuine interest in the play.

Throughout the performance, Rachel sat quite still, her eyes never leaving the stage. In spite of the anxiety she was feeling over Kitty, she found herself relaxing and enjoying the play, laughing along with the audience at the comic and witty repartee produced by the actors.

At a break in the play, Lord Kingsley leaned forward to speak to her quietly. "I'm happy to see you are enjoying the play."

"Yes, I am—very much," she replied. "After tonight's performance, without doubt, Mrs Jordan will certainly be seen as the Queen of Comedy at Drury Lane. She is wonderful in the role of Peggy, don't you agree?''

"She certainly is, although I think you do not agree with the scenario. I think I am right when I say you cannot identify yourself with Peggy, am I not?'' he asked with a glow in his dark eyes, his face not far from her own as he spoke quietly, fanning her cheek with his warm breath, speaking to her with a deep level of intimacy as each remembered the conversation they had shared by the river at Meadowfield Lodge concerning a woman's role in life.

"Not really..." she smiled "...as well you know. You are already familiar with my views on how a young lady should be raised. I cannot agree that she should be reared by her guardian—or her father or whoever it may be—in ignorance and innocence so that she may become a compliant wife. But it is just a play, after all—put on to entertain and not to be taken seriously.''

Their conversation was brought to an end by the actors coming back on stage, but all the while Rachel was conscious of Lord Kingsley's presence. His face was almost hidden from her in the gloom but she could feel his eyes on her.

The play finished early. When there was no sight of their carriage in the street, impulsively Rachel turned quickly, excusing herself on the pretence that she was missing her fan—which she kept carefully concealed in the folds of her skirts—and must have left it on her seat.

"Wait—I'll go," offered Sir Edgar gallantly, but Rachel was already going back through the door.

"No—thank you." She smiled back at him with a cheerfulness she was far from feeling. "I shall not be a moment." She ran back inside the theatre, pushing her way past the people coming out, knowing she hadn't long, so she must hurry.

Finding her way back stage, she suddenly found herself cast into a world of chaos—colourful, noisy, exciting, a world of wayward unreality. It was gaudy and bright, the warm, slightly sickly air of candles and greasepaint wrapping itself around her and drawing her into a different world—a world in which she could well envisage her gregarious sister.

Props and scenery littered the floor, leaned against the walls or were being moved by stage hands—all important elements of theatrical life. There were racks and racks of costumes—fluted, scalloped, lace, taffeta, heavy brocades, shocking and gaudy—and all manner of wigs hanging on pegs or adorning heads— long wigs, bobbed, full-curled, some straight and some elegant and stuck high with tortoiseshell combs.

Without a shred of modesty, actors struggled out of their costumes, and some, in less of a hurry to leave the theatre now the performance was over, were reciting their lines in pompous tones and throwing their arms wide in flamboyant, affected pose, oblivious to the mayhem all around in their effort to become word perfect, giving way under sudden outbursts of angry frustration and nervous anxiety when they failed to do so.

Quickly, and in desperation, Rachel made enquiries of several people concerning Kitty. Most of them knew her, some better than others, but no one could tell her why she had suddenly decided not to return to the company or where she had gone.

She stared at the picturesque presentation all around her, finding it strange, weird, almost, that all these people had known and worked with Kitty, had shared her leisure hours, and yet they had allowed her to disappear from their lives as if she had never been.

Trying to overcome the awful fear that something terrible might have befallen her sister, Rachel looked about her, lost and bewildered, knowing she must return to her aunt, who would be getting increasingly angry at being kept waiting, but she was unable to move.

With a feeling bordering on utter despair, she stood within a warm circle of light, suddenly finding it so hot behind the stage. Everything seemed to be swimming around her and she thought she would faint, but all of a sudden Lord Kingsley was beside her, a worried look upon his face. She swayed slightly and, reaching out, he placed an arm firmly about her waist, steadying her.

"I must apologise if I startled you," he said quietly. "You look most unwell. Would you like to sit down a moment before you return to your aunt?"

"No—thank you. I am quite all right."

"When I saw you dash back inside the theatre, I

followed you to make sure you were not molested. Did you make a pretence of returning for your fan in order to come back stage to enquire after your sister?''

She nodded wearily as his arm dropped from her waist, but she had been very much aware of the brief contact and experienced a feeling of regret when he relinquished his hold on her. ''Please forgive me. Everything has been suspended in my mind by Kitty's disappearance. I can think of nothing else.''

''Disappearance?''

''Yesterday, when you came to the house, I did not tell you that, when I went to see my sister at her lodgings, her landlady informed me she had left her rooms suddenly, without any prior notice and owing two weeks' rent. Can you wonder that I am worried about her? She has gone and no one has seen her since.

''Looking back to the last time I saw her, I now realise her behaviour was studied—yes,'' she said, almost to herself, ''something was wrong even then. She laughed a lot and tried to appear normal, but I now realise she was trying to create a calculated impression to fend off any worries I might have as to her health.

''Since that time, I have come to understand from the contents of her letters that she is ill. She was not specific so I do not know the nature of her illness— but I pray this is not connected in any way with her disappearance.''

''But have you enquired among the people here?

Surely, if she was with the company until before the summer recess, then she must still have friends among them. She cannot simply disappear.''

"But she has," she replied, quite distraught. "I have enquired and no one has seen her."

"Can you not think of anyone she might have gone to stay with? Relatives or friends of your family, perhaps?''

Rachel shook her head. "No. Only one thing comes to mind and it is quite, quite shocking."

William nodded slowly, seeming to understand what was in her mind. "A gentleman? Was she involved with someone?''

Rachel swallowed hard. "Yes, I believe she was."

"And have you no clue as to his identity?''

"No. Nothing. Besides," she whispered, "it would seem there are many gentlemen of her acquaintance. It could be any one of them. I suspected something of the kind when she showed no inclination to go on tour during the summer months—as many of her theatrical friends did—and by her own account had an enjoyable time even though the work was hard.

"I am deeply concerned for her health and safety. I have to find her," she said with outright anguish, with a trembling voice, struggling to repress her tears, for she did not want Lord Kingsley to see her weep. "I have to find her before her position becomes quite desperate—before something quite dreadful happens to her.''

Rachel's eyes sought Lord Kingsley's for understanding and reassurance, and she saw there was a strange expression on his face she had not seen before as he looked at her in silent sympathy and commiseration.

"What has your father to say to all this?"

"He—he knows none it. Kitty begged me to conceal it from him. She—she did not wish to cause him any distress."

"Then he must be told. You will do that?"

She nodded. "It is already done—although I am deeply concerned as to how such dreadful news will affect him in his weakened state. My aunt has written asking him to come to London immediately."

"Then let us hope for your sister's sake it will be soon," he said, deeply touched by her obvious distress, her vibrancy and physical liveliness having deserted her in her concern and anxiety for her sister. Where was the high-spirited, vital Rachel Fairley he had come to know? he asked himself. It was certainly not this maimed, scarred, forlorn creature he now beheld on the verge of despair.

Let her sister be worthy of such sisterly love and devotion, who, in her blind and wanton selfishness, had sought to gratify her own desires at the expense of her family and especially that of her sister. At that moment, overwhelming tenderness rose inside him to do battle with the anger he felt for Kitty Fairley, which shook him to his heart's core.

"Come—you are distressed," he said. "Let me take you back to your aunt."

"Yes, thank you," she said. "I need not ask that

you keep this to yourself for the time being, Lord Kingsley—at least until my father reaches London?''

''You can rely on my discretion. I am not inclined to gossip. There are secrets in most families one would wish to remain silent.''

There was such warmth in his eyes, such concern in his voice, that at that moment Rachel did not doubt his sincerity. Only later, on contemplation of his words, did she wonder if he had been referring to his own family and the peculiar behaviour she had witnessed at Mortlake Park of his stepmother.

William was deeply affected and concerned by Rachel's plight and was still wondering how he could be of help to her in tracking down her sister when his brother James arrived back in London and presented himself at Kingsley House—as though he had just returned from a jaunt around the park instead of three weeks in Kent.

William, who had not seen his brother in several months, immediately summoned him to the library and watched him enter the room with an implacable eye, asking himself—as he had done many times—if he could have directed him better. Their father's illness, followed by his death, and his own long absences in the Indies, had left James to go his own way, which had resulted in his wayward behaviour and attracted much disfavour from himself.

He was resolved to not allow James to continue in this way. He needed a purpose in life, something to bring him out of the state of lethargy he had fallen into. Not since James had been a youth had William seen excitement illuminating his eyes at some daredevil exploit.

James had always been high-spirited, thriving on excitement and danger, and his sights had been set on a military career—until his mother, unable to bear the thought of her precious son being caught up in some war or other and killed, had ordered him to put the idea out of his head. After this, James had appeared to lose heart and began spending more and more of his time away from Mortlake Park.

William was determined to try and infuse into him a new drive. He had too much intelligence, too much energy, to spend his time loitering about the clubs and taverns of London with his degenerate acquaintances, drinking and in pursuit of sexual conquests.

In stark contrast to William's dark looks, James was extremely fair like his sister. Both took after their mother. Being a slender young man with blond good looks and endless charm, James had soon adapted himself to the London social scene, becoming a popular figure in the well-to-do drawing-rooms and coffee houses.

He was elegant and immaculate in a grey cloth suit and frothing lace cravat, with lace spilling from his cuffs over long slender fingers. In fact, he was every inch a man about town, one to catch the admiring, languishing eyes of the opposite sex, who would deem it an honour to be seen hanging on to his arm. He acted nonchalant as he moved towards his brother, his manner confident, his smile guileless.

"Hello, William," he said pleasantly, in his usual placid, even-tempered tones. "It's good to see you back—although I'm surprised to see you here in London. Thought you'd have too much to do at Mortlake since your return from the Indies. Sorry I missed you before. I would have waited had I known."

"I would not be here, had you condescended to return to Mortlake instead of going to Kent, James," said his brother harshly.

James stiffened, ready to defend himself. "There was little to do in London so I went to stay with an acquaintance of mine in Rochester—who kindly invited me down to his estate for a spot of fishing," he said, absently flicking an imaginary speck from his coat sleeve. "It was just a jaunt."

"If the bills you normally run up on such excursions are anything to go by, then no doubt it will prove to have been a costly jaunt," William retorted crossly. "If you were so bored with London, why did you not return to Mortlake?

"Your prolonged neglect of your duties towards your mother is quite disgraceful. It seems you have given little thought to her or Amanda during all the time I have been absent. Your mother misses you and is forever asking what keeps you away from Mortlake for so long. What have you to say for yourself?"

At William's mention of his mother, a weariness came over James's features and he was beginning to look uncomfortable. "Only that I had much to occupy my time here in London. I saw Amanda before she went to Europe with Aunt Harriet and she informed me that Mother was quite well.''

''I suspect that is what you hoped to hear, but I can tell you she is far from it—as well you know.''

James was resentful of William's authority over him and the accusing tone of his voice, but he smiled, nevertheless—one of his best assets—in an attempt to placate his brother.

''Yes, you are right, William—you always are, it would seem,'' he said, with just a trace of sarcasm, but not enough to anger William further.

However resentful James was at times like these— when William spoke to him like his father had before him—beneath his resentment he harboured a deep love for his elder brother and always missed him dreadfully when he went to the Indies for long periods. There was many a time he would have liked to accompany him but his mother had forbidden it, convinced the ship carrying him there would be lost in a squall and she would never see him again.

He sighed, becoming subdued, his face taking on a tired, weary expression, making him look so much younger suddenly. ''I shall return to Mortlake within the week—I promise. In fact,'' he said quietly, in an abstract, thoughtful way, ''I shall be happy to.''

''I'm glad to hear it,'' said William, his expression inscrutable. ''Although I am somewhat surprised by your readiness to comply without argument, which rouses my suspicions—could it be trouble which hastens your departure from London? A debt, perhaps, or a jealous husband? Which one, James? If it is either of those reasons, then no doubt I shall find out in time.''

''It is neither,'' James replied in an offended tone, beginning to look a trifle dejected. ''Really, William, you do have a low opinion of me.''

''It is hardly surprising, is it not? The reputation of your friends cannot be recommended and you value to such a high degree your selfish pleasures more than your personal integrity. I can see you are very much in danger of falling into dissolute, amoral ways from a surfeit of indulgence.''

''I think that's a bit harsh,'' James objected, a light flush spreading over his face.

''Do you indeed? It is true, nevertheless. I am losing faith in your ability to do anything other than fritter away your time and money on idle pleasures. Do you never stop to consider the impropriety of your behaviour—the consequences of it?

''You have a casual disregard for any duty you should feel towards your family. When I returned from the West Indies, you should have been in London to accompany me back to Mortlake. As it was, when I arrived there, I found everything in complete chaos and, because Amanda had no one to guide her, she had become romantically involved with Mr Stephen Fairley.''

William's sharp eyes noticed how James paled at his mention of Stephen Fairley, that he averted his eyes and suddenly seemed extremely discomposed. Curious as to the reason, he frowned. ''You are acquainted with the Fairleys, are you not, James? They have lived in Ellerton for the past five years, I believe."

James smiled—a forced smile, William thought.

"Why—yes," he said, hesitantly, "but only in passing, you know. Mr Fairley has two charming daughters, I think. Amanda got to know one of them quite well whilst you were in the Indies—the younger one, I believe—who, if I remember correctly, was just getting over being jilted by some fellow or other. I do remember thinking at the time that he must have been quite mad—she is quite ravishing to look at."

If James had looked closely at his brother, he would have seen how his brow creased in a deep angry frown and his jaw tightened while he related this. It was not the first time William had been made aware of Rachel's lost love and how deeply wounded she had been by it.

It went a long way to explaining why, in the beginning, she had not encouraged their friendship, why she had erected a barrier about her person and displayed a cool reserve, which, he suspected, was to protect her from being hurt again. But he was determined to break down her barrier, no matter how difficult or how long it took. Although of late he had seen a softening in her attitude towards him, a lowering of her defences, which he found encouraging.

"I did notice that Amanda looked quite dewy-eyed when she came to London," James continued, unaware of the affect his words had had on William. "She told me Stephen Fairley asked for your consent to marry her and you refused."

"Of course I refused my consent. She is but seventeen years old."

"Eighteen now, William," James corrected him. "Her birthday was last month. I—I suppose you consider the Fairleys to be socially inferior?"

He seemed to ask the question with caution, once again a thoughtful, inquiring look entering his eyes as he looked pointedly at his brother—as if his answer was important to him, which puzzled William slightly. He thought little of it just then, but was to remember it at a later date.

"Come, James. You know as well as I it has nothing to do with his social inferiority. In fact, I like Stephen Fairley and consider he would make Amanda a good husband—but until this unfortunate matter of your mother's family is cleared up I cannot give my consent for Amanda to marry anyone—and I would advise you to practice the same restraint," he said meaningfully.

James had the good grace to look contrite. "Yes—of course—you are quite right, William. Forgive me. I wasn't thinking."

"And that is precisely your problem, James. You never do think. But things will have to change if you wish to enjoy the pleasures you have become accustomed to."

James looked at his brother sharply. "Change? Why—what do you mean?"

"I mean that you will have to begin applying yourself to some kind of employment. You are not free to do as you please with your life. You have been too preoccupied with your crowd of dissolute socialites to spend time with your family—and believe me, James, they will entice you into disgrace and ruin if it goes on.''

''Then what do you suggest? I strongly suspect you have a reason for this severe attack on my character.''

William sighed, his anger draining away. ''Come and sit down,'' he said, placing a brotherly hand on his shoulder and leading him to two chairs, one on either side of the fireplace, where they became seated, facing each other.

''I'm sorry, James,'' he said, in gentler, friendlier tones, ''I didn't mean to attack you and you must believe me when I say I bear you no ill will. After all, no one knows more than I how difficult it was for you growing up at Mortlake with your mother the way she was and still is—and, sadly, I have to say she is getting progressively worse. I suppose I cannot blame you for not wishing to spend your time there. But you must understand how concerned I am about the way you conduct your life.''

''I'm sorry, William,'' said James, seeming more at ease by the softening of his brother's manner towards him. ''It is not my intention to cause you to worry. But you must see that I have little else to do with my life. My mother thwarted any ideas I had of carving out for myself a career with the army—and at that time Father was so afraid of upsetting her lest it accelerated her illness that he would never go against her wishes.

''If her family had retained the plantation on Antigua, I would have seriously considered going out there—but she chose to sell it on my grandfather's death. As for Mortlake—well—I have to say I love the place. I always have. But I could not endure Mother's possessiveness any longer. I had to get away.''

William nodded. ''Yes—I know that. I do understand, James, and perhaps what I am about to say might bring a solution to the problem. I have almost concluded the sale of the plantation on Barbados, so I shall not be returning to the Indies. I did tell you that I intended finding a buyer before I returned this last time, and, as I remember, you were in favour of my doing this.''

''Yes—yes, I was. Like you, I was never comfortable with the manner in which we obtained our wealth. Slavery is an abominable practice and it is time it was abolished. What are your intentions now?''

''With the capital from the sale, I intend investing extensively in industry in this country, for the economy is buoyant enough to do this. My wish is that you will interest yourself in this and familiarise yourself with industries into which we will eventually sink our capital.''

''But what manner of industry do you intend investing in?''

William shrugged. ''Iron—steel—coal—cotton mills, whatever. More factories are being built, more coal mines opened and canals being dug. The wide range of inventions being produced is extraordinary and hundreds of new patents have been taken out in the last twenty years, bringing vast advantages to industry. Industrial output is soaring in this country and the value of exports rising considerably all the time.

"I hope you have no objection to this, James, for it will affect you and Amanda, after all. I am going to need someone I can trust to send to the north—to the mill towns and Newcastle and Yorkshire, to see how these industries are run at first hand. Come, James, what do you say? Do you support me on this? Would you be willing to undertake the duties?"

Having always left the running of things to William, James's first reaction to what was suggested was one of surprise. William observed a slight withdrawal, but there was a keen look and a light in James's eyes that he thought was the first spark of interest he had shown in anything in years. He was pleased to see he had at least managed to capture his attention and curiosity.

"I—I don't know, William. I have to admit I have given little thought to what you would do when you severed our interests in the West Indies. But surely you would be better employing someone more qualified to carry out this kind of work?"

"We will have financial and business advisers aplenty—but I want someone I can trust with me on this."

"And you would trust me with this task?"

"No one better."

"But I know nothing about industry."

"Then you can learn. You have more intelligence and common sense than you allow people to give you credit for. I have Mortlake to take care of, so I shall not have the time to travel about the country as you will be able to. Come, James, do not tell me you want to continue this degenerate kind of existence.''

James shook his head, his features set in a serious expression. "No. You are right, William. This is not what I want and I am certainly not proud of myself. I am undeserving of the trust you are placing in me, but if it is what you wish, then I will do as you ask. I shall be proud to. I shall try my utmost to re-establish myself to you. I shall try very hard not to let you down.''

"I know you will, James," said William, more relaxed, and he smiled. "I have every confidence in you. Come," he said, rising and going to where a decanter of brandy stood on a silver tray on a side table, pouring the amber spirit into two glasses and handing one to his brother who rose to stand beside him. "Join me in a toast to the success of our new venture. It's going to be an exciting time—one which will bring great changes to all our lives.''

Chapter Eight

Feeling unable to return to Mortlake Park until Rachel's sister had been located, William sent James on ahead of him, reluctant to have him remain in London any longer lest one of his acquaintances managed to tempt him to stay and he was lured back into his profligate ways.

After making his own enquiries at the Drury Lane theatre, he succeeded in gleaning some information about Kitty Fairley from a female member of the company—one Rachel had not spoken to on her visit. Acting on this information, William found himself in Covent Garden, heading for the coffee houses which, he'd been informed, she frequented on occasion.

Covent Garden was hardly a respectable place, although it was colourful and popular with actors, would-be actors, artists and writers alike. However, it was not one of William's favourite areas of London, where well-to-do had once lived in fine houses—designed over a century ago in the Italian style by Inigo Jones, until other developments further west were built and the rich and aristocratic moved out, resulting in the decline of the fashionable status of Covent Garden.

Now the houses had been converted into seedy brothels and Turkish baths. The tone of the locality was raffish and rowdy, squalid and abounding with immorality, where cheap entertainment, gambling dens and gin shops abounded behind the elegant façades of the buildings around the piazza.

William enquired in the shops and coffee houses in the hope of someone knowing Kitty Fairley. It was in the Bedford, close to the Covent Garden theatre, once frequented by well-known artists and writers such as Hogarth, Boswell, Garrick, Goldsmith and Sheridan, that at last he managed to find someone who knew her and told him Kitty was living close by with a woman by the name of Sally Pearce.

Following directions to the aforesaid woman's house, William soon found himself in the slums in the streets behind Covent Garden—in alleyways, reeking yards and dark abodes. Finding the one he had been directed to, he banged on the door. A woman of about twenty-five or so, with a fall of heavy, greasy dark hair, pulled it open, the low scoop of her stained bodice displaying her large breasts.

''Well?'' she said in a sullen tone.

There was an aura of robust sexuality about her that told William all he needed to know about her profession, for her heavily painted face and garish clothes bore all the marks of a courtesan.

It was not until she got the full measure of her

visitor that she became all smiles and sidled seductively against the door post.

"Well, well," she purred, her insolent, experienced eyes taking in his expensive and immaculate appearance from head to toe, clearly well satisfied with what she saw, for her full pouting mouth turned up at the corners and there was no mistaking her interest. "What have we here? I do declare I haven't seen so fine a gentleman in many a long day. Looking for me are you, luv?"

"Save your breath," replied William coldly. "I'm not interested. I'm looking for Miss Kitty Fairley. I've been told she's lodging with you."

Immediately disappointment caused the woman's expression to fall. "Isn't that just my luck. Oh, well," she sighed, turning her head and shouting into the dark interior beyond. "Kitty, luv," she cried, "someone asking for you—and a right coxcomb he is at that."

The young woman who appeared by her side was totally devoid of animated spirit, in stark contrast to the woman who had opened the door. Her appearance was clean and her brown hair neatly arranged. She looked at him directly without smiling, her face white and drawn, which emphasised the sombre emptiness of her dark eyes and told William she was far from well. If she was surprised at finding so fine a gentleman asking for her, she didn't show it.

"Yes? I'm Kitty Fairley," she said in a well-spoken, soft voice.

"Miss Fairley, we haven't met before. I'm Lord Kingsley. Perhaps you've heard of me?"

Both women started at the mention of his name—although why this should be he had no idea. As if she had received a terrible shock, with a sharp intake of breath Kitty Fairley's face turned as white as a sheet and her thin fingers clutched the shawl at her throat like a claw. She stepped back from him, staring out of hollow eyes at this handsome stranger, searching his features as if she hoped to see something she could recognise that was familiar to her.

"Yes, I have heard of you, Lord Kingsley," she replied in a low, trembling voice, animosity filling her eyes as she looked at him steadily. "Might I ask who sent you here?"

William frowned, a trifle nonplussed, curious as to why she should imagine anyone had sent him.

"No one has sent me. I am here purely of my own volition."

The other woman now stepped forward, having become hostile and surly, her features angry and contorted. "Why—you've a nerve coming round here with your soft words and fancy manners."

William frowned and looked at her, puzzled as to what she meant. "Have I? I am here merely to have a word with Miss Fairley."

"If I were Kitty, I'd see you on your way—that I would."

William noticed Kitty put a restraining hand on her arm. "It's all right, Sal. Go inside while I listen to what Lord Kingsley has to say."

"Aye—but I—"

"No, Sal," said Kitty firmly, her eyes fixed on William. "Go inside."

Reluctantly Sal stepped back and nodded. "Aye—if you say so, Kitty. But you're not to lay a finger on her, you hear," she spat at William. "If you do, you'll have Sal to reckon with. She's been put through enough by your lot."

Her attitude and words caused William to become even more curious. "Will you kindly explain what you meant by that remark?" he demanded sharply.

"She meant nothing," said Kitty quickly, pushing her friend back into the interior of the house. "Come, we will go to the piazza. Whatever you have to say to me, you can say there."

The piazza was buzzing with life twenty-four hours a day, seven days a week. When darkness descended, it became alive with pickpockets and trollops, where courtesans hovered to waylay gentlemen on their way from the theatres. Libertines, drunkenness and brawls abounded, and violent scores were settled in the murky depths of underground cellars.

Behind the windows of the buildings in Covent Garden, every kind of aberration could be catered for—for the right price. But as William and Kitty walked among the fruit and vegetable stalls, where carts were filled to bursting with freshly cut flowers and ragged urchins scampered about underfoot, there was no evidence of this.

"I'm sorry about Sal," Kitty said as they walked. "She's a little over-protective of me."

"Oh? And you need protecting, do you?" William asked, scrutinising her closed features.

She glanced at him sharply, preferring to ignore his question, but her look and her silence told William there was something seriously wrong, something she was keeping to herself. However, it was not for him to enquire into the nature of things—but it did not encourage him to hope that when she saw her sister, Rachel's concern for her would be eased.

"Sal has been a good friend to me. She took me in when I had no where else to go. Not that it is any business of yours, Lord Kingsley. What do you want with me? You still have not told me why you are here—although," she said quietly, her lips curving scornfully, "I suspect I already know who sent you and why."

"Yes, I think you do. I am here on behalf of your sister, Miss Fairley. She is in London at this time and is almost out of her mind with worry as to your whereabouts."

Abruptly Kitty stopped in her tracks and stared up at him in puzzled disbelief. "Rachel? You—you are here because of my *sister?*"

Frowning, William met her gaze, beginning to realise they were talking at cross-purposes. "What other reason could there be for my being here when I have never met you in my life before?"

After a moment she laughed nervously; for the first time since meeting her, William saw her relax.

"Your sister called to see you at your lodgings in Catherine Street, only to be told by your landlady of your hasty departure from her premises—that you had left without leaving an address where you could be contacted. After writing to her, stressing your urgent need to see and speak to her, can you wonder she is worried out of her mind to find you have disappeared?''

Kitty's expression became hard. "And the state of my sister's mind matters to you, does it, Lord Kingsley?'' she asked coldly.

"Yes, it does," he answered, equally as cold.

"You appear to be well acquainted with her."

"Yes I am. As friendship goes."

"I see," she said, appearing uneasy suddenly as she digested what he had said. "Did she ask you to try and discover where I might be found?''

"No. I told you, I am here of my own volition. I obtained information as to your whereabouts from a young lady belonging to the theatre company in Drury Lane."

"I see."

"You must forgive me, Miss Fairley, but I cannot help observing that you do not look to be in the best of health—and the conditions of the area you are residing in cannot be recommended and will certainly not help matters."

She smiled wanly and there was a deep sense of bitterness in her voice when she answered. "My health is not as it should be, Lord Kingsley—that I admit. But neither my health nor the dire straits I now find myself to be in are entirely my own doing." She looked at him hard, her lips twisting in a scornful smile. "How I would love to tell you more, but I fear I would only shock you and make matters far worse by doing so."

"Then if you cannot bring yourself to explain what you mean by that, is there any way I can be of help to you."

She laughed contemptuously. "You? No, Lord Kingsley, never you. You are the last man in the world who could possibly help me."

William's eyes narrowed. "I do not know the reason for your hostility towards me, Miss Fairley, and I shall not ask you to explain it, but I know your father and sister would be most distressed if they were to discover where you are living.

"Will you not allow me to escort you to Lady Brayfield's house where you will find your sister? She is most anxious to talk to you. To the best of my knowledge, your father has not yet arrived in London, but he is expected in due course, I believe."

"My father?" she gasped. "You mean—Rachel has sent for my father?"

"I believe it was your aunt's doing. Will you not permit me take you there?"

"No. Just in case Rachel has not told you all the sordid facts, Lord Kingsley, my aunt has disowned me. She no longer wishes to have anything to do with me. I am in disgrace—so, you see, I cannot go to Brayfield House. However—I would dearly love to see Rachel. Will you bring her to me—here—in the piazza?"

Her tone made the words a command rather than a

request, which deeply annoyed William. "Why not to your friend's house?" he asked with cold sarcasm, for he was angered by her refusal to ease her sister's worry, which confirmed his opinion that she was totally selfish and indifferent to the feelings of others. "I am sure she would like to see where you are living, now you no longer reside in Catherine Street."

Kitty lowered her eyes and shook her head. After her confident and independent approach to life since she had left the shelter and protection of her family to make a career for herself on the stage, she was too ashamed for her sister to see how low she had sunk.

"No," she said quietly. "I will meet her here tomorrow afternoon at two o'clock."

As William walked away from Covent Garden, promising to do as she asked, he was puzzled and confused by the meeting, which confirmed his premeditated opinion that Kitty Fairley was spoilt and lived her life placing the utmost importance on her own desires. But he was puzzled as to the cause of the animosity she had shown. What possible reason had she for being cold and openly hostile towards him?

He had intended going directly to Brayfield House until he remembered that no one would be at home, for today Lady Brayfield, accompanied by her daughters and niece, had gone to Chelsea to visit Ranelagh pleasure gardens, escorted by Edgar. Edgar had tried to persuade him to go along with them, but having already obtained information from the Drury Lane theatre as to Kitty Fairley's whereabouts, he had decided to go to Covent Garden instead.

It was a glorious day as Rachel strolled through the pleasure gardens with her aunt and cousins, with Caroline happily walking along beside Sir Edgar. Being mid-week, the gardens—popular with fashionable society—were not particularly crowded unlike Saturdays and Sundays. Usually, there was dancing by the river bank as well as in the huge rococo Rotunda, the principal attraction and centrepiece of the gardens, used for a variety of entertainments and promenading. People stopped at one of the many booths to take a dish of tea or a glass of punch, or the gentlemen to sit and smoke.

Lady Brayfield was too preoccupied with greeting friends and admiring the scene to notice how quiet Rachel was. She was becoming increasingly dejected as each day passed without any word as to Kitty's whereabouts—or as to her father's arrival in London, which did not help to ease her worry.

With the sun warm on her face, she paused beside the ornamental lake, idly letting her eyes dwell on the delicate-looking structure of the Chinese pavilion, before focusing them on the gently lapping water, and thinking of Lord Kingsley, which she found herself doing increasingly of late.

Often in anguish, but more frequently in delight, his dark eyes and sleek black brows, the attractive line of his lips when they curved in humour and the tall, athletic litheness of his body sprang alive in her thoughts.

She would lie awake for long periods at night, thinking of him, remembering the firm feel of his arm about her waist as he had reached out to steady her at the theatre, thinking she was about to faint. In dreamy contemplation, she wondered how it would feel to have him hold her—to love her.

Sighing wistfully, she shifted her eyes from the calm of the water and found herself looking full into the arrested dark eyes of the very gentleman who occupied her thoughts. Their eyes locked together and she knew he had been thinking of her too, and a wild happiness soared through her.

He was watching her in that intent, curious way of his, suave as ever, dark and splendid; when she met his gaze, his expression changed. He removed his tall hat and bowed his dark head in polite greeting, his hair gleaming in the sunlight, his physical presence almost overwhelming her. Nothing was the same between them since they had talked on the terrace at Mortlake Park.

Before either had time to speak, Sir Edgar, who had seen William approach, happily strode over to greet him.

"Well, bless my soul. I did not expect to see you here today, William. I thought you were much too busy to spare the time to come to Ranelagh."

"I have been, but my business did not take as long as I expected—and being such a glorious day, I thought I would join you after all."

"And I'm jolly glad you did."

After greeting Lady Brayfield with an engaging smile—she was delighted he had found the time to join them—William managed to single Rachel out and walk with her along the paths threading through the sun and daisy-spattered lawns. He looked at her with undisguised appraisal.

She was as slender as a willow and so perfectly groomed, dressed in fine pale blue muslin, the tight bodice emphasising her small waist and the firm swell of her breasts. Her wonderful sleek black hair was coiled under a matching hat, perched rakishly at an angle and ornamented with a soft white plume. Her eyes glowed warm, bright and welcoming as she looked at him.

"You look enchanting. You are the most beautiful lady at Ranelagh today, Miss Fairley. I'm so glad I came after all," he murmured.

Rachel paused for a moment, unaccustomed to such compliments from any gentleman. Coming from Lord Kingsley, spoken in such quiet, intimate tones, it brought an attractive pink flush to her cheeks. They were alone, yet not alone, in a park full of people, and she was extremely conscious of it. Suffering from an unexpected attack of shyness, she looked back along the path to hide her confusion.

"Perhaps we should wait a moment, Lord Kingsley. We are leaving my aunt and cousins behind."

Casually unconcerned, William glanced back, smiling at her sudden confusion. "We remain in full view of your aunt, so there is no impropriety. Besides, I see Edgar is keeping them well entertained,'' he said, walking slowly on. ''It is you I came to see, Miss Fairley, not your aunt. What I have to say to you is for your ears alone.''

''Oh?'' She felt a sudden lightness in her heart, beneath the glorious rays of sunshine blazing down on them. Observing the intimacy of the couples strolling along the paths arm in arm, she dared to hope that he might be about to utter some tender words of endearment—to declare his passion. But what he said drove any romantic notion from her mind, bringing her sharply down to earth.

''Yes. I bring you the happy news that I have managed to trace your sister.''

His words brought Rachel to a halt and she stared at him. ''Kitty? But—but—how? Oh, do forgive me. I don't understand,'' she said in a soft, breathless voice. ''How did you manage to find her—and so quickly?''

''Yesterday I returned to the Drury Lane theatre and made further enquiries among her colleagues. One young lady you failed to question gave me the information I required.''

As William looked at the dark-ringed eyes in her pale face, he could see that the nervous strain of Kitty's disappearance had almost been too much for her, and a quiet rage filled him, because she was being made to suffer for the follies of her sister. Her face turned whiter still and he laid a reassuring hand on her arm.

''Thank God. Oh, thank God she is safe,'' she murmured, relief filling her dark blue eyes. ''I have imagined such terrible things that might have happened to her. My thoughts have been intolerable. How—how is she? Is she well?''

''As to that, I cannot say—although to my mind she did not look as well as she ought—but as to the seriousness of it, I know not. She did say she would like to meet with you tomorrow afternoon.''

Rachel was uplifted. ''Yes, of course. If you give me her address, I shall call on her.''

''No—no,'' he said, much too quickly, causing her to look at him in alarm. He could not have her visiting the place where her sister lived.

Rachel frowned. ''But…why not?''

''All I can tell you is that she is lodging with a friend close to Covent Garden and asked that I take you to meet her in the piazza at two o'clock tomorrow afternoon.''

''You?''

''Yes. She realises that you cannot go alone—and, owing to your aunt's deep disapproval of her conduct, she knows she would certainly not wish to accompany you.''

Her brow puckered in a frown, Rachel looked at him. ''I have a distinct feeling you are keeping something from me, Lord Kingsley. Come—it is not in your nature to be evasive.''

''I was not aware that I was being evasive. I am merely carrying out your sister's request.''

''This—this friend you say she is living with,'' she said, averting her eyes and falling into step beside him as they continued their walk. ''Is—is it a gentleman?

Is this the reason why she is averse to my seeing where she lives?''

"No," he answered softly, smiling into her anxious, dark blue eyes. "I can reassure you on that, at least. Her friend is a woman."

Rachel let out a sigh of relief. "Then at least we can be thankful for that." She turned her head and looked at Lord Kingsley curiously. "Why did you go to look for Kitty?"

He gave a wry smile. "It was certainly not out of any concern I might feel for your sister. From what I have heard of her, I believe she is quite capable of taking care of herself."

"Then why? For what reason?"

"Having witnessed your distress at the theatre the other evening, I was both saddened and grieved," he said softly, holding her gaze with his own. "I wanted to alleviate any suffering you might be feeling owing to your sister's disappearance."

"Thank you," she murmured.

Totally unprepared for his show of kindness, Rachel's eyes filled with grateful tears—which had been too ready to flow of late. As she brushed them away, William felt a sudden impulse to reach out and take her in his arms, but he held himself in check. They walked on a little way in silence before Rachel spoke, having composed herself.

"Sir Edgar tells me your brother has returned to London, Lord Kingsley."

"Yes. After reconciling our differences, he has now returned to Mortlake, I am happy to say. Although, taking into account his fondness for the gaieties of London, it did surprise me how readily he was prepared to comply with my wishes without argument.''

"Whatever the reason, I am happy for you. But why did you not return to Mortlake with him? I was under the impression that you were to return also— that to locate your brother was your sole reason for coming to London, and that once you had found him you would return.''

"Yes, it was—until your sister went missing. I could not bear to leave you in such distress.''

"Oh,'' she said softly, a fresh wave of embarrassment sweeping over her. "You have gone to a great deal of trouble on my account, Lord Kingsley. What can I say? I don't know how to express my gratitude.''

"Oh—I think I can think of several ways,'' he murmured, his gaze sweeping over her face, his eyes fastening with hungry intent on her lips.

The intimate tone of his voice and the hidden meaning of his words caused Rachel to drop her gaze, her face growing hot and perplexed, trying to shake off the effect he was having on her—and yet at the same time not wanting to, although she was greatly afraid that she was about to be overwhelmed by her feelings.

"What—what was her reaction on seeing you? Was—was she surprised?'' she asked, suddenly, in an attempt to hide her confusion, trying not to show surprise or emotion—but William's observant eyes saw how he had succeeded in disarming her and he smiled, quietly satisfied by her feminine reaction to his words.

"Yes, you might say that—although from her attitude towards me, I would say she was not impressed. I was extremely puzzled as to what could be the cause of her hostility, which was evident to me—unless, of course," he said glancing sideways at Rachel, "she shares her sister's initial opinion of my character—without having made my acquaintance—and has taken a strong dislike to me."

"I regret that, where my sister is concerned, I have no secret knowledge which can possibly enlighten you, Lord Kingsley. However, knowing how starry-eyed she has been about the theatre for most of her life, then I doubt she has given any thought to you or your circumstances. Why, if you brought all the slaves from your plantation on Barbados and set them to work at Mortlake Park, she would never have noticed."

"To leave her home and family, to become an outcast, even, when one considers the rules that govern society—which it insists upon—then before she left the company at Drury Lane, she must have been totally devoted and committed to her work."

"Yes, she was, which is why I find it all the more curious as to why she did not go on tour during the summer months. The rules of society as we know it ceased to apply to Kitty the day she left home to become an actress. She's only happy donning the costumes she wears on stage and taking on the identity of a man in some play or other, or the guise of another woman—shedding her identity and becoming the character she plays. At these times she is no longer Kitty Fairley and she is well satisfied.

"I suppose it is rather like us when we attend a masked or fancy dress ball—where covering our faces and changing our clothes, assuming a false appearance, enables us to take on a different identity. Immediately the atmosphere becomes relaxed and causes everybody to behave in a more unrestricted and informal manner that one would never dream of adopting normally."

"Then the next time I am invited to such an event, I must make a point of asking you to be my partner, Miss Fairley," William said, turning towards her, his smile as engaging as ever.

"And I shall be happy to accept," she laughed lightly. "What was your opinion of my sister, Lord Kingsley? Did you liken her to me?"

"No, not at all. I have to say I find it difficult to believe she is your sister."

"But she is beautiful, is she not?"

An amber light glowed in the depths of William's eyes as he looked at her directly. "She is pretty, I grant you, but she does not have her sister's beauty or any of her finer qualities."

Rachel flushed and they smiled at each other. "You tease, Lord Kingsley. Please do not think I was fishing for compliments."

No, he thought, looking at her with deep admiration, anything of that nature was beneath her. She would not stoop to solicit for such worthless flattery. But he was captivated by her and she was beginning to occupy an important place in his life. That she shared his feelings he knew without being told.

"Nevertheless, I meant it as a compliment," he assured her as they continued to walk side by side along the winding, sunny path, with the other members of their party following at a discreet distance. He thought she was absolutely enchanting. What a delight it was to converse lightly with her, for her not to be on the attack as she had been on some of their previous encounters.

All those weeks ago, when William had first met Rachel Fairley, in his anger he had not felt his pulses or his emotions stir, for he had not taken the full measure of her mind or her beauty—in fact, she had irritated and angered him beyond belief. He had been furious with her but, by a sentimental turn of events, what he had come to know about her—even seeing her weakness, her tears and wretched state—had changed him completely.

Each meeting since their first had been heading up to this; now, the emptiness that had bedevilled him over the latter years was beginning to disappear, for he knew beyond any doubt that he had found someone who was to be both precious and important to his future.

They were comfortable together as they talked, content to let their relationship unfold and take its course. It was as if they were on the brink of some brand new relationship hitherto unknown to either of them—for Rachel no longer thought of Ralph Wheeler who had hurt her so profoundly at the time of his rejection.

She was aware that something was happening to her, for she was filled with a feeling of deep contentment and well-being. She delighted in Lord Kingsley's dominance and basked in the warmth of his gaze, feeling vulnerable suddenly, feminine and young—and discarding any ill feeling she still possessed in his harsh treatment of Stephen.

"You will allow me to escort you to see your sister tomorrow?"

"Yes—thank you."

"And will you tell your aunt?"

"Out of respect, and because I am staying in her house, I am obliged to be honest with her. No matter what Kitty expects of me, I will not deceive her. She deserves better than that. However, I sense a softening in my aunt's attitude towards Kitty—especially since I told her how concerned I am about her health. I shall try persuading her to allow me take her back to Brayfield House to stay for a while. At least until she is feeling better."

"When do you expect your father to arrive in London?"

"If he is well enough to travel, any day now. I know he hopes to take Harry to school and will no doubt come directly.

"So you see, Lord Kingsley, after taking me to see my sister tomorrow afternoon, you will be quite free to leave London and return to Mortlake Park. I am sure you must be most anxious to do so—and—there will be no reason for you to remain in London any longer," she finished softly, averting her eyes and pausing to wait for Emily, who was calling to them further back along the path.

Lord Kingsley cocked one of his black eyebrows and smiled, a glow burning in the depths of his eyes. "I do not think I am so eager to return to Mortlake at this present time, Miss Fairley. I think I shall remain in London a while longer—purely for my own enjoyment, of course. Besides," he said, his voice low and seductive, his eyes lingering on her upturned adorably flushed pink face, "I can think of at least one good reason why I should not leave just yet."

Chapter Nine

Lady Brayfield was far from happy about Rachel going to Covent Garden to meet Kitty in the company of Lord Kingsley. But, admitting there was nothing else for it, for Kitty must be brought back—and not wishing to discourage the relationship that appeared to be developing between Rachel and Lord Kingsley; to her observant eyes, Lord Kingsley was being extremely attentive towards her niece—she relented, giving her permission provided that her maid Celia accompanied Rachel.

"I have to say, Lord Kingsley seems to be paying you a great deal of attention of late, Rachel," she commented. "I, for one, have noticed that he never took his eyes off you during the whole performance at the theatre the other night—and when you disappeared to retrieve your fan he was not far behind to make quite sure you came to no harm. Such solicitude is to be commended.

"Today he sought you out at Ranelagh—I saw you walking close together in intimate conversation. If that does not indicate his interest in you then I don't know what does. You must have noticed, Rachel?'' she said, smiling with particular significance, which caused Rachel to stiffen; she did not like being the object of such speculation.

She knew her aunt regarded Lord Kingsley as the ideal suitor and, considering the shame Kitty's disgraceful career had brought on the whole family, thought that Rachel should think herself fortunate to have attracted the attention of a man of his standing.

''No, Aunt. I have been too concerned over Kitty's whereabouts to think about forming a close relationship with any man. Lord Kingsley very kindly made enquiries and managed to trace her—that is all. After tomorrow, when he has taken me to meet Kitty, then no doubt he will return to Mortlake Park immediately.''

Her aunt sighed, Kitty's regrettable situation driving Lord Kingsley from her mind. ''If Kitty is indeed in ill health then, no matter what my own feelings are with regards to her behaviour, she must be persuaded to return here with you so that she can receive proper care and attention.

''Heaven knows where she is living at present—or with whom,'' she said drily, ''but the outward respectability of this family must be upheld at all costs. I must say, I shall be more than happy when your father gets here—although what all this to-do over Kitty will do to his health, I shudder to think.''

Seated beside Celia, across from Lord Kingsley, Rachel was in a state of great anxiety, feeling terribly uneasy about her rendezvous with Kitty, silently praying she would be able to succeed in persuading her to return to Brayfield House with her.

Knowing her well enough to know of the tension inside her, William made little attempt at conversation. He observed her calmly, with a certain amount of anxiety over her coming meeting with Kitty, but also with a deep admiration, thinking how beautiful and composed she looked, with a clear, unguarded luminosity in her deep blue eyes and a transparency to her pale complexion, evidence of the strain she had been under ever since she had come to London in search of her sister.

When they finally reached Covent Garden, Rachel saw that Kitty was already waiting for her in the piazza, standing with her hands by her sides in the midst of a crowd of people. Leaving Celia with the carriage, she pushed and shoved her way through the throng, Lord Kingsley hard on her heels, but what she saw when she looked searchingly into her sister's face chilled her to the bone.

Kitty looked miserable and was shockingly pale and gaunt-looking, with a lacklustre, washed-out quality in her eyes, but on seeing Rachel her mouth broke into a smile and they embraced affectionately.

"Kitty! Oh, Kitty! It's wonderful to find you at last. When you were not at your lodgings or the theatre, I imagined all manner of horrid things that might have happened to you. Thank goodness Lord Kingsley found you safe."

The mention of Lord Kingsley's name caused Kitty to stiffen and she pulled away from Rachel's welcoming embrace.

"Yes—he did, but he could have saved himself the trouble," she said ungraciously, causing Rachel to look at her in puzzlement, "for I would have contacted you myself once I knew you were in London."

A mask seemed to descend over her features when Lord Kingsley came to stand beside them and Rachel saw her step back, drawing her shawl tight about her, seeing for herself the animosity Lord Kingsley had spoken of in Kitty's eyes. It was clear to her that conflicting emotions raged through her sister—she was more than pleased to see her, but she seemed overcome by a compulsion to flee from Lord Kingsley, which puzzled Rachel greatly, making her wonder at the reason.

"Thank you, Lord Kingsley, for bringing my sister to me," said Kitty coldly, "but would you mind if I spoke with her alone for a few minutes?"

Rachel frowned in puzzlement, for her voice was uncharacteristically sharp. Lord Kingsley gave no sign that he was disturbed or offended by this, but she saw his eyes narrow and his lips harden and become set in a firm line.

"Of course not. I quite understand." He looked at Rachel. "I shall wait in the carriage until you are ready to leave," he said crisply, turning abruptly and striding back to the carriage.

"Oh, dear. Did you have to sound so harsh—so objectionable, Kitty?" Rachel reproached her sister.

"Lord Kingsley has been extremely kind and considerate."

"I did not ask for his consideration."

"At least have the goodness to make an effort to be civil to him."

"I have no reason to be civil to anyone of that family. And when I recollect, you were not inclined to think well of them either not so very long ago."

"Maybe you are right, Kitty, but things have changed since then."

"So it would seem." Her eyes narrowed as she regarded Rachel curiously. "There must be a reason for his solicitude. It matters to you, does it, Rachel, what he thinks?"

"Yes, it does. In the early days of our acquaintance I did not think highly of him at all but, having got to know him a little better, I no longer feel any contempt and realise I was too hasty in forming an opinion of him. It was both harsh and unjustifiable."

"Then I cannot support it," said Kitty contemptuously. "How quickly you spring to his defence."

Rachel could not deny that Kitty was right. There was a time when it would not have entered her head to defend Lord Kingsley to anyone, but her opinion of him of late had changed considerably. Now, as their knowledge of each other grew, she knew her relationship with him was the most important, the most overwhelming thing that had ever happened to her, that he was gradually restoring her to a serene contentment that had eluded her since her unhappy affair with Ralph.

She sighed, not wishing to get into an argument about Lord Kingsley. "Tell me—how are you, Kitty? You wrote telling me you were not well—and I have to say there is a change in you. You look different, somehow. What is wrong?"

Kitty shrugged absently. "Nothing. Nothing specific, that is. I—I am tired, that is all."

Rachel suspected she wasn't being truthful and tried pressing her with further questions; when she saw her questioning was upsetting her, she resolved to let the matter rest until later. Whatever the nature of Kitty's secret, she would have to wait until she was ready to speak of it—but of one thing she was certain—it was destroying her.

"Aunt Mary would very much like you to return with me to Brayfield House, Kitty. Please say you will come?"

Kitty looked surprised. "Aunt Mary? But, surely not. I went against everything that is so important to her. She must hate me for defying convention the way I did."

"Not any longer, Kitty."

"Then it is extremely generous of her, after all the pain I have caused."

"Father is expected at any time—although I have to warn you that his heart condition continues to give us cause for concern. It is imperative that he isn't upset unduly."

Alarm filled Kitty's eyes and she became contrite. "Oh, poor Father. I'm so sorry, Rachel. The last time we met you told me he wasn't well. The last thing I intended was to cause him to worry about me.''

''I know that, Kitty, but it is natural he is concerned. Everyone is so terribly worried about your health. It is obvious to me that you are not well. Please come back with me,'' she begged. ''It does not have to be a permanent arrangement. Under the circumstances, look on it as a visit. Perhaps later, when you are feeling better, you will be able to return to the theatre—to your career.''

''No,'' said Kitty sharply, averting her eyes, but not in time to hide the pain that filled them from the sharp eyes of her sister. ''I do not think I shall ever go back.''

That was when Rachel knew something was seriously wrong, for the theatre had been Kitty's life.

''Please don't say that. Come, Kitty. Will you return with me to Brayfield House?''

Kitty looked uncertain but then she nodded, speaking in a small voice. ''Yes,'' she whispered, for she truly had nowhere else to go and was unable to continue lodging with Sally Pearce unless she had money to pay for her keep.

Of late, her health had prevented her from holding down any kind of occupation. The very idea of joining Sal in her sordid profession was abhorrent to her, but she was very much afraid that, if she did not grasp this lifeline her sister was holding out to her, she would have little choice.

''Good. Aunt Mary has had a room made ready for you. So you see—you are expected.''

Kitty disappeared to say goodbye to Sally Pearce and to collect her belongings, insisting on going alone when Rachel offered to accompany her; she had no wish for her to see the squalid rooms in which she had been living with Sal.

Clearly Lord Kingsley's presence upset her and she refused to speak all the way back to Brayfield House, which led to an uncomfortable silence between them all.

William was quiet and very polite, but his mouth was compressed in a firm line and his eyes glittered like steel flints whenever they came to rest on Kitty's stiffly upright figure across from him in the carriage, for it was clear to him that the girl was totally devoid of manners.

On reaching Brayfield House, he climbed out and assisted them to alight. "If I can be of assistance, please do not hesitate to ask," he offered, making an attempt at civility towards Kitty, but he was sharply rebuffed.

Without any attempt to control her composure, she smiled a bitter smile. "No, Lord Kingsley. I want nothing from you."

Her anger spoke eloquently, again making Rachel curious as to the reason for her strangely hostile behaviour, she wondered if she had developed some moral principles and that Lord Kingsley had been correct in his assertions—that Kitty's dislike of him was based on the source of his wealth, which enabled him to support his illustrious lifestyle.

Celia took Kitty into the house and Rachel turned

back to Lord Kingsley, who had his eyes fixed on her sister's retreating figure. She noticed how his black brows were drawn together in a somewhat troubled, thoughtful frown, his expression as hard as granite.

"Won't you come inside, Lord Kingsley? I am sure my aunt would like to thank you personally for finding Kitty."

"No, thank you," he said, his voice coldly formal. "Lady Brayfield's reunion with your sister is bound to be one of awkwardness and I would not wish to make matters worse by inflicting my presence on her. We will meet this evening; she has kindly invited Sir Edgar and myself to dine with you. I can only hope your sister's temper will be much improved by then."

"Kitty will not be joining us," said Rachel stiffly, feeling a coldness beginning to creep over her, unable to believe that, only a short while ago, her heart had been overflowing with gladness at the prospect of meeting her sister. It had all suddenly turned sour, for Kitty's disagreeable conduct towards Lord Kingsley had turned him into a cold, polite stranger.

"Then for that I am thankful; a repetition of her unmannerly conduct towards myself would only cause great embarrassment to Lady Brayfield. You are extremely tolerant towards your sister, Miss Fairley, and I wonder, after her severe condemnation of me and her disgraceful conduct, that you manage to maintain your composure. I must say that, for someone who is ill, your sister's tongue is uncommonly sharp. She is certainly ill-disposed towards me; for what reason I know not."

Completely thrown off balance by this unfortunate turn of events, Rachel felt a little surge of anger. "What can I say—except to apologise for my sister."

"To my knowledge, I have never met your sister—but I find her wanting in both civility and good manners. Her independence has taught her little but to adopt a complete disregard for the feelings of others—especially those of her sister."

"I—I am so sorry, Lord Kingsley. What must you think? I confess I am confused by her behaviour. I—it is very unlike her to be so outspoken."

Rachel's politeness, like her felicitations to her sister, irritated William almost beyond words.

"Do not feel you have to apologise for your sister, Miss Fairley. I fully comprehend that her manners, along with her dignity, have completely deserted her, which I can only hope is a temporary state. Perhaps her illness is worse than you thought—however, I sincerely hope not. Should the situation be reversed, I strongly suspect she would be singularly inattentive to you. She is totally insensitive and indifferent to the feelings of others."

"Kitty is much changed. I do not understand it."

"I must say that I find it difficult to liken her to the acclaimed actress who, by all accounts, so captivated the audience at Drury Lane in the spring—that she could inspire an audience with such delight. In my opinion, she has very little to recommend her.

"I just wonder why she has taken so strong a dislike to me. There has to be a reason for it. Perhaps I was right after all and she shares your own initial opinion of me—that her dislike stems from the manner in which I have conducted my business affairs in the past, though I doubt it. I very much suspect it to be something else.''

As offended by his attack on Kitty as she was by Kitty's rudeness to him, Rachel was both vexed and pained by it.

''Kitty has imperfections enough without you pointing them out, Lord Kingsley,'' she said sharply, ''and I have lived with her too long not to be aware of them all. I shall most certainly endeavour to discover the reasons for her uncivility. There is no accounting for her behaviour and I can only assume that something has upset her terribly. I shall do my best to talk to her—to—''

''No, no,'' he interrupted quickly, his manner brusque. ''Do not attach too much importance to the matter, I beg you. I am quite indifferent to your sister's opinion of me.''

How Rachel wished she could believe that, for he seemed extremely put out, troubled and anxious to be gone.

''I bear you no ill will, Miss Fairley—but I will leave you now. I am sure you are eager for my departure and anxious to minister to your sister.''

''Yes—yes, thank you,'' Rachel replied quietly, a sickness which was like a physical pain twisting inside her heart and becoming almost unbearable. A hard lump rose and threatened to obstruct her throat, and there was a desolation in her eyes as well as her heart. Her head was spinning as she stepped back and watched him climb quickly up into the carriage. "Goodbye, Lord Kingsley. I cannot express my gratitude enough for all you have done."

"There is no need," he said, his voice cold and brusque, an expression in his eyes Rachel had never seen before as they swept over her one last time. "I am glad I was able to be of help. Goodbye, Miss Fairley." He uttered a sharp command to his driver to drive on.

In a wretched, confused and angry state, hearing the jingle of harness and the clip-clopping of the horses' hooves as they carried Lord Kingsley away from Brayfield House, Rachel turned and went inside, feeling it most probable that because of Kitty's rudeness—her severe and unconcealed dislike of Lord Kingsley—they would never again meet on such cordial terms as had marked their meetings since they had walked on the terrace at Mortlake Park.

As William drove away from Brayfield House he was in an angry, thoughtful mood, a dark suspicion forming in the back of his mind that Miss Kitty Fairley's unmannerly behaviour towards him might in some way be connected to his brother. He recollected their meeting when James had returned to London, and his strange reaction when he had asked him if he was acquainted with the Fairleys and how he had paled, seeming nervous, and how he had fudged his answer.

He also knew James had been closely involved with an actress when he had returned from the West

Indies and James had failed to meet him in London. Was it possible that the actress concerned was Kitty Fairley, whom James had since spurned? which would explain Miss Fairley's antagonism towards himself. Could that be the reason why James had been willing to return to Mortlake Park in such haste and without argument?

And what would make an actress as devoted to her career as Kitty Fairley was choose to remain in London for the summer months, when most people involved with the stage went to work in the provinces? Could James have been the reason?

And then, feeling abandoned by James, and having no one else to listen to her complaints—all her friends having temporarily left London until the reopening of the theatres in the autumn—had she written to Rachel, playing on her emotions, her goodness, with words, in a play for sympathy, implying that she was in ill health when, in fact, it was nothing more than a fit of pique?

If this were indeed the case, then it was imperative that he returned to Mortlake Park immediately and confronted James. If there had been any impropriety in his behaviour towards Kitty Fairley, then William would have to intervene, because of his own growing intensity of feeling for Rachel, which this unhappy and unfortunate affair clarified—despite both her low social standing and her sister's behaviour.

Although Kitty had never been her favourite niece, Lady Brayfield was deeply conscious that she was her

brother's beloved, eldest child, and forced herself to
be civil to Kitty with reluctant forbearance, assuring
her that she would receive proper care and attention
in her illness—in whatever form it presented itself.
She ordered her to bed immediately and sent for the
physician.

When Rachel went to Kitty's room she found her
already in bed, pale and deflated, and was surprised
to find her weeping quietly into her pillows. Deeply
affected, she wondered at the reason for Kitty's distress, thinking it might have been brought about by
the severe reception she had received from their aunt.
Immediately she sank on to the bed beside her and
took her hand.

"Don't distress yourself, Kitty," she said gently.
"You're going to get well now we can look after you
properly. Aunt Mary has sent for the doctor and when
he has found out what is wrong with you and you
begin taking some medicine for your ailment, then
you'll soon begin feeling better."

Kitty looked at Rachel, her face blotched and her
tears trapped in the trembling corners of her mouth.
She wiped them away with her sodden handkerchief,
sighing deeply, and Rachel thought the tears had released some of the nervous tension that had gripped
her earlier.

"I don't need the physician to tell me what is
wrong with me," she murmured miserably.

"What do mean?"

"Oh, Rachel. I—I don't know how I can tell you.

You, who have always stood by me—so good—so honest.''

"What is it? Please tell me, Kitty?" she asked, suddenly terrified of what she might hear, of what Kitty had to tell her, fear taking hold of her long before her sister revealed the horror of her words. "What is it? What have you done?"

Taking a deep, determined breath Kitty met her eyes, as though she had steeled herself for this moment.

"I—I am pregnant, Rachel. I am with child."

Rachel paled perceptibly and said nothing, so shocked was she. Not in her worst fears had she imagined Kitty's illness to be anything like this—that it had been nothing more serious than the early sickness which often plagues some women in their early months of pregnancy. She could feel the awful truth stretching between them, the echo of her words hanging in the air.

"Dear God, no," she whispered at length. "What are you saying? How can you be?"

Kitty averted her eyes, so full of shame she was unable to look at her sister.

"Are—are you sure?"

"Unquestionably."

"So—this is what was wrong with you. This is why you have felt so unwell all these weeks?"

Kitty nodded dumbly.

"How long?"

"About three months."

Trying to take stock of what she had been told,

Rachel sat, looking at her sister, at her bowed head, her face almost covered by her hair hanging loose. Reaching out, she gripped her arms.

"Look at me, Kitty."

Slowly, Kitty raised her head and looked into her eyes.

"How did it happen? How did you get into this predicament? Were you violated—taken against your will?"

"No," she replied softly, with pain and despair. "The fault was mine as well as his."

"His? Who was it, Kitty? Who did this to you?"

For answer Kitty lowered her head, shaking it slowly, and no matter how hard Rachel questioned her and tried to coax out of her the identity of the man who had brought her to this state of degradation, she could not get her to relinquish his name. But whoever he was, Rachel despised him.

"I loved him," Kitty whispered. "I loved him so much—I shall never love another as I did him—as I still do, as I shall to my dying day. I believed in him—and I believed like a naïve simpleton that he was sincere when he said he loved me too."

"Is he an actor—a member of the company at Drury Lane, Kitty?"

"No. He—he's a gentleman. I—I cannot tell you his name. There will be dire consequences if I make it known."

"I would not call him a gentleman to abandon you so callously in this state," Rachel said bitterly. "Is he married already? Is that it?"

"No."

"And he knew about the child? You told him?"

"Yes—but he didn't want to know. He—he even asked me if I was certain the child was his."

"And is it, Kitty? Forgive me, but I have to ask. It is imperative that I know everything in order to help you. Has he reason to think it might not be?"

Horrified, Kitty gasped. "No. No, Rachel. There has never been anyone else. I swear it. Please—you must believe that."

Rachel sighed and looked at her. She did believe her. She could see the truth in her eyes. "Yes, of course I do. Is he rich enough to provide for the future of your child?"

"Yes."

"Then he should be made to face up to his responsibilities."

"How—how can I tell Aunt Mary—and Father?" Kitty whispered. "Oh, poor Father. What can I say to him?"

"The truth. They will both have to be told. It cannot be concealed."

"Father will be devastated."

"You gave little enough thought to Father when you left Oxfordshire, Kitty," she said accusingly, in frustration, for the seriousness of the matter was beginning to touch her nerves. Immediately she regretted her outburst, for nothing could be gained from bitter recriminations. She sighed. "I'm sorry," she relented. "I should not have said that."

"Why not? I deserve it. What you say is right, for

I realise that through my actions the whole family is likely to suffer for all time. I must tell you that I have considered keeping it from Father—not to say a word to anyone and go away until after my confinement. That way, no one need ever know.''

''And the child?''

''I—I could have it adopted.''

''And could you live with that?''

Kitty shook her head sadly. ''I don't know.''

''Why did you not remain with Mrs Gilbey? At least there you had work to support yourself.''

''Mrs Gilbey was bound to find out about my condition and would have turned me out. I could not return to the theatre because of it either—so when Sal invited me to stay with her, I left.''

''And if Lord Kingsley had not found you, Kitty, what were your intentions?''

''I have to confess that I didn't know what to do. I—I had no one I could confide in. I—I was waiting to speak to you.''

''But what about the woman you were staying with—Sally Pearce?''

Kitty smiled grimly. ''There is only one cure for such an ailment in Sal's book, Rachel. It usually means a visit to a woman who will use terrible methods to induce the pregnancy—methods which would make your hair stand on end. Oh, don't look so shocked,'' she said when Rachel gasped as realisation of what she meant registered and showed in her eyes. ''It is a common enough occurrence among women in Sal's profession.''

"Then I can only hope you have not considered this, Kitty," Rachel said severely. "It is a mortal sin—both wicked and criminal—and I have to say that I wish you had chosen someone who did not belong to so sordid a profession to stay with."

"Sal isn't so bad, Rachel. Besides, she knows nothing else. She was driven to the life she leads by cruel poverty. She is pretty and knows what she is about. Some nights, after she has been patrolling the courts in the Temple and the Strand, she does very well for herself."

"How did you meet her?"

"I got to know her when she used to wait outside the theatre in Drury Lane for the gentlemen to emerge from a performance. I'm sorry, Rachel," she sighed, "I can see I shock you, but I have seen places you cannot ever begin to understand in your sheltered life, which in your wildest imaginings you would never dream exist—squalid, revolting places, where poverty, disease, hunger and violence go hand in hand."

"I may not be as worldly as you are, Kitty," said Rachel, more sharply than she intended, "but I have no wish to see those places. I can only sympathise with those who are unfortunate enough to have to endure them. But do not forget that you chose to leave your family to make your own way in life.

"What concerns me right now is the situation you have got yourself into, how best to overcome it without causing an outright scandal—and also how best to tell Father without bringing on a seizure."

Kitty's face crumpled at the thought of telling their

father and what it would do to him. Once again she was overcome by a paroxysm of weeping, covering her face with her hands in anguish, which moved Rachel deeply, making her forget what Kitty had done—for at that moment none of that mattered. It was not a crime to love a man—but it was a crime for him to use a woman as he had done and then abandon her.

Every kind of emotion quivered through Rachel—revulsion, horror, even rage, against this man who had wronged Kitty. Filled with a compassion beyond anything she had ever known, she reached out and drew her sister's trembling, shuddering body into her arms, tender and loving, to offer some measure of comfort to her tortured mind.

"Don't worry, Kitty. Whatever happens we'll face it together. There must be no more talk of you going away, of Foundling Hospitals or that other unspeakable alternative. I will not hear of it."

Her body infused by her sister's love, by the comfort of her arms, Kitty's anguish was eased. She looked at her and a smile tugged at her lips.

"Believe me, Rachel—I did not want to burden you with this."

No, thought Rachel, maybe what her sister said was true, but she knew that, whatever happened, the burden was hers and the task of arranging what had to be done would fall on her shoulders.

"I'm glad you did. But we are going to have to be strong. When Father arrives, we will return with him to Oxfordshire and then decide what has to be done."

They were interrupted by someone knocking gently on the door. Rachel rose to admit the doctor.

Chapter Ten

When Rachel left Kitty to go downstairs to her aunt, she could scarcely believe what had happened. How could Kitty have come to this? She had vivid memories of how she had once been—Kitty was scarcely recognisable now as her beautiful, vibrant, laughing sister who had craved independence.

She had left Meadowfield Lodge and the protection of her devoted family full of the joys of life, with a confidence Rachel had envied. The sad, pathetic woman she had become bore no resemblance to her. The harsh realities of the world she had chosen to live in had treated her severely and taken the sparkle from her lovely eyes.

It was evident that her aunt knew about Kitty's condition the moment Rachel entered the room, where the physician had just left her. She was just sitting, staring at nothing, her hands gripping the arms of the large winged chair in which she sat.

The worst part was over and Rachel was thankful she had been spared the ordeal of telling her, but it was clear it had come as a bitter and terrible shock. Her face was like a marble mask and she looked much older. Rachel moved towards her, waiting for her to speak.

"How could Kitty do this to us—to your father?" Lady Brayfield said at length, speaking harshly. "He has not been the same in spirit since your dear mother died. This will destroy him. She has brought this upon herself and must face the consequences. Unfortunately, the disgrace will affect the whole family. I take it the man who got her into this unfortunate mess refuses to marry her?"

"Yes, Aunt."

"Who is the father? Has she told you, Rachel?"

"No. She refuses to divulge his name."

"I see," she said, her voice low and trembling with a quiet, controlled anger. "The manner in which she ingratiated herself into the theatrical world was bad enough, but to give her favours so willingly to a man outside wedlock is quite shocking. That she should defile her family in this manner is both shameful and intolerable. It is not to be borne.

"As soon as your father arrives, she must return with him to Oxfordshire immediately. Neither Caroline or Emily are to be told of her downfall—or the servants, for they gossip. It must be concealed at all costs. The whole family will suffer greatly for her actions and I will not see my daughters' chances of making suitable marriages ruined by any fault of hers. She has brought dishonour to us all."

Rachel hated hearing her aunt revile Kitty in this

manner, because she had fallen foul of society's rules, but she could not blame her, for her impeccable upbringing and society had made her what she was.

"No matter what she has done, Aunt, Kitty is all too well aware of the impropriety of her conduct," said Rachel, her instinct being to defend her sister. "She is deeply ashamed and full of remorse. She expects to be dealt with severely."

"And she will be."

"I love Kitty dearly and she desperately needs my help. She is my sister and I cannot abandon her at this time when she needs me most."

Her aunt's eyes softened when they fell upon her face, which was strained with anxiety and emotion, and she nodded. "No, you do not have it in you to do that, Rachel—although I have to say that it is better than she deserves. It is a pity Kitty has not inherited some of your goodness. I doubt she realises how lucky she is to have so devoted a sister."

"I am sure she would do the same for me, Aunt."

Clearly her aunt did not agree with her, but she did not say so.

"Kitty chose to challenge and rise above the conventional way of things and now she is paying the penalty of her misdemeanour," Lady Brayfield said. "No matter how she scorns the opinion of society—a society into which she was born and bred—however much she resents it, she will find it hard to bear the stigma of raising an illegitimate child.

"The child itself will suffer because of it. Her chances of securing a husband will be virtually nil, for there are few men who will take on a fallen woman and acknowledge such a child. If it is her wish to return to the stage, then the child must be found adoptive parents—otherwise your sister will lose the freedom that was so important to her."

"At the moment Kitty's hopes and ambitions of furthering her career in the theatre have been blighted by her predicament. As yet, it is too early to say what she will do when the child is born."

"Maybe—but there is no room for complacency. She must be sent away until her confinement for, if the good name of this family is to be upheld, there is no alternative. After that, what happens to the child is a matter for her and your father. It is a disappointing way to anticipate the arrival of a child into this family.

"However," she said, rising to her feet, "we will speak of it no more for the time being. We have guests coming to dinner—Lord Kingsley and Sir Edgar Mainwaring. If our respectability is to be maintained then there must be no hint of Kitty's condition. As far as everyone else is concerned, she is suffering from a general malaise for which some time spent in the country will prove beneficial. Is that understood, Rachel?"

"Yes, Aunt."

"Then go to your room and prepare yourself for dinner."

The evening got off to a bad start. The moment Lord Kingsley arrived with Sir Edgar Mainwaring,

the instant he looked at Rachel, she knew there was
to be a continuation of the coldness between them,
which had begun the moment they had found Kitty
in Covent Garden that afternoon. His mouth did not
smile and his dark eyes looked at her seriously; he
did not distinguish her with any marked interest
throughout the whole evening.

His reserve severely vexed her, although he was
attentive and polite to Lady Brayfield, whose manner
was as it always was, for she refused to allow Kitty's
misdemeanour to affect her in any way. On seeing
her, her guests would not guess from her appearance
of the terrible secret she concealed.

"I must thank you for sparing the time to look for
my niece, Lord Kingsley," said Lady Brayfield when
they were all seated at the dining table—herself at the
head of the table with Rachel and Lord Kingsley
seated facing each other on either side of her, Sir
Edgar, Caroline and Emily, happy to be gossiping
among themselves, further along the table. "We are
all most grateful."

"Please—think nothing of it, Lady Brayfield," he
answered. "I had little else to occupy my time and
was happy to be of help."

"I hear your brother has shown up at last and that
he has returned to Mortlake Park. Are you to remain
in London long, Lord Kingsley?"

"No more than a day or so at the most. I have
pressing matters to attend to at Mortlake."

"Oh!" exclaimed Lady Brayfield, clearly disappointed. "You are to leave so soon?"

"Yes. A matter of duty, Lady Brayfield, rather than will, for nothing would give me greater pleasure than to remain in town."

Rachel met his eye, unconvinced by what he said. How different he sounded from the day at Ranelagh, when he had sought her out and implied she was his reason for remaining in London. She could only conclude that now he was eager to be gone from her.

"My nieces are to return to Oxfordshire also during the next few days—when my brother arrives, of course, after he has seen Harry settled at Harrow."

"It is hoped Kitty will soon begin to feel better with a little country air," explained Rachel, her expression tense, showing the nervous strain she was under and her low spirits. It was with difficulty that she tried to induce a social lightness into her tone.

Lord Kingsley's eyes met hers across the table.

"You are eager to return to Oxfordshire, Miss Fairley?"

"Yes. The entertainments of London have never held the attractions for me that they do for most people, so I shall not be sorry to leave. Besides—my sister's health is all important to me just now."

"Of course."

"Tell me, Lord Kingsley, have you heard from your sister, Amanda? How she is enjoying her tour of Europe with her aunt?" asked Lady Brayfield.

"I had a letter from her only the other day. She is in Venice at the moment, which she is enjoying enormously. She is quite beguiled by the places she visits.

I believe they are to go on to Rome next. And your brother, Miss Fairley, have you heard from him?''

"Stephen is still in the north—although I do not believe it will be long before we see him back in Oxfordshire.''

"Then I hope I shall have the pleasure of meeting him again—and also hope my brother will take the opportunity of becoming better acquainted with him. I am sure they will have much in common. James will appreciate the benefit of his advice, I know, for he is to make a visit to the north himself shortly—to study the prospects of some investments we intend to make in industries now we no longer have any interests in the West Indies.''

"I see. Then I am sure Stephen will be more than happy to offer him any advice he might ask for,'' said Rachel, trying to stifle the disappointment she felt over his cold, impersonal attitude towards her. The tone of his voice sounded so formal, ceremonious, almost, as he uttered commonplace conventialities like a polite stranger. Her aunt remarked on it later when her guests had departed.

"It was evident that Lord Kingsley was in low spirits this evening, Rachel, no matter how politely he tried to conceal it. It seems I was mistaken in thinking he was beginning to show an interest in you, for I don't think he spoke more than half a dozen sentences to you the whole evening.''

"Yes. It would seem we have both been deceived, Aunt,'' said Rachel stiffly, trying to compose her voice to conceal her emotions and distress, which pained her terribly and was caused by his coldness towards her.

"I could not help noticing that he seemed to avoid any conversation with me at all. He was definitely out of humour—although I do not believe I have done anything to merit his disfavour. But then, considering our situation—and not forgetting Kitty's ungracious attitude towards him earlier—it is hardly surprising. In fact—I would say he was in a hurry to be gone."

As she climbed the stairs to bid her sister good night, she asked herself if she had been deceived in what she had perceived to be his growing regard for her. But how could she have been—for had her aunt not been aware of it, and Caroline and Emily, also?

She sighed sadly. If he had possessed any regard for her at all, then because of Kitty's rudeness towards him he had made it plain by his coolness towards her that she was beginning to see a decline in his estimation of herself.

As was the case with Ralph Wheeler, had Kitty ruined all her chances of forming a deeper relationship with him also, now that she realised she was falling in love with him? For—yes, she *loved* him, but there was no joy in this discovery; she could see nothing in it other than heartache and misery for herself.

In the light of her unhappy affair with Ralph, it was something she would have elected to avoid at all costs. But to have recognised this feeling, to have savoured it and dared to dream—however briefly— and to have lost it so soon, was a crushing blow.

Lord Kingsley had come into her life when she had been extremely vulnerable, when she had been hurt and disillusioned, and he was so very different to what Ralph had been. But she was beginning to realise that loving him would cause her more pain and disillusionment—far worse than anything she had experienced when Ralph had so cruelly left her.

As she stood on the threshold of Kitty's room, it was with a sad and shaky determination that she vowed she would never be hurt again—not by Lord Kingsley or any man.

Entering her sister's room, Rachel found her in bed, her face strained and painfully sad, her pale cheeks showing traces of fresh tears. She looked sick at heart and so forlorn in the big four-poster bed.

Rachel sank down beside her, her sorely tried nerves stretched taut but, on seeing her sister's continued misery, she smiled indulgently, knowing that throughout the coming weeks and months she was going to have to pay her all the sisterly, unobtrusive attention she was able to, for she was deeply concerned over the restless state of her mind.

"How are you feeling now, Kitty?"

"Never have I felt more miserable. Neither Caroline or Emily have been in to see me," she complained in a small tremulous voice, "no doubt forbidden to do so by Aunt Mary, fearful that I shall corrupt their impressionable minds. Did—did you have a pleasant evening with Lord Kingsley?" she asked hesitantly.

Rachel sighed deeply. The whole evening had been

a bitter disappointment to her, which Kitty detected from the tone of her voice and the misery in her eyes. "No—not really. After his coolness towards me earlier, I am sure he only came out of politeness to Aunt Mary. It was evident to me that he could not wait for the evening to end."

"Oh, Rachel—I can see what you're feeling. It's written all over your face. I'm so sorry. I know I haven't helped matters." She sighed wistfully. "Perhaps he does not want to be seen associating with a woman whose sister is an actress of easy virtue."

Her words, spoken with much bitterness, caused Rachel to look at her sharply and Kitty smiled thinly. "Oh, I don't deceive myself that that is what I am, Rachel, and if you must know I am deeply ashamed— but it is too late to turn back the clock now, no matter how much I would like to.

"However, if Lord Kingsley allows himself to be influenced by that, then I have to say that he has much in common with his brother," she said almost absently and with much bitterness. It was only when she met Rachel's sharp and all-at-once inquiring eyes, seeing her brow crease in an attentive frown, that she blanched and looked nervously away.

"Kitty, look at me," demanded Rachel, a terrible suspicion beginning to form in some dark corner of her mind. "What did you mean by that?"

"Why—nothing, nothing at all," Kitty replied quickly, noticing how her sister's tone had acquired a touch of hardness.

"When have you seen Lord Kingsley's brother?

Are you so well acquainted with him that you can liken the two of them? Have you seen him here in London?''

"Why—I—yes—on occasion," she answered reluctantly.

"Where?" Rachel persisted, a cold feeling beginning to take hold of her.

"At—at the theatre. He—he was often in the audience. Although—I have to say that he was already known to me before I left Ellerton," she said quietly.

Rachel fixed her eyes on Kitty's flushed face. Tension vibrated in the air between them. "And how close did you become when you were at the Drury Lane theatre, Kitty? How close?" she demanded relentlessly, unconsciously reaching out and gripping her sister's arms in a vice like grip in an attempt to force the truth out of her.

Kitty shrank back against the pillows, suddenly deflated. "Very close," she admitted with a sigh, unable to conceal what their relationship had been from her sister any longer. "An attachment and intimacy was already formed between us before I left Oxfordshire."

"James Kingsley is the father of your unborn child, isn't he, Kitty? Is this is the reason why you were so antagonistic towards Lord Kingsley earlier?"

Their eyes met and clashed.

"Yes," whispered Kitty.

The silence that fell between them was profound and complete. There was no movement from either of them—it was as if they had become petrified in stone. There was no blinking of an eye, no intake of breath,

nothing. At first Rachel's astonishment and shock was
so great that she was lost for words, but at length she
replied with caution, her face deathly white, for nothing in her life had pained her as much as the small
one-syllable word her sister had uttered.

"How could you, Kitty? How could you give your
favours so willingly to James Kingsley of all people?" she reproached her harshly, unable to withhold
her anger, for she saw her own hopes and expecta-
tions—hardly daring to imagine what might have
been—come tumbling down about her. But she must
not surrender to the full meaning of what this could
mean to herself just now. She must put out of her
mind what her future might have been had this not
happened to Kitty.

Rachel got up from the bed and paced the room,
trying to come to terms with this latest hurdle that
was going to be the most difficult of all to surmount.

"Does he know that you are carrying his child?
Have you told him?"

Kitty nodded dumbly.

"And I suspect that, when you told him, he refused
to do the honourable thing and marry you—leaving
London in some haste. Is that how it was, Kitty?"

Tears sprang to Kitty's eyes at the frank reproach
of her sister's gaze. "Yes. We—we had a frightful
argument and when he left me he was quite wretched.
I—I heard he had left London to stay with an acquaintance in Kent."

"From where he has since returned," said Rachel,
recollecting that Mrs Gilbey had spoken to her of a

bitter argument taking place between Kitty and a gentleman friend, that he had left hurriedly and not returned.

Kitty's eyes lit up with hope. "To London?"

"Yes—but he went directly to Mortlake Park. If, as I remember you saying, he has a fondness for you, then he may have refused to marry you because he did not wish to brave his brother's wrath—which would no doubt figure largely in his decision. Although why he should need his opinion or his approval is quite beyond me, for he is of age and does not need his brother's consent to marry?"

"No," sighed Kitty, "but he would want it and his good wishes all the same. Although I have to tell you that he was more concerned about how his mother would react than Lord Kingsley. His fear was always very real where she was concerned—yet he saw her so seldom, for she always made him quite miserable."

For reasons she could not explain, Rachel remembered the emotional and strained undercurrent of something being very wrong at Mortlake Park. That there was something very odd about Lady Kingsley she already knew, but it was not something she wanted to go in to just then. The most important thing was what was to be done to solve the problem facing them. Taking a deep breath, she looked at Kitty.

"It seems we have little choice but to appeal to Lord Kingsley. After all, I doubt he will want to become embroiled in a scandal any more than we do. I shall go and see him myself first thing in the morning," she said decisively. "Although after the fuss he made when Stephen sought his consent to marry Amanda, I very much suspect he will not approve of an alliance between you and his brother, with or without a child.

"Sadly, Kitty, your choice of profession and the way you shunned society is very much against you in his eyes. Also, your open attack on him earlier will have done you no good, either. You should have adopted a sense of decorum. You were too ready to slight him and should have exercised more constraint. However, something must be done and quickly. This is no time to be complacent."

"But is it wise for you to go and see him?"

"Why not? You do want James to marry you, don't you, Kitty?"

"Yes, of course I do. But is it not just a little hasty to go to Lord Kingsley and confront him with this? Should we not wait until Father arrives in London— for him to deal with the matter?"

"No. There may not be time. Lord Kingsley is to leave for Mortlake Park very soon. We must act immediately."

Kitty stared in amazement at her sister, at the determined set of her chin and the hard gaze of her eyes.

"Are you not afraid of his anger? From what I have seen of Lord Kingsley, he is a formidable man."

"No," Rachel replied, with a touch of anger added to her bitterness. "The prospect facing you—facing all of us—is too dreadful to contemplate. After what James Kingsley has done to you, he must be made to face up to his responsibilities—and it is up to his brother to make him see that he does.''

The following morning Rachel got up in low spirits, the awful prospect of what she knew she had to do having prevented any rest she might have had. As she dressed she was resolute in her decision to visit Lord Kingsley at his home in Grosvenor Square, in the hope that she could persuade him to force his brother to do the honourable thing and marry Kitty—thus saving her from total disgrace and the whole family from an open scandal.

Her sights were no longer blunted by compassion for her own feelings, which were of no consequence in the light of Kitty's predicament. The preservation of her family's good name was paramount.

On the pretext of taking a drive in the park, Rachel purposely concealed her true destination from her aunt Mary as she had no wish to involve her in this matter. It would most certainly create a degree of unpleasantness between herself and Lord Kingsley, and might result in an estrangement between Sir Edgar Mainwaring and Caroline—for her aunt had high hopes of this relationship turning into a formal attachment.

For her visit to Grosvenor Square, Rachel chose a time unsuitable for either Caroline or Emily to want to accompany her; they were to go to Bond Street to make some purchases.

With her aunt's maid, Celia, in attendance, once she was seated in the carriage—full of trepidation at her forthcoming confrontation with Lord Kingsley—

she ordered the driver to take her the short distance to Kingsley House in Grosvenor Square.

Leaving Celia in the carriage, promising she would not be very long—and ignoring the elderly lady's look of disapproval at the impropriety of her calling on a gentleman all alone, reminding her that her aunt would be most displeased if she found out—Rachel hurried from the carriage and knocked on the door of Kingsley House, considering the seriousness of her mission too important for her to be concerned about the finer feelings of her aunt's maid.

As if someone had been waiting directly behind the door, it was opened almost immediately. She was admitted by a footman who escorted her into a small reception room leading off from the hall, where he left her to announce her arrival to Lord Kingsley.

Rachel waited in an agony of suspense and anticipation, so nervous that she failed to take in the splendour of the house and its handsome furnishings. She moved to the window, looking out over the square, but so great was her agitation and the turmoil within her that she failed to absorb the view with any interest.

She was struck by the quietness of the house, which made her nervousness more pronounced, and she breathed a sigh of relief when, at last, on hearing a soft footfall on the carpet behind her, she turned to face Lord Kingsley.

Chapter Eleven

Lord Kingsley moved towards Rachel where she stood, a pale and graceful figure silhouetted against the shafts of light shining in through the long window. Her eyes remained riveted on his as he inclined his dark head in a polite bow.

The expression on his handsome features was unreadable. She had caught him completely by surprise for he was preparing to leave for Mortlake Park that very day, in the hope that his suspicions regarding any relationship existing between his brother and Kitty Fairley were ill founded.

"Miss Fairley! I have to say this is an unexpected pleasure. Although whatever the significance of your visit, it must be of some importance for you to come alone."

"Aunt Mary's maid has accompanied me. She is waiting in the carriage outside. What I have to say should not take up too much of your time."

"Where you are concerned, Miss Fairley, any time spent with you is a pleasure. Although I have to tell you that I am preparing to return to Mortlake Park shortly, so you are fortunate to find me still here. Can I offer you some refreshment?''

"No—thank you," she said stiffly. Despite his polite words there was a coldness to his manner and she felt uncomfortable beneath his direct gaze. "This is not a social call, Lord Kingsley."

"No, I did not think it was. At least, will you not be seated?" he invited, indicating a chair.

"No. I—I prefer to stand."

He nodded. "As you wish," he said, moving to stand by the window with his hands behind his back, facing her, sensing her agitation. "Your visit concerns your sister, does it not?" he said, taking the initiative.

"Yes. I realise the impropriety of my coming to see you like this, Lord Kingsley, and I realise I am taking a great deal upon myself by doing so on so delicate a matter—and that it should have been left to my father or my aunt. But my father has not yet arrived in London and I did not wish to involve my aunt.

"It is a matter that must be dealt with hastily in order to avoid a scandal of the worst possible kind, which would be disastrous for both our families. There is the need for the utmost secrecy."

Rachel fell silent for Lord Kingsley had become thoughtful. He nodded, beginning to pace the floor slowly, in measured strides, increasing her nervousness. Watching him, never had she been as aware of the love growing within her for this man as she was at that moment, but all her feelings and thoughts for herself must be repressed for the present and not allowed to intrude on the awful predicament Kitty had brought upon the whole family.

"Well? Pray continue," he said, with a touch of impatience.

Careful to guard her expression from any suspicion that she was offended by his cool manner, Rachel forced herself to look calmly into his eyes when he paused in front of her.

"It—it concerns my sister and your brother. It would seem they have formed a romantic attachment." She looked at him curiously when she saw there was no reaction from him, only a slight inclination of his head. "You do not appear surprised to hear this."

"No. You have merely confirmed my suspicions."

"I have?"

"Yesterday when I left you, after bringing your sister from Covent Garden, I knew her antipathy towards me could not be for anything ill I might have done towards her, for, as you well know, I had not made her acquaintance before coming to London. That left James. I know he has been seeing an actress of late—has formed a close attachment, in fact—and I surmised it to be your sister and that her anger towards myself had been brought about by his rejection of her."

Rachel stiffened. "Rejection! But how do you know he has rejected her?"

"What other reason could there possibly be for her anger? I am sorry if she considers she has been ill used by my brother, Miss Fairley, but I fail to see what can be achieved by your coming here to plead her cause—which is a strange mission for a woman of such tender pride," he said, irony marking his handsome features. "Your sister is a mature girl and completely self-possessed. If she is nursing a broken heart, then I am sure she will get over it in time."

Thrown off balance, Rachel stared at him in bewilderment. "You—you have it all wrong, Lord Kingsley. I admit that I have come here to plead her cause, as you so aptly put it, but not in the sense you mean. Your brother has injured my sister in the most deplorable manner. How can you defend him?"

"James has been impressionable all his life. Clearly your sister's beauty and her charms robbed him of his senses. I can only be thankful he has at last seen the defects to her character for, as I know to my cost and pointed out to you only yesterday, she has many."

"You speak of her with no more respect than a—a common trull from the back streets," Rachel said hotly.

"That is where I found her," he reminded her cruelly. "James and your sister are so very different."

"Not so different, otherwise they would not have formed an attachment."

"Nevertheless, any alliance between them would be insupportable. I hope you are not here to beg me to look on such a match as favourable—because I cannot."

"Why—how dare you!" said Rachel, stiffened by pride and growing more and more angry by the minute at hearing Kitty slighted so outrageously. His words had been devastatingly and crushingly employed. She stepped towards him, her cheeks flushed and her eyes flashing fire.

"You, sir, seem to go through life with a total disregard for the feelings of others. First, there was the matter of my brother Stephen wanting to marry your sister—which you so callously rejected out of hand, inflicting a great deal of pain on both parties—and now this. You might have the courtesy to wait and hear what I have to say before condemning Kitty outright."

William stopped and fixed her with a hard gaze, his manner suddenly one of caution and calm. "Well? What is it?"

"You do not yet know the whole of it. It is much worse than you could possibly have imagined. Kitty is with child—and—and your brother..."

She faltered, unable to finish what she had to say. William stared at her, at first with some degree of astonishment, but then his eyes became hard and glittered like pieces of coal when he realised the implication of her words.

"Are you telling me James is the father?" he asked with chill precision.

Rachel nodded, swallowing hard. "Yes."

"And you are certain of this?"

She nodded.

"And James? Did your sister tell him of the child?"

"Yes."

"And did he acknowledge it as his?"

"I—I do not know for certain," she replied, although she did remember Kitty telling her that James had questioned her as to whether or not he was the father—no doubt in order to try and wriggle out of any responsibility which might concern him. "But it is clear you consider her so lacking in morals that you do not believe the child to be his."

William responded with a chilling smile, his voice hard and cutting, his complexion pale with repressed anger. "James's reputation may be somewhat dubious, Miss Fairley, but he is still a gentleman. I am certain that, if he believes himself to be responsible for fathering your sister's child then, in all conscience, he would not have left her. Was the affair between them of short duration?"

"No. Quite the opposite. I believe it began before Kitty left Ellerton. Of her deep affection for your brother I have no doubt—and she informed me herself that he was very much in love with her."

"In love," scorned William, turning to fix his angry gaze out of the window. "My brother's romantic affairs cannot be counted. Why should his affair with your sister be any different? She read too much into it."

"Are you saying he was merely sporting with her? If so, he is completely lacking in moral principles and used her ill. His misconduct cannot be ignored."

He turned back to her. "Just what do you want me to do, Miss Fairley?"

"To intervene. To return to Mortlake Park and insist on your brother facing up to his responsibilities. To do the honourable thing by my sister and marry her. If he does not, then I fear she will be ruined forever. Through her own foolishness she has fallen into misfortune. Sadly, she is no longer the same and I am grieved over the effect it will have on my father—as you know, his failing health concerns us deeply.

"It pains me greatly to come here in this manner—to humble myself before you and beg your intervention. But if that is what it takes, then so be it—for I cannot abandon my sister to fall even further into a life of degradation."

"And I have no mind to foist a child on James with no proof that it is his. What if he has no longer any affection for your sister?"

"Kitty believes he has—for when he left her he was in a wretched state. She believes he left her so abruptly for reasons of his own—reasons he did not explain, but which she suspects has something to do with matters at Mortlake Park."

William nodded, thinking over what she had said, but not enlightening her as to what it could be that had caused James to leave her so abruptly.

"Kitty may be many things, but she is certainly not promiscuous," Rachel continued, "and would not sully herself unless she loved the man. Your brother has treated her in an infamous manner and must be brought to account. By his actions she will suffer for the rest of her life—as will her entire family, if he does not own up to the fact that he is the father of her child—while he escapes without a blemish to his character.

"He has a duty towards her. He cannot just walk away and leave her to her fate. But make no mistake, Lord Kingsley—if she were not carrying his child, then I would say that to be delivered from any connection with him at all would be a blessing indeed, but as it is, I cannot."

"After her show of anger yesterday towards myself, I would have thought that any connection with my brother was the last thing she wanted," he retorted fiercely.

Rachel's composure finally snapped and she drew herself up proudly. "You made your feelings on any alliance between our two families perfectly clear to me when my brother sought your consent to marry your sister. It seems I was mistaken in you, Lord Kingsley. I believed that being a man of considerable pride, honour and conscience, you would not allow your brother to ignore his responsibilities."

In an effort to regain his composure, William turned from her accusing eyes, for again, as was the case with Amanda when Stephen Fairley had asked him to consent to a marriage between them, he was confronted by the terrible nature of his stepmother's illness: unbeknown to anyone outside the immediate family and a few trusted servants, she had suffered from defects to her mind for many years.

He had employed the services of a Mr Hopkins to make inquiries into her family's medical background on the island of Antigua where she was raised. Until he received his report, guaranteeing there was no hereditary insanity—that the illness would not be transmitted through James and Amanda to any children they might have—he must keep the matter to himself.

However, if the child Kitty Fairley was carrying did prove to be James's then, despite the problem of any insanity being passed on should they marry, it was too late—the deed was already done.

As Rachel stared at William's smooth back, with not a crease in the material of his black coat stretched across his shoulders, she had no notion of what was passing through his mind. Anger stirred inside her, anger at herself for so readily succumbing to the attentions of Lord Kingsley like a naïve fool.

Had she not learned her lesson when Ralph had left her? Perhaps, she thought with bitter disappointment, Lord Kingsley had much in common with his brother and men like Ralph, and had been sporting with her as James had done with Kitty.

"I can see that, despite your friendliness and fine words of late, Lord Kingsley, nothing has changed from our first meeting—and I can only regret allowing myself to be so easily mollified by what I believed to be a change in your attitude towards myself."

William turned and faced her and she was surprised to see that his expression had softened and a sadness had entered the dark smooth depths of his eyes.

"Please, make no mistake, I hold you in the highest regard—as I do your father and your brother. Your sister, however, is a different matter entirely—and we will never agree on that, I fear. There is little about her character to recommend her to me.''

''You are mistaken, sir. Kitty has always been a sensible and amiable girl, and her manner has always been open and affectionate. Her anger towards you was understandable, considering the manner in which she has been treated by your brother.

''But tell me, Lord Kingsley, what is your objection? If they do indeed love each other, and your brother owns the child to be his, then what obstacle, other than my sister's choice of profession—which has so evidently discredited her in your opinion—can there be to stop them marrying?''

''None,'' William spoke resignedly and with much gravity.

Rachel's lips twisted into a wry smile. ''But clearly you would oppose it. Perhaps it would be simpler for all concerned if Kitty were to have her pregnancy terminated—which, I understand, is a method practised by many women who are faced with little alternative.''

William stared at her in horror, knowing full well to what she referred. ''No,'' he said, his eyes flashing with sudden fury, which shocked Rachel and caused her to draw back from him. ''That would never do. I have respect for human life and would not condone an abortion—which is a crime in itself. Has she considered this?''

''Yes, I am ashamed to say she has.''

''Then you must instil into her the dangers in this practice—to her own life. The methods and conditions in which abortionists work resemble butchers' shops. She must not do this.''

He sighed, his tone softening. ''I am a fair man, Miss Fairley, and I promise you that if I find my brother has a regard for your sister—and if it is proved that the child is indeed his—then I shall not stand in their way should they wish to marry. As you pointed out earlier—a scandal will not serve either of our families.''

Well satisfied, although feeling desperately unhappy and humiliated by her interview with Lord Kingsley, Rachel nodded, swallowing hard and holding her head high as she strove to retain her dignity, for he would never know how much he had hurt her by his severe condemnation of her sister.

''Thank you. I will take my leave of you now. I shall not speak of this again—and any dealings on this unfortunate affair in the future will be done with my father. Goodbye, Lord Kingsley, and thank you for sparing me some of your valuable time.''

Seeing the tears of rage and misery she was trying hard to repress in her lovely eyes as she was about to turn away, William was disarmed and moved quickly towards her, his features grave but calm, his anger gone as he was possessed by an urgent desire to protect that which she alone had aroused in him.

He could not allow discord between their families to destroy the strong emotions growing between them, emotions neither had spoken of but were each aware of, emotions they were allowing to unfold gently, to grow in intensity, until the moment that would bring them ultimate fulfilment. However, Rachel was too shaken and angry to be comforted by the softening she saw in his features.

"Please," he said quietly, placing his hand on her arm, "don't be in such a hurry to leave."

"I—I must. We have nothing else to say to each other," she said, struggling to keep her tears under control, fighting the longing to respond to the firm pressure of his hand on her arm.

"You cannot leave like this. You are upset."

"With little wonder."

"You are angry with me. Please believe me when I say that I have no desire to quarrel with you. I apologise if I sounded harsh, for I would never want to cause you any pain."

"How can you expect me to accept your apology when you speak so ill of my sister? Do you expect me to thank you politely when, by insulting Kitty, you have insulted my whole family?"

"No—not your family. Your sister, maybe, but never you. It was not my intention to offend you."

"Offend! Insult!" she cried, her emotions threatening to get the better of her if she stayed much longer. "It matters little to me one way or the other. I think you made your feelings abundantly clear."

"Again I apologise—for I desire your friendship, and more, above all else. I regret most sincerely that our families have encroached too much on both our lives—to such an extent that we are in danger of forgetting that which is important to each of us."

"How can you talk of our continued friendship after this? Your condemnation was harsh, the nature of it insulting. My sister's comfort and well-being is paramount to me just now. I have a duty to do what I can to see her through this difficult time.''

''Duty! A heavy burden to bear, Miss Fairley, but your commitment to your family is one of the things I admire about you. You have every right to be angry—but please believe me when I tell you that most of my anger is directed against my brother.

''But I have to say that I am puzzled, for James and I have always been close, and it goes against his character for him to abandon a young woman in such a wretched manner—if he is responsible for the predicament she finds herself to be in, that is. But come—we cannot allow this to cause enmity between us. We cannot allow our friendship to be ruined by this unfortunate business.''

''There can be nothing between us while this affair remains unresolved.''

''And I have told you that if it is proved beyond doubt that the child your sister is carrying is indeed my brother's, then feel confident that I will do everything in my power to legitimise their union and reduce the anxiety of your whole family.''

''How can I know that?'' she cried wretchedly, his voice—so gentle, so soothing, suddenly, devoid of all anger and mockery and sounding so comforting—weakening her. Because of the immense strain she was under, the tears she had struggled to keep in check finally spilled over her lashes and began flowing unchecked down her cheeks.

"Knowing how distasteful any connection with my sister is to you—for her then to become a member of your immediate family—I have every reason to doubt what you say. How do I know you are not lying to placate me now?"

In answer to her question, with a sigh William lowered his head down to hers, feeling her breath warm his cheek, and before Rachel knew what he was about he had placed his mouth on hers, kissing her long and deep, taking his time and savouring the moment, feeling her lips part and yield beneath his. His lips were warm and firm and she was so astonished—and at the same time filled with confusion—by his action, that she did not object.

He raised his head and looked down at her, at her tears frozen on her cheeks and her magnificent eyes looking wonderingly into his. "Now ask yourself if I was lying, Miss Fairley."

He smiled crookedly, his eyes lingering on her lips, parted and moist and vulnerable, as if he were about to repeat the action—which was exactly what he had in mind. "I do not dispense my kisses lightly—and, like my opinions, once uttered, they cannot be retracted," he said quietly, his lips so very close to hers.

This time he caught her up into his arms, imprisoning her against him in a tight embrace so there was little she could do but yield to his desire, as again his lips came down on hers. Hot and cold waves swept over her as she closed her eyes and swayed in his arms, feeling the hard strength of his body pressed to hers.

His kiss was devastating, firm and demanding, stealing away any measure of resistance she had left, blotting out her reason for coming to his house, for nothing mattered at that moment but the splendour, the joy, of being in his arms.

As her arms stole upwards and fastened about his neck, she did not struggle, she had no will to—was this not what she had wanted to happen since their coming together on the terrace at Mortlake Park?

His mouth was so warm and inviting after the chill she had endured. She was so starved of love that she responded willingly, unresisting, drowning, dissolving against him. He kissed her eyes, her cheeks, sliding his lips down the white flesh of her throat before seeking her mouth once more, eager to receive her kiss.

Feeling his hands stealing up her back to the warmth at the back of her neck, his fingers firm, strong, and yet caressing in a way that sent her senses reeling, Rachel trembled with a desire so great she thought she would die of it. He filled her body with a liquid fire that melted the freezing core in her heart, raising a hunger she had tried to deny for so long, and she yearned with a craving she had never known before for love.

When at last he withdrew from her lips, he raised his head and looked down at her face. Rachel lowered her head in confusion, the delicate pink flush on her cheeks screened by the brim of her bonnet, beneath which her dark hair gleamed, thin strands having come loose by his caress trailing about her neck.

She felt so very vulnerable, completely at his mercy, as if she hovered on the brink of passion—and the excitement of the unknown, the expectancy of it, almost overwhelmed her.

As if William divined her thought, with one arm still about her he placed the fingers of his other hand gently beneath her chin and turned her face up to his, her lash-shadowed eyes full of appeal.

He looked down at her, filled with a deep love and desire that he had been content to leave to unfold as their knowledge of each other grew, for it was too precious, too important to hasten. His thoughtful gaze caressed her face, searching and probing the misty depths of her eyes.

"Never, in all my life, have I seen eyes such as these—as lovely as these—nor have there been lips as tempting since Eve's in the Garden of Eden. I love you, Rachel Fairley—and I believe you love me too. I can see confirmation in your eyes—I felt it in your response to my kiss. Your lips do not lie."

They stood looking at each other, as if the whole world had paused in its turning to contain this special moment. William spoke with so much conviction that Rachel was unable to do anything other than stare at him in wondering awe, unable to believe he had said those things—but what he said was true.

Despite her determination never to fall prey to her emotions again after being cast aside by Ralph, Lord Kingsley's kiss had been her undoing. The way her body had quickly and wantonly responded to his lips, greedily craving for more, told her that, where he was concerned, she did not have the power or the will to control them.

She did love him, desperately, and like him she had been happy to let the love growing between them unfold. Because they felt the same, with the same longings, because they were both aware of the other's feelings and emotions, burning like a living flame between them, then there had been no need for words, no need for analysis or explanation, for they were bound by their own strange code of silence, content to wait until the moment was right for it to be realised.

What had just happened had flung open a door between them, allowing sunlight to flood in, revealing their true feelings for each other and covering Rachel in its luminous glow, so that William was almost blinded by it. Never had he seen such perfection, such radiance in any one person. She was like a flower opening and unfolding and stretching towards the light, her eyes glowing, her lips parted to reveal her shining, perfect teeth.

"Come," he said softly, restraining the urge to kiss her once more. "Are you going to deny your feelings that are so very obvious to me?"

To regain some semblance of sanity, for she was still attuned to his kiss, Rachel stepped back from him, not having realised she had been so transparent. But no matter how much she longed for him to take her in his arms, to feel his lips on hers once more, setting her skin tingling and her blood on fire, she knew she must deny the attraction drawing them closer together, the image of Kitty and her own fear of allowing herself to be hurt again standing between them.

Until she could overcome her own personal fears regarding her emotions, and until everything had been resolved between their two families, then she could not allow herself to weaken to these new sensations Lord Kingsley had awoken in her—pleasant, sensual sensations, which she longed to savour and enjoy, which were in danger of making her forget her true reason for coming to Kingsley House today.

Seeing the doubt cloud her eyes and aware of her hesitation, William frowned, becoming troubled by her reticence. "Why—what is this? Why do you hesitate? Have I expressed myself badly?"

"No," she sighed, speaking softly. "I—I think you expressed yourself very well. It is just that there are certain matters I cannot ignore at this present time. Please—you must understand—that I—I cannot allow my emotions to cloud my mind."

William wanted to reach out and shake the stubbornness out of her. "Then perhaps you have another favour to ask with regard to your sister," he said, his growing disappointment quickly turning to anger, "who seems to have an irritating habit of penetrating and dominating your thoughts so that you can think of little else."

Stung by his words, which were like a douche of cold water, returning them to an atmosphere of unrest and to their earlier constraint, filling Rachel's heart with anguish and sorrow, she stepped back, clinging to her sudden spark of anger like a shield to her emotions, pitted against his will and her overwhelming need for this man she was finding exceedingly difficult to deny.

"No. But I am happy to learn that you have not forgotten my reason for coming here." Her tone sounded harsh, but inside she was feeling wretchedly unhappy. "You cannot order my life as you do your sister's and brother's. No matter what you feel—and whatever you have read into our relationship—if you believe there can be anything between us other than friendship until this unfortunate affair has been resolved, then you are mistaken. Let it be enough for now for there to be one connection between our families."

William's face became suddenly pale and grim. His eyes narrowed and darkened and his black eyebrows drew together in a straight line. "You have every right to be angry regarding my brother's treatment of your sister—but that has nothing to do with what is between us.

"If my declaration has upset you, then forgive me. I did not wish to add to your worries; you are quite right—you have enough to occupy your mind at this time. However, having declared myself thus, and strongly doubting the truth of your denial—if denial it was—then I had hoped for a more honest answer from you. As it is, I can only regret my own declaration, which deserved better than to be rejected in such terms as these."

Rachel felt by the coldness of his voice and the

very intonation of his words that he had become a stranger—that he had withdrawn from her, and it was of her doing.

Immediately she regretted her harsh words and was swayed by his anger. She felt a sudden weakening in her resolve—and also a frightening helplessness bordering on utter despair. She wanted to reach out to him, to touch him and beg his forgiveness, but such a thing was so very difficult for her to do. Sighing deeply, she lowered her eyes to hide the misery in their depths.

"I am sorry if I offended you. It was not intentionally done—and I am not insensible to your declaration—truly—and—I have certainly not rejected you—quite the opposite, in fact."

Her words were spoken softly, with a doleful resignation and with such humility that it caused William to look at her with involuntary tenderness. She looked so piteous, so defenceless, that he sensed her distress. He sighed deeply.

"And do you still deny that what is in your heart does not equal my own? That you love me also?"

Rachel's eyes were full of tenderness and pain as she looked at him. Swallowing down the tears which were almost choking her, she shook her head. "No. I do not deny it. I cannot deny what I know to be the truth."

"Then perhaps if you were to set aside the differences that exist between other members of our families, to forget them for once and tell me what is in your heart—what it is that has caused you to raise a barrier against your emotions, which, I suspect, are of a more personal nature where I am concerned—then there might be better understanding between us. Has it anything to do with a former love—and how deeply he hurt you when he let you down?'' he asked gently.

Rachel stared at him, her lips quivering slightly, her eyes swimming with unshed tears. "You—you know?''

"Yes. Maybe if you were to tell me about him, it would ease the pain he caused you and help me to understand why you are so afraid to give vent to your true feelings—and your propensity to hide them away in your concern for others.''

"I—I'm sorry. I did not realise I did—and, anyhow—there is little to tell and—and I am sure you will think I have been extremely foolish,'' she said hesitantly.

"No—no. Never that. Come, tell me,'' he prompted gently. "In doing so, it may cease to be the tragedy it was and you will see that life is for living—not brooding over what might have been.''

"I don't,'' she said, moving away from him towards the hearth so he could not see her face. "My concern has always been to avoid being hurt in the same manner again.''

William stood very still, watching her, and it seemed that her slender shoulders drooped and bowed, which indicated to him that her hard-held defences were beginning to crumble. After a moment she turned and looked at him, reading gentle concern in his dark eyes, and knowing instinctively that he would sympathise with her. Her face became set and sorrowful, her eyes a million miles away and clouded with memory.

"Perhaps you're right and there might be better understanding between us if you know more about me, about the shame I was forced to endure when the man I loved—or thought I loved—rejected me for another. It is not a subject I find easy to talk about; it affected me deeply at the time."

"Please try. I am not as insensitive as you might think to your feelings."

"Thank you," she murmured, slowly and quietly beginning to give him an account of her unfortunate affair with Ralph Wheeler.

"When I was eighteen years old, I was on the threshold of marriage to a man I adored. At that time I thought he was the most handsome man I had every seen—who said he loved me above all else—and then he had gone. It is an age-old story, I know," she sighed, "but imagine how I felt when I discovered he had married someone else—when I discovered how he had lied and deceived me, when I knew I would never see him again. I did not think I could possibly go on living without him.

"It was only as time went by that I began to see the whole affair in a different light and realised how foolish and incredibly naïve I had been—that I was nothing but an ignorant girl."

She lowered her head when tears of misery again began to swim in her eyes. On seeing this, a flicker of pain crossed William's face.

"Would I be correct in assuming the nature of your sister's profession had something to do with it?"

Unable to deny the truth, Rachel nodded, swallowing down the hard lump in her throat. "His family belonged to the aristocracy, you understand, and became set against any connection with me or my family when they found out about Kitty."

"So—at that time she damaged your chances of marrying well, it would seem," said William, unable to keep the bitter irony out of his voice but which, in her misery, Rachel seemed not to notice. She sighed, not wishing to sound disloyal to Kitty, but the look in her eyes told William this was so.

"At first I thought it was all a mistake—that the people who told me of his sudden marriage to someone else were lying—and that he would get in touch."

"But he didn't."

"No. If he had truly loved me, then he would have defied his family. Nothing would have kept us apart. But he made no effort to see me—no offer of an explanation for his conduct. Nothing."

"And did you see him again?"

"Once. He—he was with his wife," she said quietly and with difficulty. "He—he looked at me as—as if he didn't know me—like a complete stranger. That was when I knew I would never forgive him. Oh, the pain and anguish I had felt over his rejection of me was lifted—but there was a part of me he had brought alive that shrivelled and died. That was when I came to hate him, feeling that I could never allow myself to fall in love again. I could not bear to be hurt like that a second time.''

Having listened to her simple story of pain and humiliation, William's heart began to melt with pity, drawing him from his own desolation, and his arms ached to hold her, but he must let her go on.

''So—you locked your heart and threw away the key,'' he said quietly.

''Yes—something like that.''

''But that was a long time ago and you are no longer the sensitive, naïve girl you were then. Do you still think of him?''

''No, not very often. In fact, looking back and feeling some of the emotions I believed had died being rekindled by you—then I believe the pain I suffered was a result of humiliation and hurt pride rather than the love I believed I felt for him,'' she replied, her eyes meeting his, seeing a warm light shining in their dark depths.

She became shy suddenly, which brought a flush to her cheeks and caused a faint smile to play at the corners of her mouth. ''In fact—perhaps you were right. Talking about the unpleasant affair might have exorcised him from my thoughts completely.''

''Let us hope so,'' William said, moving towards her. Placing his finger gently beneath her chin, he turned her face up to his and looked down into her glorious eyes. ''Do not judge all men to be the same after one unfortunate encounter. The man must have been a fool to reject you for another. I meant what I said when I told you that I love you. I beg you to believe that.''

''Yes—I do. I do believe the sincerity of your words—and—I love—also, more than I have allowed myself to realise. But perhaps now you can understand why I am on my guard against men's wiles— why I am so distrustful and why I have been so afraid of falling in love again.''

''I fully understand your misery, but falling in love is not an emotion easily controlled. We cannot order our hearts as we would our lives.''

The warmth in his voice was genuine, causing a joy to flood Rachel's heart. ''I know. I am beginning to realise that now.'' Feeling awkward, suddenly, and disturbed by his close proximity and the way he was studying her, his gaze focusing on her lips, she took a step back, for the powerful masculinity he exuded made her feel altogether too vulnerable.

''Please—you must excuse me,'' she said breathlessly, trying to distract her thoughts from his kiss, reading the warm glow in his eyes as his gaze dropped to her breasts, which made her feel quite naked. She thought he was about to take her in his arms again—the impulse was written so clearly on his face.

Turning from him, she moved towards the door, knowing that if she did not leave she would be powerless to prevent him from taking her in his arms again and rendering her defenceless—at a time when she needed all her wits about her. ''I—I must be going otherwise Celia will get tired of waiting and come looking for me. Goodbye, Lord Kingsley, and I hope you have a pleasant journey back to Oxfordshire.''

With an effort of will, William controlled himself from following her to the door. He smiled crookedly, a knowing light gleaming in the depths of his dark eyes, aware of her reason for taking flight and touched by her natural innocence, which, at last, he had succeeded in laying wide open.

''You will give some thought to what I have said?''

''Yes—yes,'' she breathed. ''We have both said things we need to think about.''

With her hand on the door knob, she turned one last time and looked at him. Their eyes met briefly and she dropped a graceful curtsey. His only answer was a slight bow before she turned and left the room.

Within the hour of Rachel's departure from Kingsley House, William—wrestling with the dilemma that her visit had presented him—left for Oxfordshire, more anxious to speak to his brother than he had ever been in his life. At the same moment as he was leaving London, Rachel's father arrived at Brayfield House, unprepared for the tragedy that awaited him. The following day he, too, left for Oxfordshire with his two daughters.

Chapter Twelve

When an angry William arrived at Mortlake Park it was to find James the most miserable and wretched of men—and he very soon discovered the reason for it when he challenged him about his relationship with Kitty Fairley. James did not deny anything; in fact, he appeared exceedingly relieved to have it out in the open at last.

Having had time to reflect on his despicable treatment of Miss Fairley, he was filled with a guilt so acute that when William arrived he was on the point of returning to London forthwith to attempt to repair the wrong he had done her, and to beg her forgiveness—although, he told his brother miserably when they were partaking of a glass of wine before dinner, he would not blame her in the slightest if she refused to see him.

"She is hardly likely to do that whilst she is carrying your child," William replied harshly. "The child is yours, James? Do you acknowledge it as so?"

"Yes. Absolutely."

William looked at him in exasperation, angry because his worst fears had at last been confirmed. "You knew who she was, that she was the virtuous niece of Lady Brayfield, coming from a decent, respectable family. By embarking on such a casual relationship with a girl ignorant to the world as it is known to you, you were completely indifferent to her feelings and reduced her station in life considerably. You showed her no respect."

"When you left for the West Indies, I admit that, with nothing to employ my time other than pleasure and having become acquainted with Kitty through Lady Brayfield, I found her company extremely amiable."

"And, it would seem, obliging," added his brother, his voice heavy with sarcasm.

"It was plain she took a fancy to me—and I found her pleasing enough, at first. I must confess her attentions flattered my vanity, although I had no intention of returning her regard. I am ashamed that, at the time, my attentions were, to say the least, far from honourable, and I was heedless of the consequences of such a relationship. I was careless of just how strong, how sincere, her feelings were for me; for that I am deeply sorry.

"Our friendship ended—or so I thought at the time—when she left Ellerton to join a theatrical company in Bath. It was not until I saw her again at the Drury Lane theatre that I realised how much I'd missed her."

"And you renewed your relationship?"

"Not at first. On the advice of my friends, I resisted her attractions and continued to follow my senseless amusements, but, eventually, we were drawn together and I realised how much I had come to love her. I could no longer resist her—and in those early days of her coming to London I have never been happier."

"And the child?"

"When Kitty told me, my reaction and the things I said and accused her of are unpardonable. When I left her, in my anger I did not realise how much I had injured her—but I was angry at myself, mostly, for being such a cad as to place her in a situation which could embarrass us both.

"Had things been different, I would have risked your disapproval and married her—but circumstances concerning my mother, which you are well aware of, made me afraid and prevented me from doing so. I should not have left her in the manner I did. I did her a great wrong—and my neglect of her since has been inexcusable.

"I cannot defend myself and I am deeply ashamed for any embarrassment my conduct has caused you and her family. I behaved in the most despicable manner imaginable, and since, I have been the unhappiest, the most wretched of men."

"Then I can only hope you have learnt from your folly, James," said William on a softer note, for this was the first time he had heard his brother speak his mind so profoundly, with patience and sense.

At last he was beginning to see that which he had despaired of ever seeing—that his brother was growing up. For a time, idleness and boredom had made him prey to all the vices rife in London, but his affair with Kitty Fairley, and the deep and abiding love he clearly felt for her—no matter how low his own opinion of her was—made him see that some of the values which had sustained the Kingsleys through the ages had rubbed off on James after all.

Perhaps with the responsibilities of a wife and child—and the part he was to play in the family's new investments in the industrial north—some substance and purpose would be added to his life.

"You do realise it is probable that the child will be tainted with the same illness that affects your mother, James?"

He nodded, facing him squarely. "Yes. However, it is too late to worry about that now. It is done and I have a responsibility towards Kitty."

William smiled. "Then the only way you can acquit yourself of your guilt is to marry her as soon as it can be arranged."

The ease and lightness with which William uttered these words rendered James momentarily speechless—although he had no way of knowing just then that his brother's concern was to see the matter resolved amicably for the sake of Rachel Fairley whom he had every intention of making his wife.

No matter how many angry words had passed between them on their last encounter in London at Kingsley House, after her moving tale of her rejection by a past love, had she not admitted the love she felt for him? And then there had been their kiss and her complete abandon in his arms. Once this matter of James and her sister was out of the way, there would be nothing to prevent their relationship progressing.

"You—you mean," James said at length, in genuine astonishment, "I have your approval to go and see her?"

"Yes. I have reason to believe she will be returning to Meadowfield Lodge very soon. I have tremendous respect for her father, James, and do not want this unfortunate affair to come between us, so you will repair the damage you have done by going to see him the moment he arrives back in Ellerton and asking him for his daughter's hand in marriage."

With her father and Kitty, Rachel returned to Meadowfield Lodge. She was thankful that, despite his ill health, her father had managed to settle Harry in at school and that he was not at home to suffer the gloom and despondency which descended on the house on their arrival, and prevailed for quite some time.

Her father was extremely shaken and deeply affected by what had befallen his eldest daughter—and doubly so when Kitty told him the identity of the father and that he had refused to do the right thing by her.

Lady Brayfield had been in no way sorry to see them leave London, so worried was she that Kitty's condition would become generally known and become the subject of gossip among her many friends. It would undoubtedly result in Caroline and Emily having to partake of Kitty's disgrace and ruin any chance they might have of making a suitable marriage.

Indeed, so low were her spirits since learning of Kitty's downfall that Lady Brayfield told Rachel she did not intend remaining long in London herself. Because of the poor state of her brother's health, she was also extremely concerned about the shock the news had been to him, and how he was going to cope with the situation once he was back at Meadowfield Lodge.

Since her meeting with Lord Kingsley at his house in London, Rachel cherished the moment they had shared in each other's arms, when she had been shaken to the very core by the fierce passion he had aroused in her. If it had not been overshadowed by the dreadful situation that existed between his brother and Kitty, how different things would be between them now.

Because of the identity of the two families involved in the affair between James and Kitty, there was an awkwardness to the whole situation—and, ashamed as George Fairley was to even think such a thing, he could no more blame James Kingsley for what had befallen his daughter than he could her. However, he had a duty towards Kitty and could not sit at home and ignore what had happened, hoping it would go away. It had to be faced and quickly, and with as little unpleasantness as possible.

Despite the pain and discomfort he suffered from his illness—further weakened by the racking cough that had persisted since his return from London—he would go to Mortlake Park to see Lord Kingsley and his brother, to see if something could be salvaged from the whole, unhappy mess.

If James Kingsley refused to acknowledge the child as his, then George would have to consider sending Kitty away until after her confinement. The very idea of having to resort to such subterfuge saddened him deeply, but he had Rachel to consider. If she hoped to make a suitable marriage in the future, then it must be concealed.

On her return to Meadowfield Lodge, Kitty began putting on weight and colour returned to her cheeks. Youth and her family would see her through this difficult time, but whereas she looked the picture of health, Rachel was pale and her eyes lacked lustre. However, her treatment of Kitty could not be faulted. It was one of care and consideration as she ministered to her every need—placated her when she wept, and tried to soothe her in times of fretful anger.

How their father wished Kitty would show the same consideration towards her sister, for it was plain to him that Rachel struggled on with great fortitude. He was not misled by her smiles when in the company of others; her suffering had not gone unnoticed by him—although he suspected this had nothing to do with Kitty's predicament, but with Lord Kingsley, for he understood from what his sister had told him that an attachment had been formed between them.

If this was indeed so, then he couldn't be happier—he only hoped Kitty's unfortunate situation had done nothing to jeopardise this. Rachel had already suffered one broken heart. If the same thing happened again, how would she ever endure it?

Rachel was alone with her father in the drawing-room when James Kingsley arrived unannounced at Meadowfield Lodge. Seeing her father's flushed face and weakened state and hoping to save him the from the ordeal of having to speak to their visitor, which would surely tax his strength, she offered to see James instead, but her father would have none of it and insisted on speaking to their visitor himself.

James was admitted to their presence in an extremely nervous state, as if he would have preferred not to be there, but knew he must if he hoped to win Kitty over. Rachel had hardened her heart against him and greeted him with a bitter contempt which she soon swallowed. She could not deny that she was glad that he had taken the initiative to come and see Kitty, saving her father the discomfort and humiliation of having to go to Mortlake Park.

"I have to say that I'm surprised to see you here, sir," Rachel said harshly—although, when he lifted his eyes and looked at her, she was sorry to have sounded so cold, for she was sure she had never seen more pain on anyone's face. The poor man did, indeed, look most wretched.

"Pardon me for forcing myself on you in this manner," he said, looking from Rachel to George Fairley, who was standing by the fireplace with his hand on the mantelpiece in a surprisingly relaxed pose. "I—I

should have sent a note for you to expect me—but—
I feared you might not wish to see me.''

''I am hardly in a position to refuse to see you—
considering the unfortunate condition of my daughter,'' said George bluntly.

James's cheeks flushed scarlet at being reminded
of Kitty's condition and he had the good grace to look
contrite. ''You are justified in your condemnation of
me, sir—but no amount of castigation of my character
on your part could possibly be greater than my own.''

''Then I am glad to hear it, for by your wanton
recklessness you have brought my family to a state
of degradation we did not deserve. However, if you
are here to do the right thing by Kitty—acknowledg-
ing the child as your own, of course—then perhaps
something good can be salvaged from this unfortunate
affair.''

''Yes—of course. I do acknowledge the child as
mine and I offer you my humblest, most abject apologies for any suffering I have caused.''

Unsmiling, George nodded. ''Thank you. I accept
your apologies.''

''H-how is Kitty? Will she want to see me? Will—
will she forgive me for leaving her, do you think?''
James asked hesitantly.

''Forgive!'' gasped Rachel. ''Kitty has suffered
greatly on account of your neglect. Your treatment of
her when she most needed you was diabolical—but,''
she said, a little smile beginning to curve her lips,
believing that the warmth with which he spoke of
Kitty was quite genuine and unable to watch his suf-

fering a moment longer without attempting to ease his pain, "perhaps when she sees you are indeed sincere in your entreaties—then she may see fit to forgive you."

"I love Kitty dearly and will do my best to make her happy."

"I think it is my daughter you should be saying this to. She is walking in the garden. Why don't you go and tell her yourself? Show him the way, will you, Rachel?"

"Of course," Rachel said, and as she was leaving the room she turned back to her father and smiled. Their eyes met in a glance of mutual relief that everything was to be resolved between them at last— and, it would seem, with little fuss.

The day following James's visit to Meadowfield Lodge, desperately needing to escape the restricting confines of the house and Kitty's state of euphoria since James's visit when he had proposed marriage to her, Rachel rode into Ellerton to make some small purchases from the milliners with one of the young grooms, Thomas, in attendance.

On her return journey, she left the main thoroughfare and followed the course of the river that flowed past the bottom of the gardens to Meadowfield Lodge. At this point the water was dark and deep, with dangerous, fast-flowing rapids tumbling and splashing over raised lumps of rock on the river bed. Small tributaries left the main flow to feed the lake behind a thick belt of trees, in the grounds of Mortlake Park. Thoughts of Mortlake Park brought to mind its owner.

She was unable to dwell on their last meeting without her face burning with the memory of how severely Lord Kingsley had verbally abused Kitty, making Rachel angry and bitterly hurt, before he had completely thrown her off her guard and kissed her ardently, declaring his love. How confused she had been—and how passionately she had responded to his embrace with an ardour that brought a flush to her cheeks at the memory.

A glow warmed her from head to toe as she allowed her mind to dwell on that moment in his arms, feeling a quivering, tremulous feeling in the pit of her stomach and knowing there could only be one explanation for it. She wondered when she had first started to love him—for love him she did, and deeply.

She sighed, not wishing to hurry back to the house, but, aware of Thomas's growing impatience at her wish to idle along, she told him to ride on ahead, that she would be perfectly all right, for it was a path she often took and was more than familiar with.

Thomas seemed reluctant to leave her, but Rachel insisted. Only when she was completely alone and unobserved by anyone did she slow her horse down to a gentle walk beside the fast-flowing water, and let her mind dwell on Lord Kingsley and how much he had come to mean to her.

So lost was she in her reverie that she did not hear a horse and rider approach from behind until a voice rang out. "Miss Fairley. Please—wait."

She turned and, seeing a man mounted on a large black horse galloping along the river bank towards her, drew rein and waited for him to come closer. She was scarcely able to believe her eyes when she recognised him as the man who presently occupied her thoughts.

Her heart gave a joyful leap and she watched in astonishment as he came closer, blood pounding in her temples, although she was full of consternation. There was no one in the world she wanted to see less when she remembered the intimacy of their last meeting—and yet no one she wanted to see more.

He looked so striking and relaxed astride his big horse, champing at its bit as he drew rein, with frothy white foam dripping from its mouth, its jet coat slippery with sweat. Rachel suspected he had been riding hard and would have let his horse continue to gallop free had he not seen her. His riding outfit was black with a white cravat and black riding boots. A tall hat sat firmly on his unruly black curls.

William took in Rachel's appearance at a glance. It was the first time he had seen her on horseback and he thought she looked the perfect picture of sophisticated elegance. Her cheeks were flushed an attractive pink and her deep blue eyes sparkled from the exertions of her ride.

"Why—Lord Kingsley, you—you have taken me quite by surprise," she said hesitantly, overcome by a sudden attack of shyness when she remembered the circumstances of their last meeting, and knowing from the way his eyes narrowed and lingered softly on her face that it was uppermost in his mind also. "I—I've just ridden to Ellerton to make a few purchases and thought, as it is such a lovely day, that I would ride back by the river."

"Alone?"

"No. Thomas, one of the grooms, was with me until I sent him on ahead."

"I see. Then it is lucky for me that I chose this time to ride to Meadowfield Lodge to see your father. We can ride along together. Do you often ride?"

"Yes, quite often. Tell me, Lord Kingsley, did Sir Edgar not return with you to Mortlake Park?"

"No. He may visit at a later date—but for the present..." he smiled meaningfully "...his time is taken up with forming a romantic attachment with your charming cousin, Caroline. He seems to be quite smitten by her—and your aunt seems well pleased at the way things are heading. Edgar is indeed fortunate in his choice."

"Yes, he is. In fact, it is a good match for them both, and Aunt Mary might well rejoice should anything come of it—as I'm sure it will."

They rode in silence for a while, the only sound coming from the river as the water splashed and tumbled over the rocks. William cast a glance of appraisal at Rachel as they rode side by side along the river bank.

With the reins looped between her gloved and capable fingers she rode side saddle, sitting easily, with her head erect and back straight, her shoulders square and slender—mistress of herself and her horse, a bay mare with a white blaze. Her habit was of dark blue velvet with a matching hat perched attractively atop her black hair, with a small plume dancing jauntily when she moved her head.

The simplicity and rich colour of her habit only served to heighten her beauty and the dark blue depths of her eyes. William felt an urgent stirring of desire deep inside, for he thought he had never seen her look more lovely. She had an unbelievably small waist and his eyes lingered on the soft mounds of her breasts straining beneath her jacket, and the way her round hips moved in a provocative motion with the movements of her horse.

"I am glad to have the chance of speaking to you alone. I have been meaning to ride over to Meadow-field Lodge to speak to you before now," he said, when she became aware of his scrutiny and turned and looked at him directly.

"Oh!"

"Yes. I've been wanting to apologise to you for my behaviour on our last meeting. I said many things that day of which I am ashamed. It was not my intention to give offence."

Rachel stared at him with some surprise. "Why—you surprise me, Lord Kingsley. You! Ashamed! You must forgive me if I find that difficult to believe. However—my memory of that day is not so hazy that I have forgotten the offensive and insulting things you said about my sister. You said nothing you did not mean. Let me see—what was it you said, now—'your opinions once uttered cannot be retracted.'

Correct me if my memory serves me wrong—but I believe that was what you said. So you see, Lord Kingsley, it is a little late to withdraw anything you said that day.''

She spoke lightly, but it was clear to William that she was still offended by what he had said that day at Kingsley House regarding her sister. Infuriated that she should comment on the unpleasant part of their conversation instead of what should be most important to them both, he drew his eyebrows together in an unbroken line and hardened his voice.

''Withdraw! I am offering you an apology, not a withdrawal of anything I said. It's just that, with hindsight, I wish I'd kept most of what I did say to myself.''

''With regards to Kitty or myself?'' Rachel asked pointedly.

''Your sister, of course. What I said to you was heartfelt and sincere—and,'' he said quietly, looking across at her, a merciless humour glinting behind his eyes, ''my memory is not so hazy that I do not remember your reply—or your response for that matter—for the manner in which you so ardently accommodated my embrace quite took my breath away and left me expectant for more.''

Her composure totally destroyed, Rachel's eyes met his, and what she saw—and the deep quality of his voice stroking her like a caress—made a slow, embarrassing flush rise to the roots of her hair, rendering her speechless. Her confusion brought a wicked smile of satisfaction to William's lips. They rode on in silence for a few moments before Rachel was able to speak, thinking it best for her sanity to steer the conversation away from themselves.

"Your—your brother called at Meadowfield Lodge yesterday. Did he tell you?"

"Yes. Hence my reason for riding over to see your father today."

"I cannot tell you how happy we all were to see him—especially Kitty. It seems everything is resolved between them at last. You can imagine our relief, for it is more than any of us dared hope for. We are indebted to you—I believe it is you we have to thank for the happy outcome."

"No, not at all. I cannot take any credit. It was all James's doing. When I returned to Mortlake Park it was to find him full of remorse and on the point of returning to London to find your sister and throw himself on her mercy. So you see," he said quietly, a tiny smile appearing at the corner of his mouth as his eyes caught and held hers, "do not feel you have to think better of me."

Quickly Rachel tore her eyes from his, feeling distinctly uncomfortable all of a sudden, wishing they were not so far away from Meadowfield Lodge.

"Kitty and James did not get off to a very good start," she said quickly, in an effort to hide her confusion. "But, all things considered, there is no reason why their marriage shouldn't work. I'm sure they will be very happy together."

"And your sister? How does she feel about not returning to the theatre? For I hope she realises that

it will be quite out of the question once she is married
to my brother.''

''And has become your sister-in-law,'' retorted Rachel drily, her eyes flashing across at him angrily, for
his meaning was as plain as the nose on his face.
''You need have no worries on that, Lord Kingsley.
Kitty will neither embarrass nor disgrace you.

''But not, I might add, out of any consideration she
might feel towards yourself—or because she bears the
distinguished and honourable name of Kingsley—but
because she will have little choice once the child is
born. I am sure her love for James will overcome any
qualms she might have at having to relinquish her
hopes of a career in the theatre.''

All at once William drew rein and Rachel turned
and looked at him, wondering why he had stopped.
With a mixture of anger and exasperation, he sprang
abruptly from his horse and strode towards her. Her
expression was one of puzzlement. Reaching up, he
caught her about her waist and hoisted her roughly
from her horse on to the ground beside him.

Ignoring her small cry of protest, and without re-
linquishing his hold on her arm, he pulled her towards
the shelter of the trees. Pressing her back against the
broad trunk of one of them, and after removing his
tall hat and flinging it to the ground, he placed his
hands on either side of her to prevent any escape.

Rachel stared up at him in stunned bewilderment.
His face was dark and his eyes held a frightening
glitter. Panic swept over her and she tried to stop
herself from shaking, for she was determined not to

let him see she was afraid, that his close proximity disturbed her. When she looked up at him towering over her, his whole body taut as he imprisoned her against the tree, her heart began thumping in her breast.

"Enough," he said angrily. "I am heartily tired of hearing about your sister's misfortunes. Your consideration towards her is commendable, but it goes way beyond the call of duty. She sowed the seeds of her own destruction when she decided to take up her career. You have staunchly supported her in her adversity—which I doubt she appreciates or deserves."

"Why—how—how dare you," Rachel gasped, stunned by his unpremeditated outburst of feeling. She stiffened and tried to move away, but his hands gripped her shoulders so firmly she was unable to move.

"You are not her keeper, Rachel," he said, speaking her name for the first time. "You have been forced by circumstances to share in her predicament—to comfort and stand by her, to pander to her selfishness and her needs, to sympathise when she weeps.

"But she no longer needs you. Now she has James. She is about to embark on a new life—and she will not be alone. I have to say that I am beginning to warm to the idea of her marrying James, otherwise you would spend the rest of your life dancing attendance on her."

"No—no, I would not," Rachel protested with heated indignation.

"Yes, you would. Why do you cling to her side? My own meetings with her have been less alluring, I assure you."

"She did not mean to be rude towards you—I know that—and she will apologise when next you meet."

"I can truly say I care not one way or the other. My concern is for you. Why have you let this come between us, when I thought we had sorted everything out at last? Why do you continue to fight me? I know you use Kitty as a cloak to hide your true feelings. Are you still afraid of them, afraid of letting me come too close?"

Rachel raised her head and her eyes met his proudly. "No—of course not. I am not afraid of you."

"I would not have it so—however, I know you are not indifferent to me. I felt it in your response to my kiss—remember?—on our last meeting. The truth of it is that you have held yourself in check for so long, you are afraid to give way to your feelings—afraid to admit they are equal to what my own have been for some considerable time. You told me you loved me so do not deny their existence, for I will not believe you."

"How can you be so sure of what is in my heart?" Rachel asked, her voice firm, but she was quivering inside, feeling so very vulnerable at being held in such a restricting manner with his face so close to her own. She was desperately afraid she could not maintain control of herself much longer and was furious that she should feel this way.

"Because your heart shines from your eyes," he said softly, looking adoringly down at the contours of her face, at the shine of her eyes, and marvelling in the sweet fragrance emanating from her skin.

"You, my dear, darling, irresistible Rachel, have the distinction of being the only woman I have ever declared my love for—and whether you like it or not, my feelings have not changed. You have the power to goad me to the very limits of my endurance—do you know that, Rachel? Your beauty, your intellect and wit, and your unpredictability, are just some of the reasons which I find so adorable, so attractive about you."

He sighed, his eyes darkening, drawing her closer into his arms, his voice becoming soft with passion. "Here we are alone, Rachel—just you and I—which is a wondrous thing these days. There is no Kitty, no James—no other member of either of our families to encroach on this moment.

"Despite your past hostility, your tendency to fight me whenever we meet, you have already declared your love for me, which gives me hope. Why do you tremble so? Are you afraid? And if so, of me—or yourself?"

The resistance to give in to the temptation to throw herself into his arms was so powerful—but something held her back. What was it? she asked herself.

Pride? Had he been right when he had said she was afraid? Was she afraid of him—or of herself and how her body and senses would betray her if he were to repeat the kiss he had given her at Kingsley House? But how could she call it betrayal when deep within she craved for his kiss that, because she loved him so deeply, should be the most natural thing in the world.

Unbeknown to her, her face softened its defences, and, as if waiting for just such a sign, William's arms went around her waist, her shoulders, drawing her towards him, and she felt herself pressed closer to him than she had been to any other human being in her entire life—so close that their bodies became fused together.

With her head back, limp and quite helpless in his arms, she became swamped by a warm tide of emotions and bewilderment as his eyes devoured the wonderful exciting beauty of her eyes, her lips, the very curve of her cheek, and the soft hollow of her throat where a pulse throbbed gently beneath the surface of her flesh. Her eyes were wide open like those of a kitten, with a fire burning in the luminosity of their depths.

His breath hot on her face, William's lips hovered above hers, almost touching, but not quite, and she wanted them to. She wanted him to kiss her like he had on that other occasion. But when his lips finally sought hers and they stood pressed together in warm, dark rapture, his kiss was nothing like the one before.

With her mouth against his, Rachel uttered a long shuddering sigh of love and longing, yielding her lips to his and opening them the more to appreciate his kiss, which was long and deep, soft and caressing, evoking feelings and disturbing sensations she had never known existed.

She raised her hands in a feeble attempt to push him away, but instead of breaking his embrace they stole upwards around his neck, her fingers becoming fixed and lost in the mass of black curls crowning his head, pulling his face ever closer to her own, surprising herself at the wantonness that gripped her with a passion such as she had never known, wiping everything but this one blessed moment from her mind.

She moaned to the accompaniment of the water tumbling along its rocky bed, and when his mouth left her lips to travel down the length of her slender throat, to kiss the place where the pulse was beating madly, tantalising him, she wanted to speak, only to find his mouth again covering hers.

Eventually their lips drew apart and they stood looking at each other while their breathing slowed, their eyes fastened together, devouring and intense, their hearts beating in unison, the torrent of feelings each had awoken in the other having taken them both by surprise. Rachel stared at William with mute longing, with a half-suppressed gesture of appeal, her lower lip quivering, and at last those wonderful eyes fixed on his were naked and quite defenceless.

Suddenly William's eyes looked past Rachel and became alert, his hands dropping to his sides. She looked at him in puzzlement, turning slowly and following his gaze, gasping when she saw Stephen sitting astride his horse behind them, watching them, his expression one of absolute horror and amazement at finding his sister locked in so passionate an embrace with Lord Kingsley.

Chapter Thirteen

In a state of shock, and still under the influence of the spell cast on her by the passion awoken in her by Lord Kingsley's embrace, Rachel stared at her brother as one mesmerised, her face still flushed, her eyes still glowing, and her lips parted and moist.

"Stephen!" she whispered, her head reeling, still unable to comprehend that he was there, having had no idea he had arrived home. She was frozen with horror, embarrassment and shame—that her brother should find her in such a delicate situation with Lord Kingsley of all people.

What could she tell him by way of an explanation that might excuse her conduct? But she could think of nothing. He would not understand anything she had to say when his own eyes had witnessed the truth of the incident. "This—this is not as it appears."

William regained his composure almost immediately, bending to retrieve his hat and dusting it down before casually placing it back on his head. "Yes, it is," he said, contradicting what she said firmly, not in the least put out at being discovered in a compromising situation with her by her brother.

"I observed for myself the way of things," Stephen replied, dismounting, not quite sure what stance he should take.

It was right he should appear to be outraged on finding his sister being taken advantage of in such a scandalous manner—and perhaps if Rachel had not found such obvious pleasure in Lord Kingsley's embrace then he might be. But there had been no protestations on her part, so he could only assume there might be some kind of understanding between them that he knew nothing about.

The situation was one of extreme delicacy. Had it been anyone other than Lord Kingsley he had found embracing his sister, he would have reacted with anger, but as it was he suppressed any displeasure he felt. Apart from Lord Kingsley's refusal to give his consent for him to marry Amanda, he had no reason to think ill of him, and his knowledge of him was that he was a gentleman, for he was held in the highest regard and valued in the circles in which he moved.

Was it possible he had been deceived? He knew not what to think, but, urged by an instinctive bid to protect Rachel, knowing it was important that her reputation should remain intact, then Lord Kingsley or not, he had to ask him of his intentions.

He cast a severe, critical eye at his sister. "Your conduct and the impropriety of such wanton behaviour disturbs me, Rachel. And you, sir," he said, shifting his gaze to Lord Kingsley, who was not in the least contrite or put out in any way—in fact, he seemed amused and quite at ease with the whole affair.

"I have to say I am surprised that you, of all people, should take advantage of my sister's innocence in this manner. It is fortunate that no one other than myself came by this way, otherwise she would be publicly disgraced. By all accounts, the situation between Kitty and your brother is bad enough—but for Rachel to find herself in the same situation with another member of the Kingsley family would be too much. I have to ask you to explain yourself, sir."

Surprise continued to leave Rachel speechless and she stared from one to the other in anguished apprehension.

Leaving her side, William moved towards Stephen. "I fully comprehend you—and you are right to ask me to explain myself. Were the situation reversed and had I come upon you and Amanda in such a delicate situation—then I would have behaved with less dignity," he said in a voice which was perfectly calm, not in the least perturbed by Stephen's apparent displeasure and the embarrassing awkwardness of the situation. "I apologise. I know how it must look to you—but I have the utmost regard for your sister's reputation and would not tarnish it in any way."

"Then what are your intentions?"

"I wish to marry her."

Neither of them heard Rachel gasp from where she stood a few paces away, or saw the incredulity of her expression. Stephen stared at Lord Kingsley with absolute astonishment, unable to comprehend at first what he heard, and then his face broke into a smile of absolute relief.

"Indeed! Well—who would have thought it? I—I have to say that changes matters somewhat."

"Of course, I shall have to seek your father's consent."

"There will be no objection there. My father holds you in the highest regard—and will deem it a great honour to give his consent to a match between you and Rachel."

From where she stood, Rachel could not believe her ears. She had been swamped by shame at Stephen finding her in such a situation as this and, on observing Lord Kingsley's reaction to it, which was one of dispassionate unconcern, vexation also. How could he be so nonchalant after what had just happened between them?

Tears smarted her eyes and she wanted to cry, but she swallowed them down, anger being her only outlet for her overstretched nerves as she listened to them discussing her as if she were of no consequence.

"Why—how dare you," she cried, stepping towards them.

William turned and looked at her flaming cheeks, raising a sleek black eyebrow questioningly. "Why— is something wrong?"

He was so cool, so self-assured. His light airy tone whipped up Rachel's anger further.

"I have listened to you discussing my future as if I did not exist. How dare you?" she fumed, the savagery in her tone startling both men. "You are discussing me as—as though I were some kind or property to be bartered at will. Your arrogance and impudence never ceases to astound me, Lord Kingsley. One kiss and you take it for granted that I will marry you. You might at least show me some courtesy by asking me first."

Beginning to see the funny side, Stephen smiled. "Come now, Rachel. Why this show of outraged modesty? It appeared to me you were rather enjoying Lord Kingsley's embrace."

"Oh—no. Never." She fixed her blazing eyes on William. "You have shamed me, sir, and in front of my brother. Oh—I—I will never forgive you for this. Never."

Not troubling to hide his amusement, William laughed outright, which infuriated her further. Her cheeks flaming red and too angry to say anything further, Rachel crossed to her horse. William strode after her and, before she knew what he was about, had placed his hands on her waist and lifted her up into the saddle with remarkable ease.

Too angry to bring herself to look down at his handsome face, at his black eyes dancing with merciless merriment, she rode off without another word, without even a backward glance. This was a blessing, for if she had, her anger would have intensified at seeing the smile of amusement that passed between her brother and the man who wanted to marry her.

"Oh, dear," said Stephen, watching her retreating figure. "My sister's fury is unequalled when roused—

as I know to my cost, having been on the receiving end of her tongue on many occasion. But I have to say, it is the first time I have seen her so angry, so discomposed, for some time. Clearly you have touched a raw nerve, Lord Kingsley.''

''Not for the first time. From the very start of our acquaintance she made it known there is nothing meek or pliable about her. Her tongue is oft laced with acid.'' He chuckled softly.

''I fear she means what she says.''

''I don't doubt that—but not only will she forgive me, she will also remember the episode with a great deal of pleasure.''

Stephen fixed him with a serious gaze. ''Forgive my asking, sir—but it is only right that I should, Rachel being my sister—but...you are serious about marrying her?''

''Yes. Now I've compromised her so outrageously,'' he said, walking towards his horse, ''then she'll have no choice but to marry me.''

''And is Rachel aware of the sincerity of your intentions?''

''Not yet,'' said William, moving towards his horse. ''But she will be. Come—seeing as I've been deprived of the company of your delightful sister, ride with me to Meadowfield Lodge. There is a matter I have to discuss with your father.''

Stephen stared at him aghast. ''About Rachel? Forgive me—but I had not thought you would speak to him quite so soon.''

William laughed. ''No. There is another wedding

to be arranged first—between my brother and your sister, Kitty.'' He cast him a cursory glance. ''Ah—I see you already know of this matter.''

''Yes. My father enlightened me on my return. It would seem much has been happening whilst I have been in the north.''

Together the two men followed Rachel in the direction of Meadowfield Lodge, but already she had disappeared from sight.

Over the days following the episode between herself and Lord Kingsley, Rachel maintained an enforced silence on any mention of him. No matter how ardently Stephen was tempted to tease her on the matter, she would not be drawn, for the impertinent manner in which he had arrogantly assumed she would marry him, without bothering to ask her first, continued to anger her.

From the beginning of their acquaintance, there had been so much that had kept them apart. Now, when everything had been reconciled between them, were fresh obstacles to be erected—and were these obstacles to come from Lord Kingsley himself? It seemed that, in his egotistical male pride, he was fully convinced he was the right person to make the decisions about her future, without even pausing to consider her opinion.

And yet the memory of his embrace brought a softening to her senses. Whenever she thought of his kiss, which had been so ardently and expertly given, then her face crimsoned with a mixture of shame and em-

barrassment at the wanton abandon with which she
had yielded, bringing a warm tide of pleasure flooding
within her heart.

He had awakened her to all the pleasurable sensations she had only ever dreamed of, primitive, rapturous sensations she had always associated with being in love. She felt no shame in this, for she could
not escape the fact that she adored him.

The overwhelming temptation to go to Mortlake
Park and throw herself into his arms and allow him
to do as he wished with her, to carry her off, almost
proved too powerful to resist—was this not what she
wanted more than anything else—for him to love
her—to want her? But she restrained any weakness
she might have; she would not yield to the temptation
to abandon herself to him without thought. She too
had her pride, and if anything was to grow between
them, then he must have respect for her feelings and
her right to make her own decisions.

Lord Kingsley made all the necessary arrangements
for the marriage between James and Kitty, which was
a quiet affair at Ellerton Church. Apart from the bride
and groom, the only other people present were Lord
Kingsley, Rachel, Stephen and their father. Lady
Brayfield and her daughters would have been present,
but they had not yet returned from London.

All parties, knowing of the delicacy of the circumstances that called for haste, were eager for the wedding to be over and done with and Kitty once more

accepted—as much as she ever could be—back into the realms of social respectability.

After a few months travelling in the north of the country with her new husband—who would be acting as agent for his family, seeking advice and gleaning as much information as he could into which industries the Kingsley fortunes could be the most profitably invested—she would spend some weeks before her confinement staying with relatives of her father's in Leeds. Eventually, she would return to Oxfordshire with her husband and child—and, hopefully, the whole unpleasant episode of her time spent as an actress would be forgotten.

It was the first time Rachel had seen Lord Kingsley, at the brief ceremony in Ellerton Church, since the unfortunate episode when Stephen had come upon them that day. Although she tried not to show it, she was in a state of nervous apprehension, wondering how he would receive her after she had left him so angrily on their last encounter.

Sadly, now her anger had left her and her heart had softened towards him once more, her regret over the whole episode clouded any enjoyment she should have felt on her sister's wedding day.

Lord Kingsley was in a serious mood. Throughout the ceremony, she ventured to glance at his tall, darkly handsome figure, letting her eyes linger on the way his black hair curled over the collar of his black frock coat. His expression was gravely serious as he became absorbed in what was taking place: Kitty and James exchanging their marriage vows.

It was impossible to read what was going on in his mind. Was he disappointed that James was marrying someone so far beneath him socially? she asked herself. Although, in all fairness to Lord Kingsley, there had been times when his manner and behaviour towards herself had almost convinced her that none of this mattered to him.

He did not approach her until afterwards, when they returned to Meadowfield Lodge to partake of a small wedding breakfast before James and Kitty left for the north. Rachel took the courage to look directly at him and he looked back, his eyes expressionless. Gradually he moved towards her, his voice politely formal, and the subject on both their minds was not alluded to.

"It is a satisfactory outcome, don't you agree?" he said, referring to the happy couple about to leave for the north.

"Happy—as well as satisfactory, I would say," Rachel responded softly.

"Your sister seems much changed," he commented, "and her manner towards myself is a good deal improved, I am relieved to say."

"It is hardly surprising—now she has married your brother, Lord Kingsley. Any ill-disposed feelings she might have had for you have been eased considerably by recent events. I only hope she has remembered her manners and apologised to you for her unpleasant behaviour of late."

"Yes, she has."

"And you forgave her?"

He glanced across the room at Kitty, who was glowingly hanging onto his brother's arm with easy assurance, with cool deliberation. "As to that, I cannot say. Maybe in time I will be able to overlook her deficiencies and become reconciled to her as a sister-in-law—although I doubt I shall ever feel true affection for her. However, I bear her no ill will and would not wish for any unpleasantness to come between my brother and me."

"How charitable of you," Rachel replied with a hint of sarcasm to her tone. "I am sure Kitty will be more than grateful for any consideration you might show her in the future. She will not disgrace you, if that is what you think."

William looked at her sharply, but before he could reply, James, having crossed over to them, gained all his attention.

When Kitty and James had left for the north, Rachel, in silent mortification regretting having so upbraided Lord Kingsley, watched him leave Meadowfield Lodge, believing all was indeed lost.

It would seem that her anger and the way in which she had left him on the day when Stephen had come upon them had been the end of their acquaintance. After his declaration of love and her angry refusal to listen to his proposal of marriage, then he was hardly likely to suffer the indignity of a second rebuff.

But that did not stop her from ardently hoping he would ask her again. She desperately wanted to tell him all that was in her heart, but the opportunity for doing so did not arise. When he left Meadowfield Lodge, his cool indifference told her there could never be anything between them. It was plain he no longer cared for her and she was fully convinced he would not come again.

William's reasons for not calling on Rachel, and his cool austerity on the day of the wedding, were of an entirely different nature and had nothing whatsoever to do with her. His stepmother's mental defects prevented him from leaving Mortlake Park. Doting on James as she did, his presence since returning from London had comforted her, but his marriage had not gone down at all well, and his departure for the north had unhinged her mind completely.

She had become unreasonable and violent, and the door to her room had to be permanently locked, for there was no telling where she might wander once outside the house—or what she might do to herself or others who tried to apprehend her. Each day she showed increasing signs of becoming more and more unbalanced and one never knew in what form her madness would emerge. With great reluctance, William was forced to summon the physician, who finally declared her insane.

It was an enormous relief to William that Mr Hopkins arrived from Antigua at this time, with the long-awaited and welcome information about the medical history of his stepmother's family.

Unfortunately, the information he had to impart was overheard by Lady Kingsley herself—who, in one of her more lucid moments, had cunningly out-witted her maid and escaped the confines of her room. Finding her way downstairs, she quietly hovered in the half-open doorway and listened with silent interest to what was being said between her stepson and his visitor. Only when they had finished speaking did she turn and slip like a shadow out of the house.

It was not until Mr Hopkins was leaving that one of the servants came to inform Lord Kingsley that his stepmother was nowhere to be found.

However hard Rachel tried to conceal it, her dis-appointment over Lord Kingsley's coolness towards her, and the fact that he hadn't called on her at Mea-dowfield Lodge, was evident to Stephen.

In an attempt to cheer her, he was relieved to see how she brightened considerably when he suggested they ride over to Ellerton Hall to visit their aunt Mary, who had returned from London, and to congratulate Caroline on her recent betrothal to Sir Edgar Main-waring. Unbeknown to either of them, they set off for Ellerton Hall on the same day that Mr Hopkins went to Mortlake Park to see Lord Kingsley.

Having left their aunt in a state of shock after re-lating the details of Kitty's marriage to James Kings-ley, and incredulous on discovering he was the father of Kitty's unborn child, they were riding back to Mea-dowfield Lodge in happy spirits.

The day was extremely cold but, thankfully, the heavy rain that had fallen constantly over the previous week had stopped at last and the clouds had broken to reveal huge patches of blue sky. Following the path that followed the course of the river, in a moment of high spirits Stephen turned to his sister.

"Come, Rachel—I'll race you back to the house. Let's see who can be first into the stable yard."

Rachel laughed, for they never failed to race back to Meadowfield Lodge after riding over to Ellerton Hall. It was a rare occurrence for Rachel's docile mare to beat Stephen's large, high-spirited stallion, but she always rose gamely to the challenge.

"All right, Stephen—but as usual you have an unfair advantage on your mount. He's a good deal faster than my own and you know it. At least have the generosity of heart to give me a start."

He grinned back at her. "Very well—just a few lengths, if you think you need it," he conceded graciously.

Happily, Rachel rode on ahead but Stephen soon caught her up and, with a victorious whoop, overtook her, leaving her trailing behind. Riding hard in an attempt to regain some ground, out of the corner of her eyes Rachel thought she saw a flash of something white on the opposite side of the river. At first she thought her mind was playing strange tricks but, glancing across, she saw someone emerge from the trees and stop on the bank of the river.

Slowing her horse to a walk, she fixed her eyes on the figure of a woman who, despite the extreme cold of the November day, was scantily clad in what appeared to be a nightdress, the hem lifting as she moved to reveal her bare feet.

Rachel stared in disbelief, sure she was about to cross the river—which was shallow at that point—until she saw Rachel and hesitated, standing still for just a moment, hovering on the brink of indecision. It gave Rachel time to look at her and recognise the pale features of Lady Kingsley, her white hair hanging loose down either side of her face.

Quickly she turned and ran back into the shelter of the trees, leaving Rachel staring after her. At a loss as to what she should do, in desperation she looked ahead to see Stephen just disappearing round a bend in the path, galloping hard in order to be the first into the stable yard.

"Stephen," she called above the noise of the river. "Stephen, wait."

Unfortunately, he was too far ahead to hear her. She was undecided about what she should do, but in the end her concern for the well-being of Lady Kingsley overcame her desire to follow Stephen, for she could not let the poor woman go wandering about the woods in a state of semi-undress.

Gingerly, she urged her horse down the river bank and looked with unease at the churning water, for after the heavy rain the river was running high, forcing horse and rider to pick their way across the slippery stones with care. Once on the other side, she rode into the trees in search of Lady Kingsley, curious as to the reason for her strange behaviour, and what she could be doing running about the countryside in such cold weather with so few clothes on to protect her.

There was no sign of her in the wood but, undaunted, Rachel rode on through the gloom, following a track between the trees. They began to thin out and presently she emerged into the sunlight. At last she caught sight of Lady Kingsley, but her heart almost ceased to beat when she saw she was heading for the calm, still waters of the lake.

Rachel called out and Lady Kingsley turned and peered at her, making Rachel's blood run cold when she beheld the expression on her face.

Lady Kingsley's eyes were wild, her face one of anguish, and her mouth gaping wide open in a silent scream. Her look was one of madness—as if she had completely lost her senses—and then Rachel knew that she was mad, that this was the terrible secret which Lord Kingsley had tried to conceal from her and the world. The fact that his stepmother suffered from a severe mental disorder explained so many things.

Lady Kingsley turned from her and stepped into the water, and did not appear to be aware of the intense cold as she began wading out towards the centre. Again Rachel called out to her, but it was no use. Quickly she dismounted and ran to the edge of the reed-infested lake, calling and looking around in frantic desperation, startling the birds on the surface of the water and causing them to take noisy flight.

What could she do? she asked herself. She could not let her go further into the water—she would surely drown. But, she thought suddenly, horror striking at her very soul, was that what she wanted? Was she so unhappy that she wanted to take her own life?

This thought filled her with despair, for in all conscience she could not let her do that—she must get help from somewhere. But how could she? There was no time. The great house of Mortlake, reflected in the gleaming waters of the lake, was too far away. By the time she summoned help from there, it would be too late.

Without thought for her own mortal danger—unlike Stephen, she had never learned to swim—she began wading out into the lake, shuddering when the cold water invaded her shoes. Her feet stirred up the muddy silt on the bottom, which clouded the water about her. With her eyes fixed on Lady Kingsley, she shouted for her to come back, but Lady Kingsley carried on, paying no heed to her entreaties.

Despite being hampered by her heavy skirts, Rachel managed to get close to her and tried to measure the distance between them and the degree of strength she would require to pull her towards her. Reaching out, she managed to grasp the white material of her gown but, with a groan of despair, she felt it slip from her grasp when the ground beneath her feet suddenly disappeared where the lake shelved.

Feeling herself floundering, sheer terror gripped her, and a fear that she was going to die. She was frightened, more frightened than she had ever been in her life.

She did not see Stephen emerge from the trees—having come back to look for her when he realised she wasn't following, thinking her horse might have lost a shoe—and nor did she see the people running down the hill from Mortlake, or hear one of them calling her name in frantic desperation.

Flinging off his jacket as he ran and pulling off his boots before diving into the water, with powerful strokes he began to swim out to her across the lake.

Death stared Rachel in the face as she went under the water, her legs, as they thrashed about, becoming entangled and held fast by long trailing weeds, resembling the long black strands of her hair that had become unpinned. It was like a nightmare from which there was no awakening—because of the water she could not cry out.

She managed to surface briefly and gasp for air—at the same time seeing Lady Kingsley disappear, her hair floating on the surface of the water like a pale, beautiful halo of light.

Gradually Rachel became unaware of the intensity of the cold seeping into her, of the numbness taking over her entire body. She closed her eyes, aware of water in her mouth, her eyes, her ears, pulling at her, taking her further and further down to the murky depths of the lake.

It would be so easy now to give way to weightlessness, so easy to surrender, to give herself up to the darkness waiting to claim her completely. A pleasant stupor stole over her and time lost all meaning, but from somewhere in the centre of her mind the instinct for self-preservation made her fight the darkness in one last scramble for life. She flailed her arms, struggling to the surface and gulping for air as her head surfaced again, before darkness claimed her one more time.

Just when she thought all was lost, when she thought all the breath had been driven from her and her lungs would burst, she was sure she heard someone calling her name from up above, commanding her to live, and she felt herself being grasped and pulled upwards, strong arms encircling her waist. Again her head appeared above the water and this time someone was holding her, making it impossible for her to sink back into the slimy dark abyss of the lake.

Briefly her eyes flickered open and her heart soared when they became focused on William's familiar, beloved features. She was in no condition to ask what miracle had brought him to her when she needed him most, to snatch her from the very jaws of death. It was enough for her that he had come.

Barely conscious, Rachel heard more voices as a boat was brought alongside and more arms reached out and pulled her up out of the water. Only when she felt the hard boards of the boat beneath her back did she give a long shuddering sigh and surrender to the mist swirling all about her.

Chapter Fourteen

Rachel felt herself being lowered onto the ground, overcome by a fit of convulsive coughing as she tried to rid her lungs of the water. William knelt beside her, cradling her head in his arms, unwinding her long sleek hair which had become tangled about her body.

Her eyes were closed and circled with purple shadows, emphasised by the deathly pallor of her face. He shouted for someone to find something warm to wrap her in and a blanket was quickly produced, which he wrapped around her, wiping her wet hair from her face before gripping her shoulders.

"Rachel—open your eyes. Please—I implore you."

Hearing his voice, Rachel felt her lips move, but no sound came for she was trembling too much. The excruciating terror of her ordeal had seeped into the deepest places of her mind and she was too weak, still too terrified, to do anything other than shake.

Again William shook her in an attempt to get her to open her eyes, the hideous fear which had gripped him when he thought he might lose her beginning to recede when he saw she was breathing. "Rachel— look at me. For God's sake, open your eyes and let me see you are all right."

Gradually Rachel came out of the darkness, hearing a buzz of voices all about her. Opening her eyes, her vision was obscured by mist, but she saw a blurred outline of someone bending over her.

"Thank God," said William, feeling that nothing could be compared to the joy he felt. His voice and the expression on his face gave evidence to the relief he felt on seeing her open her eyes, but he cringed when he saw they were wild with terror. Death may have receded, but fear would take longer.

Feeling a surge of deep compassion he drew her into his arms, holding her tight in an effort to convey to her some of his warmth—his love. In her fear and desperate need for comfort he felt her press herself against him.

"Be still, my love, be still," he murmured gently, placing his lips on her brow, speaking the words naturally, for never would he know such anguish, such agonising pain, as he had felt when, on searching for his stepmother, his instinct had drawn him down to the lake.

When he had seen Rachel following her into the water, all the demons in hell had broken loose inside his head. It had been too late to save his stepmother— and a moment longer Rachel, too, would have been lost to him forever. He had managed to bring her back from the brink of death. Never would he be parted from her again.

"I will take care of you. Don't be frightened. Come—calm yourself—you're all right now—you're safe. It's all over. I'm going to carry you to the house, Rachel. There you will be tended to. Do you understand what I am saying?"

Rachel managed to nod her head, the mist receding from her eyes, making his face clear to her. She saw his clothes were wet, his shirt clinging to his skin and his black hair glistening with droplets of water. Her eyes left his and became fixed on the glassy, rippling water of the lake, so calm now, giving no evidence of the tragedy which had taken place within its depths just a short while before. Immediately her thoughts turned to Lady Kingsley.

"L-Lady Kingsley?" she managed to ask hoarsely, searching his eyes for the answer.

"She is no longer in the lake, my love. We managed to recover her body. She is at peace now—which is a blessing after her torment of the past years."

Rachel closed her eyes, unable to prevent the warm tears from oozing out beneath her lids as she was overcome with a deep sorrowful sadness. William picked her up and carried her, as effortlessly as if she weighed nothing at all, up to the house. She clung to him, shaking uncontrollably, trying to speak but her words were disconnected.

As William carried her, with an anxious Stephen walking beside him, her terror and trembling seemed to lessen as she became comforted by his warmth, by his strength—and his love, which stole over her, giving her warmth and security.

As her fear lessened and the tension inside her began to relax, she wept softly, her face hidden against his chest, feeling her despair being washed away and replaced with love and hope as she was carried by this man she adored above all else, wondering how such exquisite happiness could have been born out of such a grievous tragedy.

Rachel was put to bed at Mortlake Park and the doctor sent for, who insisted she remain in bed until she was recovered from her ordeal. There was no question of her returning home to Meadowfield Lodge for the present, so Stephen left to fetch their father while Rachel gave herself up to the ministerings of the two maids Lord Kingsley had selected to look after her.

When William saw her after the doctor had left, and he had bathed and changed into some dry clothes, he could see the ordeal had taken its toll. Her face was drawn and as white as the pillows against which she lay; the full horror of Lady Kingsley's death— which was almost certainly suicide—was still to be seen in her lovely eyes.

He sat beside her and she came into his arms gladly, almost like a child seeking comfort and reassurance, for she was still prey to her haunting fears. He placed his lips gently on the crown of her shining black hair, which snaked its way down her back like a silken sheath.

"How are you feeling now?" he asked quietly.

"A little better," she whispered. "Oh, William—it was so terrible. I truly believed I was going to die."

William's arms tightened around her, for there had been moments when he had thought this also. "I know," he said hoarsely, overcome with emotion. "Thank God I saw you—that I managed to reach you in time. Another moment, my love, and I fear I would have been too late. I was searching for my stepmother, who had gone missing. Imagine how I felt when I saw you in the water—what horrors I suffered."

Rachel leaned back in his arms and looked at him. "How did you know to look for her down by the lake?"

He shrugged. "Instinct mainly. Although she had a fascination for water, which may have had something to do with her being brought up on Antigua. Her home was very close to the sea."

"Please tell me about Lady Kingsley. Help me to understand why she did that terrible thing—what drove her to it. She—she did mean to kill herself, didn't she?"

William sighed and took her hand, becoming thoughtful as he raised it to his lips, his eyes meeting hers. "Yes. Seeing at first hand the torment she went through, how much she suffered, then I believe she did. But are you sure you want to hear what was wrong with her now? Perhaps it would be wiser to wait until tomorrow—until you are feeling better."

"No—please tell me now. I—I feel so sorry for her—so sad. She must have been terribly unhappy."

William nodded, sighing deeply. "Yes, she was. But the sadness of it all was that there was nothing anyone could do to help her. Just the day before James married your sister, the doctor declared her to be insane."

Rachel's expression of relative calm changed to one of deep concern and her white face became even whiter. She already suspected that his stepmother had suffered from some kind of disorder of the mind—but insanity? Surely not. This was too dreadful to contemplate.

"Insane?"

William nodded.

Rachel was stricken nearly insensible, the pupils of her eyes enormous as she stared at him wordlessly in growing horror of what this could mean to Kitty's unborn child—of what it would do to Kitty.

"Oh, no—no—dear Lord." Her voice was agonised as she whispered a frantic prayer in her throat. "I—I don't understand," she said in appalled terror, her eyes staring into his with silent appeal when the full force of what he had said struck her like an ice-cold blast—that Kitty's child might be tainted with the same insanity.

"Dear God, William," she cried, gripping his hands, very much afraid suddenly. "Tell me it is not true—for I know it is said that insanity in a family can be passed on through the generations. K-Kitty's child! Oh, when my sister discovers this she will be devastated. I know there will be no consoling her."

"Hush, Rachel," William said, gathering her up into his arms and cradling her trembling body closely as he prepared to allay her fears, alarmed by her reaction and beginning to wish he'd kept it from her until she was stronger. "Don't torture yourself. There's no need."

"But how do you know? How can you know?" she cried, quite distraught, staring at him with searching inquiry as she tried to comprehend what he had told her—and the terrible legacy Lady Kingsley had left to Kitty's unborn child.

"Please—calm yourself. What I have to tell you will offer reassurance—I promise."

"Then tell me," she said, her eyes fastened on his—for him to tell her that everything would be all right. He had to. He must.

"Some time ago I employed a Mr Hopkins to go to Antigua to make enquiries into my stepmother's family background. He has since returned to England and came to Mortlake this very day to tell me of his findings."

"W-which are?"

"That there is no history of hereditary insanity in her family whatsoever. This being the case, the doctor who certified her death has told me it is highly unlikely that whatever caused my stepmother's mental disorder will be passed on to future generations."

"But how can he be certain of this? How can anyone know?"

"Unfortunately, mental disorders are still a dark territory. I have made a study of the illness and very little is known of the human mind. The physicians I have talked to have explained as much as they can—and how, if the illness is hereditary, it passes from one generation to the next.

"Through his investigations, Mr Hopkins did discover that my stepmother suffered a serious fall from a horse a year before she met my father—and that she was rendered unconscious for several days. The doctor believes this may have had something to do with her condition. If so, it will go no further."

Rachel stared at him, a flicker of hope stirring within her. "Can he be certain?"

"No—nothing is certain. But it is highly likely."

Swallowing hard, Rachel looked at him steadily. "Then that is what I shall believe."

William nodded. "Yes. We all must. Before knowing any of this, it was natural that I was afraid the illness might be passed through James and Amanda to their offspring. I hope this will explain why I could not give my consent for Stephen to marry Amanda—and the shock it was to me when you told me Kitty was carrying James's child. Knowing what I did, it would not have been fair to Stephen to give my consent until I knew more.

"However, where Kitty and James were concerned, it was too late, for the deed was already done. But because of the stigma attached to mental disorders, I preferred to keep the matter to myself until it could be guaranteed the illness was not hereditary. Do you understand?''

''Yes—I understand perfectly—and you were right to conceal your fears that such a terrible illness might be passed on. Although, had I known that your refusal to consent to a marriage between Stephen and Amanda had nothing to do with my family's social inferiority, I would not have judged you so harshly. I can only thank God everything has been resolved—but what a dreadful worry it must have been for all of you.''

Because the doctor had certified Lady Brayfield's insanity just the day before his brother's wedding, it also explained to Rachel that this could be the reason why his manner had been so austere, so remote. ''How long was she ill, William?''

''For several years—although over recent months her condition became much worse. My father knew long before his death—soon after his marriage, in fact—that something was happening to her, for she suffered constantly from headaches and always appeared stressed.

''Gradually, her behaviour became more and more irrational over the years—her moods erratic. When my father died, she became much worse and became obsessive about Amanda—and especially so about James. She became quite demented when she learned he was to marry. She hated to let him out of her sight for a moment—which, sadly, became one of the reasons why he spent so much of his time away from Mortlake.''

"So—it would seem her condition had nothing to do with your father's death. I—I know she came from Antigua—that she did not come to England until she married your father. Did she find it difficult to settle at Mortlake?"

"Yes. Oh, she tried to make the best of it and liked it well enough, especially when James was born—but she always yearned for Antigua and always said how she envied me each time I went over to Barbados. It broke my father's heart when he saw what was happening to her but, of course, like all mental disorders and because of the stigma attached to any disease of the mind, he went to great lengths to conceal what was wrong with her."

"Will you write to Amanda—telling her of her mother's death?"

"Yes. I shall have to let her know, of course. No doubt she will want to return immediately."

"And James?"

"Yes, James, also. Although I doubt he will return to Oxfordshire until after the child is born."

"What will you do if Amanda's feelings for Stephen are unchanged? Will you still refuse to give your consent to their marriage?"

William smiled crookedly and his dark eyes twinkled. "My darling girl—I am hardly likely to do that when I have designs on his sister. When we are married—"

"Wait," gasped Rachel, a spark of the old Rachel showing through. "There you go again. Your impertinence will never cease to astound me, Lord Kingsley. Don't you think you should ask me first?"

He laughed, drawing her into his arms. "You are quite right, of course—and I stand rebuked. But I must warn you, my love, that I will not take no for an answer. When you went after my stepmother into the lake, I almost lost you. I do not intend doing so again—and I shall not release you until I receive a satisfactory answer," he said, tightening his arms around her. "So, come. What do you say? Do not keep me in suspense a moment longer."

Within the protective circle of his arms, Rachel tilted her head up to his, looking into his eyes, which had become dark and serious, knowing there was nothing she wanted more in life other than to be joined to him for ever.

"Yes," she whispered, "I will marry you. I love you, William. I shall be proud to be your wife."

The funeral of Lady Kingsley was a sad and quiet affair attended by few. She was interred in the family vault at Ellerton Church along with her husband—and after a respectful period of mourning, William and Rachel were married and she went to live at Mortlake Park.

Amanda returned to Mortlake deeply saddened by her mother's death and the circumstances of it, but her grief was relieved by Stephen's presence, his support and gentle solicitude. Their feelings for each other remained unchanged—in fact, the long separation had increased their love. Anyone seeing them together could be in no doubt that another wedding uniting the Kingsley and the Fairley families could not be too far away.

Darkness had fallen and William and Rachel were alone in the room they shared, having retired for the night. They lay side by side on their rumpled bed, William leaning on his elbow and looking down at his wife's face, flushed pink in the soft glow of light that bathed the room.

Having fallen into a light sleep as she often did after their love-making, which always left them both blissfully fulfilled, her eyes were closed and he remained unmoving, afraid to break the magic of the moment, pride almost bursting his heart as he looked down at her sleeping face.

She was so beautiful that he was mesmerised by her sheer perfection. She looked fragile, faun-like, her body as slender as a wand; he was often afraid he would break her in the passion of his embrace. He never ceased to marvel at the fact that she was his wife, that she belonged to him completely—and that she gave herself to him with a passion and intensity that equalled his own and brought them a wondrous awe.

Since their marriage there was no longer any need for reticence between them. Here, within their own private room, they came together night after wonderful night in timeless enchantment, in blissful union, two people, a man and a woman who loved each other unconditionally and unashamedly.

It had not taken Rachel long to settle down at Mort-lake Park and think of it as her home, although it would be a long time, if ever, before she would be able to look at the calm waters of the lake without remembering it had almost claimed her life as well as that of his stepmother.

She stirred and opened her eyes sleepily, smiling up at him, happiness giving her an inner glow that shone through. With a happy sigh of contentment, she nestled closer to him.

"What are you thinking?" she murmured.

"How lucky I am to have such a beautiful wife—and how amiable you have become, my love," he teased gently. "There is scarcely a trace of the con-trary young woman I came to know in the early days of our acquaintance."

"Do not be deceived, for she is still there—lurking somewhere in the background." Rachel smiled softly, stirring within his arms, sighing and lifting her bril-liant eyes to his, letting them feast on his handsome features. She adored this man, her husband, and ev-erything about him, and she had come to know him like she did no other—the smell of him and every muscle and contour of his fine body.

His ardour had taken away her inhibitions and she always gave herself to him with unrestrained delight, but how she wished he would not remind her of those early days of their acquaintance when she had treated him so abominably.

Reaching up she placed a gentle kiss on his lips, sighing and nestling within the tender and protective circle of his arms. "How I have agonised over my rudeness, my preconceived and ill-founded opinion of you in the early days of our acquaintance. My ignorance as to the merits of your character has caused me to reproach myself many times."

"Then I must beg you not to," he murmured with his lips against her hair, breathing deeply and drawing in the delicious fragrance of her body. "You sincerely thought your opinions to be well founded, and I did little to enlighten you—to give you any reason to think better of me. I deceived you knowingly into believing that what you had heard regarding any defects in my character to be the truth.

"It was both cruel and indefensible, so if there is any blame to be attached to anyone then I must take my share of it also. But all that is in the past—let us forget it. Come," he said, rolling her on to her back and kissing the lips she offered, "there are other, more important matters to interest us now. I want to hear you say you love me."

Rachel smiled happily, putting her arms about his neck and drawing his face closer to her own, seeing the need in his eyes that matched her own—a need that would not be satisfied until the sweet, agonising moment of fulfillment.

"Of that you need not ask. Have I not convinced you of it many times?"

Harlequin Romance ®

Delightful
Affectionate
Romantic
Emotional

Tender
Original

Daring
Riveting
Enchanting
Adventurous
Moving

Harlequin Romance®—
capturing the world you dream of…

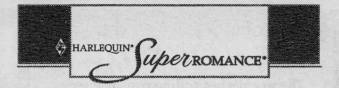

HARLEQUIN *Presents*

The world's bestselling romance series...
The series that brings you your favorite authors,
month after month:

Helen Bianchin...Emma Darcy
Lynne Graham...Penny Jordan
Miranda Lee...Sandra Marton
Anne Mather...Carole Mortimer
Susan Napier...Michelle Reid

and many more uniquely talented authors!

Wealthy, powerful, gorgeous men...
Women who have feelings just like your own...
The stories you love, set in exotic, glamorous locations...

HARLEQUIN *Presents*

Seduction and passion guaranteed!

HARLEQUIN®
INTRIGUE
WE'LL LEAVE YOU BREATHLESS!

If you've been looking for thrilling tales of
contemporary passion and sensuous love stories
with taut, edge-of-the-seat suspense—then
you'll love Harlequin Intrigue!

Every month, you'll meet four new heroes
who are guaranteed to make your spine tingle
and your pulse pound. With them you'll enter
into the exciting world of Harlequin Intrigue—
where your life is on the line
and so is your heart!

THAT'S INTRIGUE—
ROMANTIC SUSPENSE
AT ITS BEST!

HARLEQUIN®
Makes any time special ®